Beyond the Storm

Other books in the Quilts of Love Series

A Wild Goose Chase Christmas
Jennifer AlLee
(November 2012)

Path of Freedom
Jennifer Hudson Taylor
(January 2013)

For Love of Eli
Loree Lough
(February 2013)

Threads of Hope
Christa Allan
(March 2013)

A Healing Heart
Angela Breidenbach
(April 2013)

A Heartbeat Away
S. Dionne Moore
(May 2013)

Pattern for Romance
Carla Olson Gade
(June 2013)

Pieces of the Heart
Bonnie S. Calhoun
(August 2013)

Raw Edges
Sandra D. Bricker
(September 2013)

The Christmas Quilt
Vannetta Chapman
(October 2013)

Aloha Rose
Lisa Carter
(November 2013)

Tempest's Course
Lynette Sowell
(December 2013)

Scraps of Evidence
Barbara Cameron
(January 2014)

A Sky without Stars
Linda S. Clare
(February 2014)

Maybelle in Stitches
Joyce Magnin
(March 2014)

BEYOND THE STORM

Quilts of Love Series

Carolyn Zane

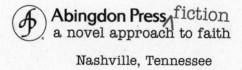

Abingdon Press fiction
a novel approach to faith

Nashville, Tennessee

Beyond the Storm

ISBN: 978-1-4267-4597-3

Published by Abingdon Press, P.O. Box 801, Nashville, TN 37202

www.abingdonpress.com

The persons and events portrayed in this work of fiction
are the creations of the author, and any resemblance
to persons living or dead is purely coincidental.

All scripture quotations are taken from the Common English Bible.
Copyright © 2010 by the Common English Bible. All rights reserved.
Used by permission. (www.CommonEnglishBible.com).

Cataloging-in-Publication Data has been requested from the
Library of Congress.

Printed in the United States of America

1 2 3 4 5 6 7 8 9 10 / 17 16 15 14 13 12

For my sister, Judy

Acknowledgments

Thankfully, I have never been in an actual tornado, so I had to lean heavily on the expertise of others and on detailed historical documentation. Any errors made regarding storms are due to my own lack of understanding on such matters, not misinformation from my experts. My second cousin, Nancy McKenney, was a first responder for the Red Cross in the recent Tuscaloosa, Alabama, tornado, and she told me many firsthand accounts of the devastation she encountered there. I also interviewed a number of friends from the Midwest who shared their memories of rushing to the basement, a tornado at their heels. Thank you, Elizabeth Kelley, Linda Schuck, Harold Maycumber, and Jill Foster for sharing these memories.

For the basic plot and idea, I have to thank my sister, Judy Pierce. For her many prayers, our brainstorming sessions, the Spurgeon quotes, her enthusiasm for this project, and our countless phone calls devoted to discussing details, I have to say that this is her baby, too. Also, thank you, first readers: My husband, Matt Pizzuti; parents, Doug and Pat Tope; my daughters, Madeline and Grace Pizzuti; niece, Charlyn Pierce; and my good friends Betty Springer and Wendy Warren, who were so encouraging and gave awesome critiques and notes.

I must also acknowledge the nonfiction books I pored over for the hair-raising details of the real thing: *And Hell Followed with It* by Bonar Menninger, *Storm Warning* by Nancy Mathis, and *5:41: Stories from the Joplin Tornado* by Randy Turner and John Hacker are among some of the best. YouTube also has amazing firsthand video of recent post-storm devastation in Joplin and Tuscaloosa and other regions, which reduced me to tears more than once.

For pure inspiration as to what it looks like for a person to be sold out to and in love with Jesus and his Word, I thank my pastor, Brett Meador, for his fine example. His book-by-book, verse-by-verse Bible teachings can be found online on the Athey Creek Christian Fellowship website (http://www.atheycreek.com).

I can't begin to explain the chain of miracles that led me to write this book without saying a huge, heartfelt thank-you to my award-winning agent, Sandra Bishop of the MacGregor Agency, and to my editor, Ramona Richards, who conceived the Quilts of Love series. Thank you both, for believing in me.

And, of course, first, last, and forever, Jesus Christ, my co-author and redeemer: I love you.

PART ONE

THE EDGE OF THE STORM

All afflictions are not chastisements for sin;
there are some afflictions that have
quite another end and object.

—C. H. Spurgeon

1

7:00 a.m.

"Good morning Rawston, heart of the American Midwest! We've got seven a.m. straight up on your Saturday, May 3rd, and you are listening to Mike and Julie on 101.5 K-RAW. Keep it right here for traffic and weather on the tens as head meteorologist Ron Donovan's got some breaking news about a thunder boomer headed our way, right after this!"

—∞—

The bell over the Doo Drop-In Hair Salon's front door jangled as it opened. "I got wings!" Isuzu Nakamura shouted as she did every morning when she arrived for work. As usual, she gave the door a healthy, window-rattling slam.

"Mmph." Twenty-eight-year-old Abigail Durham, the salon's owner/operator jerked awake and blinked around the break room. Ah, man. She'd been dozing. And the day hadn't even begun. What on earth had possessed her to stay out so late last night? Isuzu's massive purse crashed onto her workstation table and moments later, Abigail could sense her standing at the door, frowning as she sat up and peeled a granola bar wrapper off her cheek.

"You look terrible."

Abigail yawned up at Isuzu-fresh-as-a-lotus-flower-Nakamura. She might be tiny in stature, but the dainty Japanese national was as tough as the acrylic she used for her customers' French-tip nails. Isuzu rummaged through the cupboards. "I make more coffee. You stay out too late at Kaylee bachelorette party last night?"

"Golly, mom. Why do you ask?" A person would never guess that Zuzu was three years younger than Abigail, the way she acted like such a granny at only twenty-five.

Isuzu dropped the metal coffeepot into the sink and turned the water on, full blast. "You wear two different shoe."

"Oh?" Abigail frowned at her feet. "Oh. Don't worry. I'm not actually here yet. I just came down to check my appointment calendar. I don't have anyone till 8:30."

The smell of the coffee beans Isuzu had ground began to tease Abigail awake. "So? How was party?"

"Kaylee hated it . . . so, it was fun." Dancing and party shenanigans had never been the virginal bride's bag. Probably would have left before the whole thing started, but Kaylee wasn't one to hurt anybody's feelings. Had Kaylee been an animal, she'd have been a dainty, coal-black poodle, all soft curly hair, soulful brown eyes, and perfect manners.

"Too bad you miss Friday service at church last night. They dedicate big, fat baby to Jesus. Baby cry and smack pastor in nose. Blood everywhere. Very exciting."

"Ah. Yeah. Well. Next time." *As if.* Abigail ducked her head and crossed her eyes. Church on Friday night? Isuzu needed to get a life. Sunday morning was enough for any normal person and even then, only if one couldn't come up with a good excuse for sleeping in.

The door jangled again, and Isuzu glanced up. "I do prom nail for my niece, Brooke, this morning. She invited to prom dance with nice boy tonight. Fresh coffee in two minute, okay?" Isuzu pointed at the hissing machine and then rushed to greet her niece, leaving Abigail to mull over memories of last night while she waited for her java to perk.

Kaylee's bridesmaids had gone all out. A piñata filled with party favors and gifts, line-dancing lessons, and some dude named Bob Ray Lathrop—part-time personal trainer—had dressed as a cop, arrested Kaylee for "breaking hearts everywhere," and then proceeded to do a dance that had everyone howling. They'd all taken a turn on the dance floor with Bob Ray, and he'd passed out business cards and coupons for one free personal training session down at his gym, The Pump.

But, to Abigail's way of thinking, the best part of the night had arrived too late. "*Whoooie!* Get a load of the Marlboro man!" one of Kaylee's bridesmaids had shouted over the blaring country music, just as Abigail staggered off the dance floor and flopped into a chair to rest up. Craning to see, Abigail had snapped to attention. *Oh, my. Yes, indeedy. Cute, cute, cute. Real cute.* He wore his plaid shirt untucked, and his Levi's and cowboy boots gave the impression that he'd just climbed off the rodeo bull. In her professional opinion, he could use a good haircut, but it was hard to tell as he'd covered most of the offense with a backwards ball cap. She ignored the niggling voice of caution that cried, *Anybody that good-looking has to be a womanizing jerk. Don't you have enough scar tissue on your heart from meeting guys like him in places like this?* Feeling rebellious, Abigail had pointed her fingers, like twin revolvers, at cowboy-man and pulled the trigger, then blown at her fingertips.

"Abigail! He saw you!" the bridesmaid had shrieked and ducked her head in a fit of laughter.

"Uh-oh," she'd said and laughed. Right about that time, the bride, killjoy-Kaylee, began making noises about heading home. Seemed the bachelorette had family arriving from

Seattle over the weekend and wanted some beauty rest. Plus, her fiancé had called her twice, which Abigail had razzed her about, teasing that he was probably worried about Kaylee's virtue.

"Marlboro," as the girls had nicknamed the newcomer, stood just inside the door, arms folded—making it obvious he spent time in the gym—and surveyed the joint for a few minutes. Then, much to the bridal party's delight, he strode across the room and asked Abigail to dance. It had been like something out of a movie.

"My hero!" she'd shouted for the benefit of the girls. They'd all catcalled and whistled as she'd skipped out to the dance floor after him. Abigail's hands had felt feminine in his work-roughened ones, but his touch had been gentle and polite and his smile genuine. He was all beautiful teeth and twinkling eyes and five o'clock shadow. He'd taken enough time to slap on a little aftershave that morning. Armani. It wasn't cheap. Abigail knew this because she carried it at the salon. *Mm-mm.* Such deep blue eyes. And eyelashes? Long enough to sweep her off her feet.

As she reminisced, Abigail found a mug and poured herself a cup of coffee.

"Come here often?" he'd asked in a deliciously rich baritone.

She'd leaned back in his arms and grinned at the dopey line. "Nope. You?"

"To be honest, the only reason I'm here now is because I just finished some work I was doing on a charity project and I'm starving. If I come here at all, it's usually with a group of work buddies for burgers and to catch the game scores."

"Sounds fun." *Charity thing. Yeah. Sure. Whatever.* It was true, however, that Low Places offered burgers as big as your head and a trough of fries for a song.

"Your boyfriend mind me asking you to dance?"

She'd laughed. "No boyfriend. No husband." He'd seemed inordinately pleased, which pleased her. Inordinately. "You?" she ventured.

"None of the above." He was probably feeding her a load of baloney, but she was a sucker for a pretty face.

"Ah. What about a girlfriend or wife?"

"Nope. I'm relatively new to the Midwest. Haven't lived here a full year yet."

"Welcome to Rawston," Abigail murmured and smiled into his shirt. *Oh, yes.* He was a great dance partner. Nice and tall, which made her 5' 6" plus heels feel perfect.

Just as things were getting interesting, Kaylee appeared at her shoulder and announced that the clock had struck midnight and she was leaving the ball. And, since Kaylee had driven most of them, it was time to bid Prince Marlboro adieu. Abigail's friends were all laughing as they pulled her off the dance floor.

"Goodbye," Abigail had mouthed and thrust out her lower lip in disappointment.

"Next Friday?" he'd answered, seeming just as disappointed.

What the hey? Maybe this time it would be different. Maybe he was that rare combination of good-looking and unmarried good guy. *Eeh.* Probably not. But she'd nodded anyway, grinned, given him a thumb's up, and that had been that.

Abigail couldn't wait for Friday. She opened the fridge for some creamer and suddenly remembered.

"Oh, no," she muttered and stared at the refrigerator door. "I forgot to ask his name!"

"What?"

"Nothing. Hey, Zuzu? I'm gonna go home and shower." She headed toward Isuzu's nail station. "I'll be back in by 8:15 for my first appointment. Aunt Selma is scheduled for 8:30. Oh, and if she gets here before I do, put her in the chair and give her a magazine."

"Okay. Look at this polish Brooke pick. Nail going to be perfect for tonight." Isuzu held up a bottle of sparkly color and waved it at Abigail.

"Hey, Brookie-cookie. How you gonna dance without any ice under your feet?" The Olympic hopeful and her figure-skating twin brother were the local celebs. "Excited?"

Brooke snorted and laughed. "Uh, yeah? To finally dance with a normal boy, and one who won't be tossing me into the air and then not catching me? Totally."

"What's his name?"

"Nick Gleason." Her face flared crimson, and Abigail had to wonder if there was more to the story than that. "He's my best friend."

"That's cool. Friendship is more important in a relationship than the mushy stuff, trust me." Abigail sighed. "Not that I'd know. I haven't had a date with a friend in . . . ever. But hope springs eternal."

7:10 a.m.

"It's time for weather on the ten's with head meteorologist, Ron Donovan."

"Thanks, Jack! Right now, we've already got 72 degrees; looks like it's gonna be a sizzler today. There's a cold front moving in from Canada, bringing a strong chance of a thunderstorm arriving by six or seven o'clock tonight. Possibility of some hail and lightning, so park in the garage and keep the kids and pets inside this evening. Stay tuned here for any changes in the storm's severity and direction. Traffic and weather brought to you by Quilty Pleasures Quilt Shop."

"Thanks, Ron. Hey folks! If you're looking for some family fun, be sure to head over to the 17ᵗʰ annual Rawston Quilt-o-Rama May 17th and 18th. That's just two weeks away, so be sure to put it on your calendar. My family went to that last year, Julie, and I gotta tell you, the quilts are beautiful, but the food? Oh, man. Good eats down there at the Rawston Taste!"

The thing Justin Girard appreciated about living in a small town like Rawston was the charm, he thought as he snapped off his radio and pulled the keys from his truck's ignition. Partially because the city planners insisted on it and partially because the shopkeepers down here had a ton of civic pride, all the shops in the entire Old Town area were required by city ordinance to have western storefronts and covered wooden sidewalks. Barrels and baskets of flowers were encouraged, as were benches, twinkly lights, and alfresco seating for diners. The stores all had catchy names like Quilty Pleasures, Quick Draw McGraw's Art Supplies, and The Sarsaparilla Soda Fountain. The trees that lined the streets were huge and shady and a hundred and fifty years old if they were a day. The area was so quaint and welcoming that even in times of heavy recession it flourished.

This friendly, slow-lane lifestyle was new to Justin. Last summer, he'd transplanted from the East Coast to escape the rat race and a failed relationship and also because he needed to be closer to his grandparents. They still lived by themselves but were now in their eighties and beginning to have some health problems. Since he was the only one in the family who wasn't saddled with a spouse and kids, Justin had been elected to head out to the Midwest to help them and to keep an eye on things.

For the most part, small-town, middle-American life really agreed with Justin, except that he missed his friends and family. Although he had to admit, venturing out on his own for dinner last night had been a step in the right direction. The place he'd selected? Normally, he avoided the bar-and-grill scene in favor of a drive-thru window. And dancing had certainly been the last thing he'd expected to be doing. But the smell of charbroiled burgers wafting from Low Places had been more than his rumbling gut could ignore as he'd driven home late last night, so he'd given in to his hunger pangs and pulled into the crowded parking lot.

Loud country western music greeted him before he even got out of his rig, and he'd followed the thrumming bass through the front door. When he'd entered the room, a tall, curly-headed blond was jumping to the beat and was obviously the life of a bachelorette party. Even from across the room, he could see she was different. A real spitfire, yes, but there was something else. Something unpretentious and oh-so-joyful. As he'd laughed out loud at her antics, he decided that he had to ask her to dance before the night was over.

Her huge green eyes seemed to miss nothing, and she had a single, deep dimple in one cheek that only appeared when she laughed. Her hair was wonderful—wild, shoulder-length blond stuff done up in a big old mess of curls that was losing its gravitational hold with every jerky dance step. Like a compass needle to due north, her carefree abandon had drawn the attention of every guy in the place. He'd zeroed in on her, a decision that had given him second thoughts in the middle of the night. A pang of guilt had him regretting his promise to meet her next Friday night. Just because he'd lived here for a year and hadn't met some nice girl who shared his beliefs didn't mean he had to start looking in bars.

He shook his head. *Focus on business, Girard.*

The pungent smell of hair chemicals assailed him as he stepped into the upscale hair salon.

"I help you?" A petite Asian lady sat painting the toenails of a kid who he assumed was her daughter. They were both pretty as porcelain dolls.

The nail lady eyed him with suspicion. Must not get a lot of guys in tool belts looking for hairdos and nail jobs. "Uh. Yeah." Justin fumbled in his shirt pocket for her info. "I'm supposed to talk to somebody named . . . uh, Abigail Durham. She around?"

"Abby? No. You just miss her. She go home for little bit. Maybe one hour. I give message for you or you come back later."

Coming back held no appeal. "Yeah. Okay. Tell her Justin Girard stopped by?" He dug around in his shirt pocket some more and produced a business card. "I'm donating the labor for the Quilt Fair food cart? I hear—since Jen Strohacker is having a baby any day now—Ms. Durham is taking over her job for the high school booster club."

"Yeah, yeah. Abby doing that. She used to be Rawston Rah-Rah so she think she qualify for running little restaurant." The nail lady seemed to find that hilarious. "This long message. You want to wait and tell her? Sit there." She waved at a comfortable grouping of chairs in the corner. "Sit, sit, sit! She be here later to work."

"Oh, no. I just wanted to tell her that I ran into a bit of a permit problem, and we need to talk before I put on the awnings. City ordinance won't allow us to build it the way it's designed without more fees. It's going to be expensive, so we need to discuss options. Have her call that number when she gets a chance, okay?"

"It's 8:10 here at K-RAW 101.5 FM. Hey, Julie, don't know about you, but I'm already sweating. Feels like you could just grab the air and wring it out, huh?"

"Yeah, Mike, you know I've been thinking about starting a new fad and making all my clothes out of beach towels. Attractive, yet functional."

"Hey, that'd be cool! Make me something fetching?"

"Aaanyway! We've got a set of concert tickets for the fifth caller in our Name That Hair Band contest sponsored by Doo Drop-In Hair Salon! So let's wake these sleepyheads up with some rock and roll! Who's performing this oldie but goodie?"

A refreshing shower, some fruit, oatmeal, and a huge cup of coffee later, Abigail felt as if she'd rally. She lingered another moment on her back balcony lounge chair, knowing that in a few minutes she'd be inside for the rest of the day. It would be too hot to do otherwise. Feet propped on the deck's railing, she jotted down a quick grocery list as she watched a small cloud, like a puff of meringue, float across the crystal clear sky. Ron Donovan predicted a T-boomer, huh? Wouldn't be his first misdiagnosis. Wouldn't be his last. Seemed like he'd been wrong every day this week. Even so, she added batteries to her list. Her flashlight was dead.

Man. It was gonna be a hot one. Tiny beads of sweat were already collecting on her upper lip. She'd changed out of her sweats and mismatched shoes and into a bright, flowery mini-skirt, a periwinkle blue tank top and flip-flops. Wielding the blow dryer in this heat would no doubt make even this skimpy ensemble too much by midday. A quick glance at her watch told her Aunt Selma was due any minute now. She was notoriously early for everything.

Standing, she stretched and then paused, straining to listen to a low rumble in the distance. *What was that?* Leaning over the railing, she glanced up and down the street, looking for the semi-truck that sounded as if it was rumbling by. But there was none. She eyed the lone cloud with skepticism. Wasn't thunder, that was for sure. Must be traffic from the next street over.

Skipping downstairs to her salon, Abigail headed to her whitewashed, antique lobby desk. A quick scan of the appointment book told her she had five haircuts, a perm, a complex color job, and two prom up-dos. Busy day. She dropped the pencil on her blotter and stepped back to survey the newly decorated room. The cream n' java paint she'd chosen for the lobby walls last month looked perfect. Chic. Especially with the brown and blue curtains she'd made herself. She'd splurged on a fabulous blue vase for the coffee table and kept it filled with fragrant white roses. A special shelf held her *North American Hair Stylist of the Year* award and other trophies, certificates, and honors. Abigail was good at her craft. And people knew it.

It had taken her three years to achieve this magazine-cover perfection for her shop. Three years of garage-saleing and sanding and scraping and painting and arranging everything just so. But it had been worth it. Between her creativity with the shears and the beautiful salon, she was attracting new business in droves. Luckily, she was able to add two part-time stylists and a manicurist last year to deal with the overflow. She was even thinking about renting the spare room to a masseuse.

Then again, though Abigail loved her salon—and Rawston—an offer hovered over her, never far from her thoughts. Abigail had received a call from an exclusive salon in Los Angeles, one that catered to a number of celebrities. The money would be great. And it would be nice to finally bust out of small-town USA with the small-town busybody mindset. But she'd miss her aunt. And her friends. And her clientele. Some more mulling would have to happen before she made a decision that drastic.

Just outside her plate glass window, Selma Louise Tully's 1972 Oldsmobile Cutlass Supreme, driven by Selma herself, jumped the curb for a moment before settling back into the parking spot in front of Abigail's salon. The car was an ungainly machine that seemed to drive Selma, rather than vice versa, and had more than one dent to make that case. Riding so low in her seat that she had to peer through the spokes of the steering wheel, Selma regularly drew goggling stares from folks who thought the car careened down the road without a driver.

Selma was as saucy as a plate of spaghetti and never failed to infect everyone she met with her unbridled enthusiasm for life. Though she was eighty-seven, she was still glass-shard sharp, and her dry sense of humor and boundless energy made her seem decades younger. She'd just renewed her driver's license for another five years and ran the quilt shop two doors down—Quilty Pleasures, one of the most famous quilt shops, among the quilting set at any rate—in America. She wore her white hair in a close-cropped cap, and her clothing was usually gaudy enough to glow in the dark. She claimed it kept folks from stepping on her.

A blast of hot air charged into the room along with Selma. "Hi, honey. I'm early. Came straight here from home. Wanted to give you some extra time to turn me into a bombshell for the Quilt Fair. I have to look good for my adoring fans." She grabbed Abigail into a crushing embrace and standing on tiptoe, noisily kissed her cheek. "Hey, Zuzu," she called and climbed into Abigail's hair chair.

"Hi, Auntie Selma," Isuzu called back as she guided Brooke to the blue light machine to cure her nails. "You getting ready for quilt people to come mob you?"

"You know, I've been doing this thing for years, and I still get butterflies."

"That's because every year fair get bigger."

Isuzu was right. Selma's darling shop was a seriously big deal in Rawston and not simply because of her huge selection of vintage fabrics and notions. Nor was it a destination point because of the treasure trove of beautifully crafted quilts that hung from every wall and the high rough-hewn ceiling rafters. Though those things were true, the real reason for the shop's notoriety was the annual Quilt-o-Rama Selma founded seventeen years ago. What had started as a little quilt show was now an event that literally took over the streets of Rawston as quilters from all over the nation flocked to partake of the festivities. Quilts dangled off railings, gutters, rooftops and any other thing that sat still long enough to act as a display stand. The carnival atmosphere consisted of a nationally renowned quilt contest, sack races, pie-eating contest, Mrs. Grandmother America pageant, quilting bees, and more.

Abigail was rummaging in her closet for a cape for Selma when Isuzu shouted, "Oh, Abby you have message from handsome guy who come in for you."

"Seriously?" For a second Abigail thought it might be the guy from last night, until she remembered they hadn't exchanged names. "What'd he want?"

"He leave his card. Call him. City won't allow you to build booster food cart. You fix. Very expensive problem."

"*What?*" Abigail moved to the door and stared at her, completely flummoxed. "You have got to be kidding me! The Rawston Taste is in two weeks! And we don't have our new *food cart?* For the love of—" Spinning around, she gave Aunt Selma's cape an agitated snap before she fastened it around the old woman's neck. As if she didn't have enough to do already for this Quilt-o-Rama booster club deal. Now she had to fix the food cart?

"Try not to let the stress get to you," Selma clucked sympathetically. "You just do what you can do, and then let the rest go. It seems like every year there's a crisis. Which reminds me, you know each year I host the team speed-quilting contest?"

Zuzu's niece, Brooke, laughed from across the room. "That just sounds hilarious."

"Oh no, missy. This is serious stuff. Even an Olympian such as yourself hasn't *seen* competition until you've witnessed a dozen teams of quilters come in from all over the United States and start quilting Saturday morning and not stop until Sunday night. The prize is six thousand dollars for the charity of your team's choice. The quilts are all auctioned off for that charity, too."

"Whoa." Brooke was impressed.

"Yeah, whoa. Well, anyhow, The Rawston Raw-Edges have not won in six years, and we're tired of eating crow. We've all been trying to come up with a great theme, but so far," Selma stuck out her tongue and blew, "*Ppfft*. Nada. Zippo. Thelma Edwards suggested a garden patch theme with flowers. Mae Dewsbury suggested berries or grapes. I'm thinking those are just . . . oh, what's the word?"

"Mind-numbingly dull?" Abigail yanked her shear drawer open and stared inside. What was she looking for again? *Ooo, this food cart thing honked her off.*

"Okay. I might not put it that way, but sure. Anyway, I don't know what is wrong with me, but this year I just can't seem to think of a winning theme. Nothing seems to . . . to . . . to just *jump out* at me, you know?"

"That's cool." Abigail was only half listening as she was still fuming about the guy who'd just dumped the food cart problem in her lap. Thank heavens Jen Strohacker was coming in at ten. Maybe she could help her untangle some of this mess.

"I know God will eventually show me the perfect idea, because I've been praying over it for some time now," Selma said. "I'm sure that I'll know it when I hear it."

Abigail closed her eyes so Selma wouldn't see her rolling them. *Like anyone—let alone God—cared about cool ideas for quilts.* All her life, Abigail had listened to Selma natter on about the tedious subject of quilting. All those little pieces of material, making all those little designs and filling them with all those little stitches . . . Just thinking about it had her falling into a coma on her feet. Because, *come on. Who cared?* A quilt was a quilt was a quilt. *Booooring.*

"*Quilting isn't just sticking pieces of material together,*" Selma liked to say, "*it's about putting the pieces together.*" Abigail wanted to ask, "*Putting* the pieces together? *Sticking* the pieces together? What did that even mean? And why should I care?" But she didn't because she loved her quirky aunt, and so she tried to listen and feign interest.

The bell over the door jangled. Isuzu's sister-in-law was here to pick up Brooke.

"Hey, Mieko." Abigail put on her professional façade of tranquility, though on the inside she still fretted. "You guys have something going on today?"

"I've gotta get the kids up to the Southshire ice rink for a training session with their coach," Mieko said.

"On Saturday?"

"Every day." Mieko sighed. "Monday through Friday the kids practice from three to seven, then we have to drive back in time for school. It's a hassle."

"Wait, you're talking three *a.m.?*"

"Yeah."

"Wow! And you and your husband still have to work all day at the restaurant?" Abigail occasionally ran over to the Sakura Garden for sushi. As far as she knew, aside from Isuzu pulling some evening shifts in the kitchen, Mieko and her husband were the only people who worked there. "When do you guys sleep?"

"Sleep?" Mieko laughed. "What's that? The kids sleep in the car to and from, and I doze while they practice. It all works out. And, in the end, God willing, it will be worth it. Come on, Brooke. Tyler's waiting in the car and he's hungry. Let's go!"

Abigail looked back and forth between mother and daughter. "Are we still on to put your hair up this afternoon for prom?" she asked Brooke.

"Oh, yeah!" Brooke was wriggling like a puppy.

Mieko's smile was exhausted. "Four-thirty. Okay. Zuzu! You coming to help roll sushi tonight?" Isuzu answered in Japanese, but because her head was bobbing, Abigail figured that's where she'd no doubt go after closing.

"And I thought I had a busy schedule," Abigail deadpanned as she began wetting down Selma's still thick, snow-white hair.

Selma tsked. "They are too busy. Everyone is these days. Busy, busy, busy. No time to sit back and enjoy the splendor of God's creation. The devil must get a real charge out of all this stuff we think we need to do."

"You preach, sister!" Isuzu shouted from her station.

"Who needs it? I'm telling you, Zuzu, I miss the good old days. The days where people turned off the boob-tube and went outside and visited with their neighbor—"

Abigail tuned the sermon out. Nobody ever said anything about her having to help build the stupid food cart. That was *his* job. For pity's sake. She was a volunteer. She had already put dozens of hours in on this project, and all she ever got was complaints. Well, this was the last time she was ever gonna step up to the plate. Let some other poor slob take the heat. Just as soon as Selma was out of here, she was going to call this goon and give him a piece of her mind.

2

8:30 a.m.

"Mike! We've got Elsa Lopez on the line! She says she knows who performed that last Hair Band number from 1988! Come on, Elsa! Tell us who it is!"

"Guns N' Roses?"

· Horns blared and Mike and Julie shouted in jubilation. "That's right, Elsa! Who are you going to take to the concert with you?"

"My mom."

"Your mom must be awesome!" Julie shouted. Elsa's giggles and heavy breathing cracked over the phone line. "How old are you, Elsa?"

"Sixteen."

"You weren't even born when Guns N' Roses performed that hit! Congratulations, Elsa and Elsa's mom! What are your plans for the day, kiddo?"

"I'm going to prom." More giggling.

"Prom! That's right. Tonight is the big night out at Rawston High, huh? Have fun, Elsa! And, don't forget to keep an eye out for some rocky weather this evening. Bring an umbrella, because you won't want to get that prom dress wet, okay?"

"Okay." More giggling.

Twenty-year-old Heather Lathrop was sitting in the kitchen of her single-wide mobile home, feeding her toddler son, when her husband staggered into the room and yanked the cord to the radio out of the wall. Without glancing at them, Bob Ray plugged in the blender and began to assemble the ingredients he needed to whirl up a batch of his special protein drink. He spent hundreds of dollars on that stuff and the majority of his time in the gym, sculpting his beautiful body. Heather eyed his bulging muscles with distaste.

Whenever they argued about how little time and money he spent on his son, Bob Ray would claim that his body was his investment. Without it, how would he support her and the brat? He acted like his massive biceps were the gold that would someday get them out of the trailer park and into the good life.

"Morning." She forced herself to smile at Bob Ray.

"Da-da!" Robbie shouted and smacked the tray with his spoon.

"Shut him up, will you?" Bob Ray grunted.

Heather touched Robbie's lips with her fingertip. "Shushie, Robbie." How typical. Bob Ray was not a morning person. And, since the baby had been born, he wasn't an afternoon or evening person either. "Are you going to be around today?" Heather asked as she snapped the lid on her two-year-old's sippy cup.

"No! I'm not going to be home today!" His tone had lost any pretense of civility about a year ago.

"Tonight?"

"No."

Bob Ray spent every day down at The Pump where he served as a personal trainer to bored and lonely housewives and young singles in pursuit of a bikini bod. Heather knew the women who congregated there were young and slender and eager to steal her man.

"Da! Da! *Da!*" Robbie held his arms out and squirmed, anxious to be noticed by his father. But Bob Ray rarely touched the kid anymore.

"Here, honey." She poured some Cheerios into a cup for Robbie to mangle. The blender screamed, and Bob Ray's batch of miracle juice was born.

Heather knew that Bob Ray saw Robbie and her as an anchor around his finely sculpted neck. She had yet to lose the baby weight she'd gained with Robbie, and there never seemed to be enough money for her to go out and get some new clothes or a haircut. She was a mess—and she knew it—a mere shadow of the Rawston Rah-Rah who'd stood on the high school football field's sidelines and cheered for Bob Ray only three short years ago.

Heather tried not to think about the pretty, starry-eyed, college-bound girl she'd been. The future had been filled with the thrill of untapped potential. That is, until junior year when the tiny plus sign appeared on the pregnancy test stick and life as she knew it changed forever. Within a month, she and Bob Ray had bowed to her daddy's demands and married the day after Bob Ray's graduation. Robbie had been born at Christmas. Seemed Bob Ray wasn't wild about his gift.

Heather peeled and sliced a banana for Robbie, and he clutched a chunk of it until it squished out between his fingers. "Robbie gave the pastor a bloody nose last night at his dedication."

Bob Ray snorted as he poured himself a drink. "That's my boy."

"I'm sorry you weren't there. It was really very sweet."

He slammed the glass blender pitcher on the counter, and Robbie jumped. "Climb off, will ya? You know I have to make a living, okay?"

Robbie's face screwed up and his lower lip stuck out. He glanced at mama to make sure everything was okay.

Heather patted his slimy fist before she bowed her head and squeezed her eyes shut. *God, give me strength not to throw this butter knife at Bob Ray. Please love him for me. Please love him through me. Because I can't stand him, and he's the father of our son.*

Bob Ray was even more miserable than she was, she figured, as she watched his Adam's apple bob. They'd had to grow up so fast. The stress was horrible. But deep in her heart she believed that it didn't have to be this way. They'd been happy once—best friends since she was in first and he was in second grade. With a little effort, she believed they could be again. She didn't even want to think about trying to raise Robbie on her own. "Sorry. Anything you need at the grocery store? I thought I'd head out this afternoon. We're low on milk."

"Just don't spend any money, okay?"

Heather frowned. What was she supposed to spend? A number of ludicrous ideas flitted through her mind: Dirty diapers? Bob Ray's golden muscles? Rocks?

Moving to the sink, she rinsed and wrung out a cloth to mop up the mess under Robbie's high chair.

Bob Ray finished chugging the magic elixir that kept him beautiful and then belched. He left the room without a word.

8:55 a.m.

"Remember to be thinking about that speed quilting idea for me," Selma called as she left Abigail's shop. "Something snappy, now!"

"Right," Abigail called back. *Not gonna happen.* "See you at lunch." She waved at her aunt, then scanned the business card that Isuzu had given her. **Justin Girard, owner, J.G. Construction Company**. But the address was Dan Strohacker's Lumberyard. *Must have an office there?* She stabbed his phone number into her lobby's desk phone and drummed her nails on the tabletop while she waited for him to pick up.

"Hello?"

"Oh. Uh. Hello." *Now what.* She hadn't really thought out how she was going to express her dismay. Touching her tongue to her suddenly dry lips, she glanced at the card again. "Is this, uh . . . er . . . Justin Girard?"

"Yes, ma'am. What can I do for you?"

Didn't he just sound chipper? "This is Abigail Durham? You were in my hair salon a little while ago?"

"Right!"

"I understand that the food cart for the Quilt Fair's Rawston Taste is not finished yet."

"That's right. There are some permit issues. In fact—"

"Why am I only just now hearing about this?" Her eyes narrowed at his business card.

"*Beee*-cause the county just told me?"

"Well," the fact that he was innocent only exasperated her further. "How'm I supposed to get it to the field and set up on time if it's not already done? The fair is in less than two weeks. We can get this permit thing squared away in two weeks, right?"

"Actually, no. The city planning commission is really cracking down on food carts lately. They have new, very particular ordinances and—"

"Excuse me?" Abigail wound the phone cord around her finger so tightly the tip began to turn blue. "What . . . *ordinances*?"

"As long as the awnings are supported by the cart, it's fine. But, the minute the poles touch the ground, it becomes a structure. And, if it becomes a structure, you are looking at permits and other costs, and the permit process is . . . involved."

"*What?* You have got to be kidding me! That is the stupidest thing I have ever heard! We are trying to *raise* money, here, not *spend* it. And we can't wait around for some stupid awning thing to be . . . to be . . . *approved!* The booster club just spent their last dime on tortillas and frijoles. Plus, we have to use this thing for football and baseball games in the future. I don't want some skimpy old shrimpy excuse for awnings! I want the big ones we planned for! Can't you just build the thing the way we originally designed it, and I'll deal with the commissioners when, and if, they catch us?"

"No can do. Besides, the fines would be more than the permit fees."

A pang of guilt had her suddenly feeling less like a volunteer and more like a criminal. Her face flamed. "May I ask just what am I supposed to do with the wandering mariachi band and the tables and . . . and chairs and stuff? They'll cook out there under the sun! We will fry like . . . like . . . something *fried!* And in the fall, we'll get soaked! I don't know if you've been down to the Rawston High Football field lately, but there is precious little shade, okay? And you know what, I—"

"Look, lady. I can see you're getting a little hot under the collar."

Lady? He'd interrupted her to call her . . . *Lady?* It might have been the humidity. It might have been a touch of sleep deprivation. Then again, it might have been a pinch of PMS. Whatever the cause, Abigail was in no mood for this clown. "You bet I am, buddy! This whole thing got dumped on me, and it's been a pain in my neck since day one, okay? Last week, it was the salsa guy, recalling the salsa because of *e-coli!* Before that it was the price of—"

"Okay. I can see we're not gonna get anywhere over the phone."

Again, with the interrupting! Abigail's lips screwed into a wad of agitation. Was he even *listening* to her? Shocking herself—as well as him, she suspected—Abigail slammed the phone down. She snatched her shears off the lobby table and welcomed Guadalupe Lopez to follow her back to her chair. Eyes wide, Guadalupe folded her magazine and stood. "You're not going to take your frustration out on my hair, are you?"

———

"Phone ringing," Isuzu called from where she bent over Kaylee Johnson's bridal nails.

"Don't answer it." A glance at caller I.D. told Abigail it was one Mr. Justin Girard calling, and she was too embarrassed to pick up, so she smiled in the mirror at Guadalupe Lopez instead. "What are we doing for you today?"

"Something short, but stylish. My daughter, Elsa, wants you to make me look like a glamour puss, okay?"

Abigail gave her the thumbs up. *This would be distracting.* Guadalupe was short, stocky, middle-aged and just this side of frumpy. "You'll be ready for your close-up."

Guadalupe jiggled when she giggled. *No wonder Aunt Selma loved working with her at Quilty Pleasure*, Abigail mused. She had this wonderful, huge laugh that made Abigail smile. And today? That was saying something.

———

Justin fumed as he spun the screwdriver in circles on his desktop and waited for the crazy Ms. Durham to pick up. He had no idea who this broad was, but she must have had a bowl of rusty nails for breakfast. *"Hello, this is Abigail Durham at the Doo Drop-In Hair Salon. I'm with a customer right now, so if you'll leave your name, number, and the best time to call, I'll get back to you as soon as I can."*

He hung up and hit redial. Message machine. Again. This was a business. She could hardly take her phone off the hook. So, fine. Two could play this game. He'd just keep calling until she went berserk. Or answered the phone. Either way was fine with him.

⸺⸺

"Phone ringing." There was irritation in Isuzu's tone.

"Don't answer it."

"Okay." Abigail could hear Isuzu's heels tap in irritation across the room where she picked up the phone. "Doo Drop-In and Zu-Zu Nail. I help you?"

"Zuzu! I said don't!" Abby hissed.

"Easy on the hair." Guadalupe giggled. "My daughter just won concert tickets on the radio, and she's taking me out next Saturday night. So . . . I'll need hair."

Isuzu's voice took on a distinctive purr. "Oh, yes. I remember you. Yes. Yes, she very sorry and want to speak to you right now. Abby, Mr. Girard on line one." The light on the phone in her hair cubicle began to flash. She'd kill Isuzu later. Finger aloft, Abigail smiled at Guadalupe. "One moment," she whispered and winked.

Guadalupe held up both hands. "Take your time. All the time you need."

Abigail snatched the phone from the cradle, and growled, "Hello?"

"So, I have about an hour this afternoon to sit down with you, show you what the inspector said, and give you some ideas I have for getting around the whole awnings issue." The fact that she could tell he was grinning only served to agitate her more.

"Where?" she asked, tone clipped.

"Why don't you meet me at Dan-the-Handyman? There is a little hardware store in front of the lumberyard?"

"I know where it is. What time?"

"I'll be locking up for Dan Strohacker tonight. He's got an ultrasound up near the hospital in Southshire with his wife after work tonight, so . . . six?"

"Fine."

Justin smiled at his phone as he dropped it into the cradle. This town was filled with some pretty interesting women. He wondered what this one looked like.

"Abby? She's cute. Kinda reminds me of a tall Tinker Bell."

Justin laughed at Dan Strohacker's description of Abigail Durham. They were outside in Dan's lumberyard and had just finished loading Justin's truck for a job he was starting today. If Justin trusted anybody's take on another person, it was Dan's. In the time he'd known him, Dan had never said a bad word about anybody. But he was a great judge of character. What he had to say about people went a long way toward helping you understand exactly who they were.

Dan was a great big teddy bear of a guy. An ex-marine, he was intimidating to look at with his meaty fists, barrel chest, silvery military buzz cut, and salt and pepper goatee, but on the inside? Dan was pudding. Rescue pet commercials on TV would regularly reduce him to tears, and if you were in need, you could always count on Dan to give you not only the shirt off his back but also the rest of the outfit, including his shoes.

"Tinker Bell, huh? You sure you don't mean pit-bull? She doesn't bite, does she?"

Dan rested his forearms on Justin's tailgate and squinted. "Not that I know of. Why?"

Justin dabbed at his temples with his wrist. Man, it was hot. He couldn't understand how a big guy like Danny could look so cool. Must be the fact that he grew up in this sauna. As he squinted off in the distance behind the lumberyard, the panorama was so flat, Justin thought he could see the earth's curve in the horizon. Spring wheat crops were just beginning to fuzz the ground and irrigation sprinklers shot water in an arc like the swish, swish, swishing tail of a horse. Cicadas whined in a high-pitched drone the way electricity charged across power lines, and overhead the sky that had been so blue only an hour ago, had taken on a hazy quality.

Turning his attention back to Danny, Justin gave his shoulders a jerk. "We had a little tiff on the phone today. She wasn't happy about the new awning codes for the food cart. I don't think I can get her permits in time for the Quilt Fair's Rawston Taste, and she was bent out of shape. Sounds like the boosters are low on dough."

"That's why you donate the labor and I donate the wood, my friend."

"She didn't exactly come across as grateful," Justin grumbled and pulled off his leather gloves and slapped them on his thigh. "What's her story, anyway?"

"Sorta hard to explain in just a few minutes, but she had it kind of rough, growing up. She was in my youth group at church. Always asked me a lot of the questions a kid would normally ask her dad." Dan pushed away from the tailgate of the truck, pulled his own gloves off and tucked them into the back waistband of his jeans. "She was raised by a single mom. Karen Durham's not that much older'n me. Late forties to early fifties. Lives in California now. Abby's daddy left on her eleventh birthday, which I get the feeling she never got over. He sold TV's and stereos out there at Dave's World on Fisher's Mill Road. Still lives on the other side of town, but as far as I know, Abigail never sees him. Even after all these years, she's havin' a hard time forgiving him."

"What'd he do, tell her he couldn't put an awning on her doll house?" Justin smirked.

Danny laughed as he plucked a red plastic flag from a cardboard box and tied it to the end of the longest board sticking out over Justin's tailgate. "Wish it was that simple. Nah, I know Dave is the first one to admit he made mistakes. He's been a guest speaker at our men's Bible study more than once, so it's pretty common knowledge that he used to be a bit of a player. Ran around on Karen and ended up fathering a child with the kid he hired to clean the stereo shop after school. Was quite a scandal."

"Ouch. No wonder she's mad."

"I know this sounds nuts, but Dave's a real good guy. He was another one with a rough childhood. Those things can be a generational coil. Old Dave started going to church and cleaned up his act, but Abby doesn't trust him anymore."

"Can't blame her."

"You ever hear the saying about not forgiving someone is like drinking poison and waiting for the other guy to die?"

Justin smiled and shook his head. "Can't say that I have."

"That's why Abigail can be a tad edgy sometimes. Dave has tried to mend the fence more than once, but she suffered because of him. Now, she wants him to suffer."

"She's good at what she does," Justin said sardonically.

"Maybe, but I don't think it gives her joy or peace, because she's regularly in tears after a good sermon on forgiveness, when she manages to show up at church. Give her a chance.

She's been a great friend to Jen over the years. She's an amazing woman, and the good Lord isn't done with her yet, I'm sure. Worked her way through beauty college. Built her business all by herself. Even bought the building and at only twenty-eight, that's an accomplishment. She's funny and creative and sharp as a whip. But there's something else. When you meet her, you'll notice it. She draws people to her. Even complete strangers. She's a little like a flame that way. And the rest of us? Moths."

"Just so I don't end up on the grill of her rig." Justin climbed in his truck, slammed the door, and left Danny standing in the parking lot laughing.

3

10:00 a.m.

Oh, thank heavens you're here!" Abigail rushed to greet Jen Strohacker as she entered the salon.

Jen smiled in confusion as she waddled back to Abigail's chair for some high and low lights and a good cut. Once the baby came, she'd told Abigail, the Lord only knew when she'd find time to get back. "Is my hair that bad?"

Abigail laughed. "No, no. I just have some stuff going on with the booster club's food cart, and I need to pick your brain about something."

"Oh. Sure. Shoot." Jen grabbed the arms of the chair and, with some awkward maneuvers, lowered herself into the seat.

"Do you know somebody named Justin Girard?"

"Justin? Oh, yeah. He's probably Danny's closest friend."

"Danny? Our Danny? *Your* Danny?"

Jen laughed at the sour expression on Abigail's face. "You've met?"

"The food cart guy? No. And, I'm thinking I don't want to."

"Oh, then you're missing out. He's a great guy." Jen was as easy-going as she was beautiful. She owned Tantastic, a tanning shop about a mile away in the strip mall, and they shared a lot of the same clients. Abigail set to work, digging Jen's hair colors out of her cabinet. "So, he's not one of those contractors who takes the money but doesn't finish the job, huh?"

Jen blew a raspberry. "Justin? No. He's put a lot of work into that thing. And to think, he donated all of his labor—"

Abigail froze. "He . . . *donated* it?"

"You didn't know that?"

"No!" Her eyes slid closed and she groaned. "I took my permit frustrations out on him. *Ohhh*, I am such a loser."

Jen grinned. "He'll forgive you."

Abigail snorted. "So how come you know this guy so well and I've never met him?"

"I'm surprised you don't know him. He goes to first service at our church."

Abigail colored. No wonder she hadn't met him. She never went to first service and rarely went to second. "Oh. So, where'd he come from?"

"Well, *hmm*. He's originally from the East Coast, but he's got some family out here. Grandparents, I think. Last Christmas, Danny and I met his mom and dad and they're really sweet. He's got . . . uh . . . two brothers, both married with kids. We haven't known him quite a year yet, but I think he's become the younger brother that Danny always wanted but never had."

"Oh, that's right, I forgot. Danny's an only child, like me." Abigail didn't count the fact that she had an eighteen-year-old half-sister out there, somewhere. They didn't run in the same circles.

"Mm. And you know what's weird about that? Both of Dan's parents were only children. And now, most likely," she patted her belly, "this guy will be an only child. I'm pretty sure that's why Danny married me. I come from a big family."

"That and the fact that you're a babe," Abigail teased. It was true. Jen was a tall, willowy beauty. At over forty, she was still turning heads. "You're the youngest, right?"

"Of eight. Danny was Brett's—my older brother's—best friend when we were kids." Jen's gaze followed Abigail's hands as she set up a veritable chemistry lab.

"I think that's what Danny has always wanted more than anything else, beside his relationship with Jesus and with me. Family. A family of his own."

Abigail nodded. Danny was renowned for his two passions. Jesus and Jen. He carried his bright red Bible everywhere and knew it frontward and back. And he could tell you the coolest stories and trivia. If he'd been so inclined, Danny was probably the only guy she knew that could carry a Bible into a bar for a meeting of the atheist society and have everyone fascinated and clamoring for more by the end of the evening. Abigail didn't attend church as often as she should, but when Danny subbed for the regular pastor, she never missed.

"Looks like it won't be long before he gets that family, huh?" Abigail said, referring to Jen's advanced pregnancy as she worked.

"Doctor says I'm due in a little over two weeks, but it could be any time."

"You guys must be excited."

"Over the moon. You don't wait so long for something like this without getting a little stupid. You should see the baby's room, and I'm still not done. In fact, I'm going to go visit your aunt about making a quilt for the crib. I ordered a Noah's Ark pattern that will take me the rest of my life to make." She was beaming with excitement over a *quilt*—just like Selma would do. Abigail didn't get it.

Anyone who knew the Strohackers very well knew that they'd been trying to conceive for at least sixteen of their twenty-year marriage. They'd spent a fortune on fertility and *in vitro* treatments, which had all failed. And then, when they'd given up all hope and Jen was in perimenopause—surprise! That "stomach virus" was going to be a boy. "My sister, Sarah, is an ultrasound tech. She's working me in after hours tonight for a private ultrasound at her clinic across from the Southshire hospital. Dan can't wait to get a look at his son."

"That is so sweet." Abigail smiled as she began to section out Jen's hair and twist it up into clips. "He's gonna be a great dad, huh?"

Jen patted her belly. "He already is."

⚬⚬⚬

"Hey, beautiful, where are you?"

Kaylee sighed and smiled. Just the sound of Chaz's voice in her phone could turn her knees into jelly. "Hey, sweetie. I'm just popping home for a minute to change some sheets before I head in to work. This afternoon, I'm going to go pick up Mama and Aunt Lydia at the airport. I can't believe how much there is to do before the wedding." Kaylee moved a stack of brand new, monogrammed towels off the couch and to the overflowing coffee table so that she could sit down. The dining and living rooms of her apartment were literally stuffed with wedding gifts.

"And it's only seven days away. Seven more days until heaven." There was a teasing note in his voice that left Kaylee giggling. The news had spread that they'd both been saving themselves for their wedding night, and it was a bit of a running joke among their friends. And, though there were those that mocked and jeered, most people were impressed— as well they should be. It hadn't been all that easy at times.

"Seven days," he whispered, "ten hours and twenty-seven minutes. . . ." He was panting and snorting into the phone.

"Stop it," she giggled. "You're getting my ear all wet!"

"Hey, now, that's interesting." Chaz's rich laughter rumbled in her ear. They'd always been able to make each other laugh. Sometimes it could get almost painful—this knack they had for cracking each other up. It was a wonderful face-and-bellyache that she hoped they'd share with their children in the future.

"What are you doing today?" she asked.

"I'll be down at the cleaners pulling a shift for my dad." Chaz's father, Ernest E. Edwards, owned the Tripoli Cleaners across from the convenience store in the strip mall about a mile from Old Town. Chaz worked at Tripoli during the day and on his law degree up in Southshire by night. He and Kaylee had just bought a house north of town so that they'd be halfway between both places.

"What time you getting off?"

"I can probably be out of here no later than six-thirty. Seven at the latest. Why?"

"I was just wondering when I should have dinner ready. Mama and Aunt Lydia are looking forward to seeing you."

"Plan on seven. What time are they landing?"

"I have to be in Southshire by three-thirty. Their plane is landing at just after four, and I don't want to keep them waiting, in case they're early. They're going to help me get a jump on thank-you notes and reception favors. When Daddy comes in on Friday, he's gonna rent a truck and help us move everything over to the house."

"Sounds good. Don't wanna take 'em line dancing, huh?" he teased.

She groaned. "Pul-eeze. I was always facing the wrong direction and smacking into somebody."

"I like the way you line dance, baby. You can smack into me anytime."

"Get to work, silly boy." It felt as if her grin could just swallow her face whole.

"You want me to pick up some sushi next door at the Sakura Garden, since you'll be on the road with your mama? I can bring it over to your place for dinner tonight."

Was he the most thoughtful man on earth, or what? "Oh, that's a good idea. Mama loves sushi. It's a date. I love you, Chaz."

"And, I love you, Kaylee Johnson, soon to be Kaylee Edwards."

Justin backed his tailgate up against the loading dock at the rear entrance to The Pump. The owner had contracted for a sauna in the men's locker room. Though he'd never say it, Justin wondered why the men didn't just go outside and sit if they wanted to sweat. Seemed like a waste of money to build a special room for it. Sweat for free, right outside. Whatever. Jobs like these paid his grocery bill, so he wasn't going to complain.

The backdoor swung open and Justin glanced up and grinned. Well, if it wasn't the half-naked arresting officer from Low Places last night. "Hey, Bob Ray! I hardly recognize you without your badge."

"Shut up." Bob Ray laughed and leapt off the dock and into the truck's bed to give him a hand unloading bundles of cedar and stacks of 2x4's. Justin didn't know Bob Ray as much more than a workout buddy. He seemed to be a likable enough kid. A little on the cocky side. The guy who owned The Pump trusted him to handle a lot of the managerial stuff, so he must have a reasonable work ethic.

"So, you have to go to the police academy to learn those moves?"

"Learned everything I know from Rawston's finest," Bob Ray joshed as he hefted a load of cedar up to the dock. Justin chuckled and handed another bundle to Bob Ray. Together they began to slide stacks up onto the dock.

"Heather know you moonlight as a gigolo?"

"What mama don't know, don't hurt her."

Justin didn't let Bob Ray see him wince. He'd heard that the kid had to marry his girlfriend when they were still in high school. And he didn't doubt that Bob Ray's days of sowing his wild oats weren't over yet. If there was one thing Justin was eternally grateful to his folks for, it was that they demanded that he and his brothers treat women with respect. He didn't envy Bob Ray's being caught in a teenage marriage, but just because he'd had to man up at a young age was no excuse to go AWOL on his wife.

He wondered what Danny would say to Bob Ray in a situation like this. Justin wished he had his friend's knack for always having just the right advice or Bible story or something perfect to illustrate the direction somebody oughta be headed. If Justin tried to quote some Scripture to the kid, he'd come off sounding like a phony. Most likely because, though he believed what Danny would say to Bob Ray, Justin didn't exactly model it the way Danny did. Someday, Justin hoped to be more like Danny. Especially for times just like these.

He grabbed a stack of 2x4's and shoved them onto the dock. In spite of feeling inadequate, Justin felt a strong urge to pursue the subject. "Gotta be tempting, being around those beautiful women all night, every night. A lot of 'em seemed to like you."

"Yeah, well, I didn't ask to be a married man at only eighteen, so she's just going to have to deal."

"That how old you were when you two got married?" Justin continued stacking 2x4's while Bob Ray pulled bundles of cedar out of the truck's bed.

"I was almost nineteen. Heather was seventeen, almost eighteen."

"Ouch."

"Yeah, ouch. I go from fullback to fatherhood in less than a year. And now? I live in a single-wide trailer and have to work two jobs to keep her and the kid in Cheerios."

Justin worked for a while, thinking. "Life's weird, huh? Dan Strohacker, you know him?" Justin stood and rested for a second.

"Oh, yeah. He's . . . he's . . ." Bob Ray dragged a hand over his face. "He's a real good man." There was a flicker of something on the kid's face at the mention of Dan's name that Justin couldn't pinpoint. Respect? Probably. And something else. Guilt?

"He really is. Anyway, he and his wife tried to get pregnant for years. I mean, they tried everything and spent a ton of money. They were old enough, financially secure, and have a beautiful home. You'd think God would go, 'Okay, Danny boy, I hear your prayers. You'd make some kid a great dad. I'm going to bless you with a baby.'"

"And here I am, just some chowderhead football player, knocks up his girlfriend when they're using birth control." Bob Ray's grin didn't reach his eyes. "Don't make a lick of sense to me."

"Not fair, that's for sure. There has to be something in there, don't you think? Cuz neither of you got what you wanted. Both of you . . . It's like you're being tested."

"Well, if that's the case, I have a sinking feeling I'm not passing." Bob Ray climbed out of the truck. "Come on. I got a couple of ice cold Gatorades inside. Let's drink one before we haul this stuff inside." He led Justin to the employee break room and pulled a couple of bottles out of the fridge. He tossed a bottle to Justin, then twisted the top off his own bottle and drank deeply. With a grunt, Bob Ray flopped into a chair at the break room table and stared at the Gatorade label.

Pulling a chair out and spinning it around, Justin straddled it. They sat in companionable silence for a moment, although Justin sensed Bob Ray was wrestling with something. He didn't speak, figuring the kid would spit it out if he wanted.

"Dan and his wife?" Bob Ray finally began, and Justin nodded. "They were gonna adopt our son, Robbie." It was obvious this topic wasn't easy for Bob Ray.

Expression as neutral as he could make it, Justin hoped his slow nod hid his surprise and, at the same time, encouraged Bob Ray to continue.

"It was my idea. Danny was the youth group leader back when I used to go to church. Since my dad died, Dan was like a father to me. Always came to all my games and stuff. Tried to pound some religion into my bony head. You can see how well that worked." Bob Ray's laugh was mirthless as he began to peel the label off his Gatorade bottle. "My dad died when I wasn't much older than Robbie is now. I don't remember that much about him, but the whole thing left its scars. I didn't want my kid to end up living without a guy like Danny around. I sure wasn't ready for the responsibility, but Dan and Jen were."

Bob Ray's eyes closed, and he sighed. "They'd have been awesome parents." When he opened his eyes, Justin could see the emotion sparking, igniting a pain that still simmered beneath Bob Ray's arrogant façade. "Heather even agreed after a while. But her old man . . ." Tears lurked behind Bob Ray's gaze. "Her old man was mad at me. Wanted me to take responsibility. I was eighteen, man. I was scared. Scared of him.

Scared of everything. So, we got married. And I gotta tell you . . . the kid is real cute and everything, but if I had to do it all again . . . I wouldn't."

Justin nodded. That's all he could do. Didn't have words. But he guessed that was good, as Bob Ray didn't seem to want or need words.

4

10:30 a.m.

"Hey everybody, Ron Donovan here with the latest on a super-cell cloud formation that may bring a tornado watch with it, later today."

"Ron, is it just me, or does there seem to be more bad weather than usual?"

"It's not just you, Julie. This has been the wildest spring we've had in this area in over fifty years, and we don't see any signs that it will ease off in the foreseeable future."

11:10 a.m.

I got my tan at Tantastic! Kaylee speaking, how may I help you?"

Jen grinned. Kaylee liked to tell people that she and Chaz got their velvety dark skin color here at her salon. It never failed to make people laugh. Jen dropped her purse behind the counter and waved at Kaylee. She was going to miss seeing her bright smile every day. But she and Danny had decided a long time ago that she'd be a stay-at-home mom. So Kaylee was going to take over as manager here just as soon as she returned from her honeymoon. They both agreed that having an African-

American woman running the place would give Tantastic a fun advertising angle. And Kaylee was just beautiful—not to mention nutty—enough to make the *"I got my tan at Tantastic"* gimmick work and infuse new life into the business.

"This afternoon? Uh . . . sure. What time? No, but I have a slot at 1:45. Fifteen minutes? Sure. Okay. Name? Uh-huh. Okay. Thanks. Bye." Kaylee threw down her pencil and spun around in her chair. "Wow, your hair looks awesome!"

"Thanks. Abigail does a great job, huh?" Jen sat in one of their well-padded lobby chairs and motioned for Kaylee to come join her for a spell. Kaylee grabbed them each a bottle of juice from the mini fridge and they took a break.

"Abigail is going to do my hair for the wedding," Kaylee told her as she burrowed into the loveseat and kicked off her pumps. "She's going to build this elaborate Celtic knot and then work the veil in at the back—it's gonna rock!"

"You'll be beautiful."

"I'll feel that way, anyway." Kaylee laughed. "Are you on your way to lunch?"

"Yes, but I'll be back in plenty of time to let you head to the airport. After lunch, I'm taking Danny shopping for the baby, so I'll see you between 1:30 and 2:00. Okay?"

"Cool." Kaylee propped her elbow on the squishy armrest and regarded Jen thoughtfully. "You and Danny are so happy."

Jen gave her head a little side bob and smiled. "Most of the time, yes."

"You've been through some pretty emotional stuff, what with waiting so long for your baby and everything."

"I think every marriage ebbs and flows. Yours will, too."

"Yeah, but how have you done it? I mean, what is the secret behind staying happy through the rough patches?"

Jen exhaled slowly as she mulled her answer. "You already have the two most important ingredients. Number one, your marriage will be a triangle—God at the top, you and Chaz at the corners. That is a very strong shape for any marriage. And number two, you guys can make each other laugh. Hang on to that wonderful sense of humor and you'll be just fine."

11:45 a.m.

"Ron, Julie and I were wondering if you could take a minute out of your busy schedule and tell our listeners what's going on out there today with this horrible heat and any ideas when it might lift?"

"Well, Mike, in layman's terms, I can tell you that we've got some hot, wet air trapped down here by a layer of colder air coming down out of Canada."

"Sounds like tornado weather."

"Hard to say. It's true that when two air masses like these begin to move, they cause a friction that literally begins to roll the air into a cylinder. Rolling air charged with energy like that is called a supercell. Supercells are the formations that lead to twisters."

"Ron, for a couple of months now, seems like we've been preparing for tornados that just don't happen. Do you think people might be getting immune to the warnings, the 'Cry Wolf' syndrome, if you will?"

"No doubt about it, Mike. Aside from the actual twister, complacency is probably the most dangerous thing of all."

12:34 p.m.

Selma's Quilty Pleasures simply oozed charm. Aside from absolutely everything a serious quilter could ever dream of needing, there were knickknacks and ornaments and aprons and hot pads and more—all quilted and stitched together with love. If it could be quilted, a customer could be certain that Selma carried it in her shop. Abigail had grown up with the scents of potpourri, candles, new fabric, and orange-oiled wood; and—though she wasn't into quilting herself—nothing filled her with contentment faster than a lunch hour with Aunt Selma in her homey shop.

In her aunt's cluttered quilting classroom Abigail was finishing the last of the sub sandwich that she'd shared with Selma while she listened to her pitch some ideas for her speed quilting theme.

"So, you're saying 'no' on the candy theme, 'no' on the pumpkin theme, 'maybe' on the wedding ring theme, and a 'don't-make-me-barf' on the baby animal theme, right?"

"Eh," Abigail said and shrugged. "Auntie Sel, I'm the wrong person to ask. Don't hate me, but I just don't see why people get so excited over a blanket made out of a bunch of scraps when you can just go to the store and buy a comforter already made."

Selma stared at her. "And you came from my sister's daughter's loins? You come from generations of quilt masters, and yet, you don't appreciate the wonder and beauty of telling a story and painting a picture with fabric? Who *are* you?"

Abigail leaned back and hooted at the fierce expression on Selma's face. "I like to tell a story with hair?" she offered as an olive branch.

It was Selma's turn to laugh. "What would you think about a quilt called 'hairstyles through the ages'?"

"I'd *love* it!" Abigail sat up at that idea. Now Selma was speaking her language. "I might even buy a bunch of those raffle tickets! I might even," the creative wheels were suddenly turning in her head, "have some sketches of hairdos you could copy—"

A ruckus out in the store interrupted her train of thought. There was a whole lot of giggling going on out there. "To be continued," she called after Selma, who'd gone to see about the noise. Curious about the laughter echoing from out front, she gathered up her paper plate and napkins, tossing them in the trash on her way after her aunt. A smile bloomed on her lips as she wove through the tightly packed rows of merchandise to discover that the source of the silliness was big, silver-headed, Dan-the-handyman Strohacker balancing sixteen-year-old Elsa Lopez on his feet and counting as Elsa giggled, a hapless rag-doll in his arms. "One, two, three, one, two, three . . . Get it?"

"No!" Elsa fell into more gales of laughter.

Selma, along with her employee, Guadalupe—who was also Elsa's mother—and Jen were hooting and catcalling as Dan did his best to teach Elsa to waltz to the Muzak piped in through the store's stereo system.

"Dan," Jen called to her husband, "put the kid down. We all know you are just trying to get out of material shopping. Come on. I have a quilt to make and curtains to sew."

Abigail squeezed between Selma and Guadalupe for a better view. The absurdity soon had her giggling nearly as hard as Elsa. "Shucks, Danny, you are a regular twinkle toes!" Abigail called. Seemed like just yesterday it was her balanced on Dan's feet and learning to waltz, just before prom. How the time did fly. He blew a raspberry at her and Abigail whooped.

"Come on, girl!" Dan commanded. "Put some backbone into it!"

"I can't," Elsa's hilarity came out in shrieks and gasps and her head lolled limply back on Dan's arm. He swung her into a row of material bolts and knocked them on the floor.

"Now look what you made me do," Dan said, razzing Elsa for his clumsiness. She was laughing too hard to respond.

"Dan," Jen chastised when she could speak, "let the poor kid go. We have material to choose!"

"What? And let her go to the prom not knowing how to waltz?"

"We don't *waltz!*" Elsa hollered as Dan steered her down the notions aisle. "We slow dance."

"Well, why didn't you say so? Slow dancing is easy. I'm great at it, just ask Jen."

Jen shook her head until Dan glanced her way and then she nodded vigorously.

"So," Dan said, "first off, you stand in one room and the boy stands in the other."

"No!" Elsa giggled. "Teach me for real."

"Okay. For real. Stand right here in front of me. Now then. The boy should put his hand here at your waist and not one inch lower, or I want you to use the pepper spray I'm gonna give you."

Elsa shrieked.

"He's so sweet to do this for us," Guadalupe said to Jen. Abigail knew Elsa's daddy had been deported last year, so she didn't have very many moments like this.

"Anytime," Jen murmured and patted her husband's Bible. She was cradling the heavy book in her arms, as if it was a baby.

"Practicing for the real thing?" Abigail teased, pointing to the Bible she bounced.

"Oh!" Jen grinned. "I've been doing that to everything lately. Instinct, huh?"

"That's a unique cover," Guadalupe noted and brushed the bright red fabric shot with heavy threads of primary color with her fingertips. "Handwoven. Mexico?" Guadalupe was Selma's go-to gal when it came to fabric history and type.

"Yes, it was a gift to Dan, when he was down there building houses as a teenager. He built most of one woman's house and she was so thrilled that she wanted to give him something special in return. She saw that his Bible was getting kind of beat up, so she made it just for him." Jen opened the book to the inside flap. "See this? It's a prayer pocket. She told him that people always promise to pray, but forget. So, he was to write the prayer request down and put it there, and then he'd never forget to pray." She fished her finger around inside. "There's a paper in here," she murmured.

Abigail and Guadalupe leaned closer. "What's it say?" Abigail asked.

Tears brimmed at Jen's lower lashes and her smile was tremulous. "It says, 'Remember to pray for Jen and my son today.'"

5

1:00 p.m.

Justin leaned against the door of his truck as he finished jotting a list of supplies he needed to bring with him on Monday. He was checking it for anything he may have forgotten when a distant rumble had him looking up. It wasn't the sound a jet would make. If the sky hadn't been cloudless, he'd have thought it was thunder. *Didn't you have to have clouds to make thunder?* There were no clouds, but the sky had taken on a sickly color. As if it were pale and sweating. Feverish. Dying. The air, the sky, the sound . . . everything felt terminal.

He wondered how Rawhide was doing and figured he'd better head home, let him out, and make sure he had plenty of water. Danny had talked Justin into taking the dog after he'd seen him featured on a morning news show. Poor, mangy old Rawhide was allergic to everything and had chewed his hind end half off. Jokingly, Justin had called him "Rawhide from Rawston" when he first got a good look at the mixed breed dog, and the name had stuck.

A quick glance at his watch told him he had just enough time to take an icy, refreshing shower, play with Rawhide, and eat some lunch before he had to head back to the lumberyard and take over for Danny. He ducked back inside to let Bob Ray know he was going to head out.

"Okay," Bob Ray grunted from where he lay at the bench press, straining against some massive weights that rattled at the ends of his bar. After his last rep, he shoved the bar into its holder and sat up. "I'm headin' out in a few minutes, myself. Gotta put in a shift out at Low Places later."

"Gonna arrest anyone?" Justin joshed.

"No dancing tonight." Bob Ray grinned. "I'm just going to be stocking the bar and some other grunt work." He lay back down and prepared to lift another set of vein-popping reps. "See you Monday."

3:00 p.m.

Heather paused at the mailbox. The poor thing listed slightly toward the road, as if it yearned to follow the outgoing mail. Not that she blamed it. The flat, dusty, broken-down Barnaby Estates was the last place she'd have thought they'd ever call home. Everyone called it "Beer-belly Estates," which she had to admit fit. Aging single- and double-wide trailers were crowded side-by-side, sharing the shade of an occasional tree. Driveways were crammed with junk and junker cars and even junkier washing machines and junkyard dogs that were chained to stakes in the dirt. Heather guessed it was just a step above prison, or maybe hell, but she and Bob Ray could afford the rent and, at this point, that's all that mattered. When she reached inside the mailbox, the usual stack of bills awaited her perusal. Bills, and of course, junk mail. All of it advertising stuff she and Bob Ray could never buy. Looked like there was a $29.99 deal for cable TV this month. She'd love to have that. Anything to break up the tedium of sitting all day in the single-wide with Robbie.

Heather's parents were still pretty glacial regarding her "shame," and had refused to grace her with a visit, let alone a handout. The message was clear. Mrs. *Persona Non Grata* and her baby would sully their upscale digs, and they wouldn't be caught dead here at Gap-tooth Gulch. Though, she had to admit, her mom had started to thaw recently. They'd run into each other at the grocery store on Heather's side of town several weeks ago, and Mom hadn't been able to stop staring at Robbie. Her mother's smile had been more than a little wobbly, and she'd fingered Robbie's sticky hands with a look that spoke of deep regret. It had been a sweet, fleeting moment, and Heather was homesick for two days after. What had Mom been doing, shopping over here on this side of the tracks? Had she been watching them? Did Daddy know?

Heather had been dying for news but had been too proud to ask, and her mother had been too stubborn to tell. But she wondered just the same.

With a sigh, she tucked the mail under her arm and headed back to the house. It seemed to her that the sky was starting to look pretty weird. There was an almost yellowish cast to the light, giving her an eerie feeling deep in her bones. The trailer park, usually alive with dogs barking and the steady whine of grasshoppers, was oddly silent, too. The screen door slammed shut behind her, and instantly, she knew that Robbie was up from his nap and up to no good. "Robbie?" She could hear a steady stream of water rushing in the bathroom.

"Uh-oh!" he shouted.

Heather began to run. "Robbie? What on earth?" Water was flowing down the hallway now. A guttural growl filled her throat. She should have known better than to stand there and shoot the breeze with old lady Carmichael before she headed to get the mail, but she'd so longed for a touch of adult conversation—no matter how addled—that she'd tarried.

"Uh-oh," Robbie repeated. He cast her a delighted smile as she rounded the corner into the bathroom. It looked like he'd filled the toilet with several rolls of toilet paper and some toys and towels, and then tried his hand at flushing them away. When that had grown tedious, he'd turned to the tub, and it, too, was overflowing.

"Robbie, oh, Robbie. No, son. This is a big no-no." Huge no-no.

"No!" Robbie shouted. "No, no!"

"That's right, little man." Dropping the mail in the sink, she shut off the tub's faucet, pulled the stack of soggy towels away from the drain, and turned her attention to the toilet. She didn't have a clue, so she shut the lid, grabbed Robbie, and headed for the kitchen to call Bob Ray.

Didn't it just figure that no one had seen him at The Pump. She sighed and reached for her phone book. She scanned the list of handy people she knew—who also gave a rat's hind-quarters about her and Bob Ray—and came up with Danny Strohacker. Danny would know what to do.

Once she'd explained the situation, Danny chuckled. "Oh, boy. I'm gonna be having these kinds of problems myself here real soon, huh? Okay, first off, don't panic. On the wall, behind the toilet, there are two shutoff valves. Go twist 'em until the water stops. I'll swing by later with a snake for the toilet and a shop vac and some fans and stuff, and I'll get the toilet unplugged and your floors dried out."

"But don't you have to go to Southshire tonight?"

"Yeah, but it's only . . . 3:30 now, and getting you squared away shouldn't take long. I'll finish up a quick delivery and then head by the lumberyard to pick up the stuff I'll need and—"

"Danny, no. This is too much." Heather was beginning to feel guilty about pulling him away from his special evening.

And Jen had told her how excited he was about seeing pictures of his baby boy.

"Don't be silly. I wouldn't have it any other way. Jen won't mind. She's got stuff to do at her job anyway. I'll let her know that I'll be swinging by your place in say . . . an hour and a half or so. Don't go anywhere."

"Okay." Where would she go? Bob Ray had their piece-of-junk car. She had the 1973 single-wide "Challenger" style mobile home. Never could figure out what the "mobile" part was supposed to mean. The old girl was anything but mobile. It was, however, decades into some serious "challenges."

Everything leaked or sagged or stunk. The carpet was so horrendous that Heather had to spread sheets across the living room floor so that Robbie could stay clean. On most days, she sat on a broken-down divan in the living room, texting an old friend about her miseries. Not that Sophia could do anything about her woes from her college dorm room, but it felt good to vent just the same. Sophia had urged her to pack up and leave Bob Ray more than once. And she would have, too. Except for the night of what she thought of as her "miracle." Something strange and wonderful had changed her attitude about a lot of stuff.

Robbie had been only a couple weeks old and colicky. It was late. Close to midnight. Bob Ray still wasn't home, which was fine, because, hey, Heather was no longer at the end of her rope. Oh, no. Nope. She'd fallen clean off the rope, and the rope had slipped away to tie itself into a noose. While she contemplated the sweet relief that ending her life would no doubt give, she just sat there, holding her son and wailing right along with him. And the more she cried, the larger the self-pity grew.

Nobody cared. Seriously. No. Body. Cared. Her mother and father didn't care. She'd been unable to live up to the expectations of their legalistic religion, and they felt obligated to teach her a lesson. Bob Ray didn't give a hoot. She was a wife and mother, not the centerfold material that he helped sculpt down at the gym.

Even God didn't care. And she told him. Loudly. "You don't *care!*" she'd burst out between great heaving sobs. "I don't get it!" Face contorted with anger, she'd thrown back her head and implored the ceiling. "Why do You love *every-one* but me? Why do You curse me? Why do You hate me? Why don't You ever, *ever* talk to me? Can You hear me at all?" Her voice grew snarky, filled with all the vitriol of too much responsibility and not enough help or sleep. "I hear all those people at church saying, 'Oh God gave me a word about this, or God told me to do that,' but You won't ever talk to me! You *hate* me!"

As she thought back over her life, all she could see was the enormous burden of trying to appease her parents and their merit-based religious views by being good. But as hard as she tried—she was never good enough, and they always . . . *always* let her know it.

By this point, she'd been shrieking and sobbing so hard, Robbie had stopped crying and was staring up at her. She'd wiped her nose on his blanket. "You don't care about me. If You did, You'd give *me* a word. But You won't. I'm nothing. I'm a *sinner!*" she'd jeered. "I give up. I give up . . . because You . . . don't care. You don't care. You don't care about me." Running out of steam, she sat rocking and repeating, *"You don't care. You don't care. You don't care about me . . ."*

Over and over she chanted, until Robbie's pale pink eyelids slid closed, and she could see the blue veins moving as his eyes darted about, searching for the deep sleep of an exhausted infant. Finally, he grew heavy in her arms, and Heather staggered to his crib and put him down. She had to move a book out of the way to lay him flat. Strange, because she hadn't left a book in his bed, and no one else had been in the house that day.

She knew that Jen had mailed it to her after Robbie was born, but she hadn't had the time or energy to read it. The next day when she'd asked, Bob Ray claimed he hadn't put it there, and she believed him because Bob Ray wasn't much on reading. Once Robbie was settled, she took the book to her bed. It was a devotional. Like a journal with a verse-a-day to memorize and then some Scripture and encouragement stuff written underneath. Curiosity had her opening it to that day's date. And there, she found the words that changed her forever:

Throw all your anxiety onto him, because he cares about you (1 Peter 5:7).

She had gasped and sat up, wide-awake now. Not just because the verse hit her like a bolt of lightning between the eyes, but because the second half of each day's devotion was divided into parts. Morning. Afternoon. Evening. And this verse had been for the evening. Incredulous, Heather had started to laugh, and she laughed until she cried deep, cleansing tears of sweet relief. Because those simple words were to her. Straight from God. He *cared*. God hadn't forgotten her. He was there, just for her. Out of all the people on the planet, he was chatting with her. On that date and in that time zone. Her eyes devoured that afternoon's devotion:

But God shows his love for us, because while we were still sinners Christ died for us (Romans 5:8).

While she was yet a sinner, a failure, Christ died for her? How could that be? Sobs welled from the depths of her soul. Because she was a sinner, her entire family and most of her friends had abandoned her. And—the irony was impossible to miss—because she was a sinner, the Lord died for her, Heather Bancroft-Lathrop. This dawning illuminated a life-long darkness that had held Heather captive. Sweet relief flooded her, and suddenly it no longer mattered what her parents thought.

In the days that followed, Heather found a group at Jen's church that catered to married women and their struggles. That was where she had really gotten to know what a wonderful person Jen Strohacker was. Jen could have been mad about Heather not going through with her plans to let her and Dan adopt Robbie. But she wasn't.

Instead, she offered to babysit sometimes and brought over care packages. Not just the stuff they needed around the house either, but personal, fun stuff, too. Girlie things like bath salts and hand lotion. Sometimes, Jen would stop by just to give Heather a word of encouragement. The woman, who couldn't have a baby of her own after years of trying, came to encourage her. They'd formed a fast, mentor-style friendship, and Jen had taught Heather what it meant to lean on Jesus. So Heather clung to her faith believing that God would lead her not only through the valley of the shadow but also out the other end and into blue skies. If she cast her cares on Him, things would get better. They had to. Couldn't get much worse.

4:00 p.m.

"We interrupt this broadcast to bring you an up-to-the-minute storm warning with our head meteorologist Ron Donovan. Ron?"

"Yes, we're getting reports that Lincoln County is experiencing some severe weather, which is manifesting itself in nonstop thunder and lightning strikes. We're looking at a pretty high risk of fire; in fact, right now a small house is burning just south of Suffolk County. Also, if you're headed out to Jefferson County, you might want to hold off. We're getting reports of hailstones the size of golf balls right now. If you look out the window, you can see the weather beginning to change locally. Keep it tuned here to 101.5 K-RAW for up-to-the-minute storm-tracker advisories and tornado watch reports. Right now all signs are pointing to severe storm activity arriving around 6 or 7 tonight."

6

4:30 p.m.

Happy hour was in full swing by the time Bob Ray arrived at Low Places to begin stocking the bar. The Buffalo wings and cocktail weenies were hot, and the girls who lounged across the bar, teasing and flirting with him, even hotter. Already, the joint was jumping.

The mood—to put it mildly—was jovial. Saturday nights at Low Places practically came with a guarantee: Get there early enough and trouble will follow you home. Bob Ray bit back a grin. Tonight, trouble was wearing short shorts and cowboy boots and a top that revealed just about everything but her navel. The busty redhead had been posing at the bar, smiling at him, watching his every move as he pulled the empties and unloaded fresh boxes. He'd worn his T-shirt one size too tight and, because of an afternoon spent pumping some pretty heavy iron, he knew why she stared. Bob Ray had seen her in here with a group of her ditzy friends before—the last four Saturdays in a row, actually. Tonight, she was alone.

"You come here often?" she asked, when he came over to fill the pretzel bowl.

He laughed, making sure his biceps bulged as he rolled up the pretzel bag. "Often enough to keep a paycheck coming."

Elbows together, she leaned forward and grinned, her full plum-colored lips revealing a Cheshire grin. "Ever get out from behind that bar to play a little pool?"

Bob Ray pushed the pretzel bowl toward her and braced himself on his forearms. "Sometimes." Their noses were only about six or seven inches apart now. She smelled like spearmint. His heart accelerated as he wondered what it would be like to kiss her. This was a small town. Undoubtedly, people thought he'd already cheated on Heather. And it wasn't that he hadn't seriously considered it. It's just that so far, he hadn't been able to find the time or the place. Or maybe . . . the guts.

He and Heather went way back. They'd known each other since grade school, and he had harbored a secret crush on her—on and off—since then. Even though he resented his marriage, Heather still starred in the title role as his first "everything," not to mention being the mother of his son. As much as he longed to bust free, for some lame reason, he just couldn't seem to cross the infidelity bridge. Yet.

His gaze slid from the bombshell's lips to her eyes. Those were some bedroom eyes just loaded with an invitation. A long slow smile pushed a come-hither dimple into her cheek. Then again, if he just kissed her . . . just once, Heather would never be the wiser.

4:40 p.m.

"Tantastic, Jen speaking. How may I help you?"

"Hey, Mama. It's Daddy."

Jen smiled down at her burgeoning belly. "Hi, Daddy. I was just going to call you." She tucked the phone between her ear and shoulder so that she could continue folding a clean pile of tanning bed towels.

"I've got a little job to do over at Bob Ray and Heather's place. Seems Robbie got a toy and some towels stuck in the toilet, and the place is flooding. I'm heading over to the lumberyard to pick up a shop vac and some fans and plumbing supplies now."

"Oh, poor Heather," Jen laughed. "Well, it'll be good practice for when your kid does something like that."

"Yeah. That's what I said."

"Oh, your son wants to speak with you, okay?" It was a dumb game they started playing the day they found out she was pregnant. Jen set the folded towels down and put the phone to her belly. She could hear the tinny echo of her husband jabbering some silly baby talk.

"Hi, there, buddy boy. Daddy loves his little man. You giving Mom some good kicks?"

"Yes!" Jen said loud enough so Dan could hear. His chuckle filled her hand. The baby must have heard him, too, because he kicked or punched at the phone. "Guess what!" Jen pulled the phone back up so she could talk. "He is listening to you on the phone! I'm not kidding, he just kicked the phone."

"I'm tellin' ya, he's gonna be a soccer star." The pride shimmered across the line.

Jen had never known a man more excited about becoming a father. She was so blessed. "You know, I'm so lucky to have these precious moments with you. You are such a sweetheart, and you're going to be an awesome dad."

"Hey now. What brought that on?"

She wasn't going to tell him that she'd been snooping in his prayer pocket. "I don't know. You. It's just . . . you. Who you are. The way you are about everything. Even now, going over to Heather's house to dig baby toys out of her toilet. You're special."

"Thanks, honey. Right back atcha."

Awkwardly, she bent to tuck the newly folded stack of towels under the front counter. So many of the women in the

mother's group at her church didn't have such a great partner. She sighed. Heather Lathrop was one. "What time do you
think you'll be done over there at Heather's place?"

"In plenty of time to get you up to the clinic, don't worry.
Make me a sandwich or something for the ride up there, okay?"

"I have a better idea. I'll make you dinner instead. I'll defrost
some chops."

"We won't have time."

"Yeah. We will," Jen said and heard her breath gust in the
phone's mouthpiece, "Sarah called and canceled. There's a
tornado watch for our area. They just announced it on the
Weather Channel, and she doesn't want us to take any chances.
She'll reschedule after the weather clears up."

"Oh . . . bummer. Well, I guess that's the nice thing about
having an ultrasound technician for a sister, huh? You can get
in just about whenever you want."

"True." She could hear him deflating and wondered what
she might do to cheer him up. A gallon of rocky road usually
did the trick. She'd stop by the Quick In Go next door on the
way home. "So, it'll be just the two of us tonight. One of our
last romantic evenings together before the baby comes. You
can help me cut out the baby's quilt."

"Sounds good to me."

"You *are* a good man." She laughed. "While I'm waiting for
you, I'll try to wrap up a bunch of loose ends here in my office.
Between Kaylee's wedding and me having a baby, neither of
us is going to have much time to get anything done for the
next two weeks." Jen squinted out the salon's front window.
The glass was tinted sunshade blue, giving the sky an unusual,
bright green cast. Funny how it almost seemed to glow. "The
weather already feels odd. The storm they're reporting must be
on its way. Be careful out there, okay? "

"Will do. You, too."

"I sure love you, Daddy."

"Mm. I love you, too, Mama."

4:30 p.m.

The door jangled as Isuzu shooed their last customer of the day out the door. She flipped the Open sign over to Closed and turned to inspect Abigail, who was sweeping up a pile of hair. "You wear that to meet Handsome-business-card-guy?"

Frowning, Abigail glanced at her flip-flops. "What's wrong with what I've got on?"

"At least you wear two same shoe." Isuzu harrumphed as she strode to her workstation and sprayed the table down with disinfectant. As she scrubbed, she said, "Handsome-guy is good catch. I know I see him sometime first service on Sunday with Dan and Jen Strohacker. Mae Dewsbury from Doozy Juice say he build her new kitchen. She say he very hard worker and tell me Handsome-guy is honest guy with ugly dog who love Jesus."

"I'm confused. Who loves Jesus? Handsome-guy or ugly dog?"

Isuzu rolled her eyes. "I think you need go get him now."

"You've certainly done your research." Abigail dumped her dustpan of hair into the garbage pail. "If he's that great, why don't you go get him?"

"I prefer man who love Jesus *and* speak Japanese. Easier for me at home. But, if no man from Japan show up soon," Isuzu shrugged, "and you not interested in this Handsome-guy—" brows arched, mouth downturned in thought, she seemed to consider her plan, "—I will sit by him at church and flirt. Maybe," she waggled her brows, "I teach him some Japanese." Isuzu's family emigrated from Japan when she was a teenager, and she and her older brother—Brooke's father—still preferred to hold most of their conversations in Japanese.

"You really don't like what I have on?"

Isuzu brandished her bottle of disinfectant spray. "It very casual."

"So?"

"Fine. Whatever you do, take umbrella. I look at sky just now and I see rain up there. Radio say big wind and hail, too."

"Yes, mom. I've got a sweater in my car."

5:00 p.m.

"You're in luck!" Danny said as he plugged the shop vac in and handed the nozzle to Heather.

"Why doesn't it feel that way?" Heather gave him a bleary stare.

Danny's chuckle was filled with empathy. "I'm talking about my helping you get this mess cleaned up. Jen's ultrasound appointment was canceled, so I can help you get dried out." He turned to Robbie. "How did a squirt like you get so much water on the floor?"

"Uh-oh," Robbie shouted and pointed at the small lake that had swallowed his feet.

Danny tickled his bare belly and teased him till Robbie was squealing with laughter. "Did you do all this 'uh-oh' stuff all by yourself, Mr. Mister?"

Heaving a long, tired sigh, Heather followed the direction of Danny's curious gaze with her own. There were still standing puddles in the bathroom and down the hall, and the living room carpet made squishy noises as she walked across. The air was hot and damp, like the steam room down at The Pump. She'd soaked up as much as she could with bath towels and then wrung them outside, but that was hard, slow work made even tougher because she had to keep an eye on Robbie at the same time. Lord only knew what the squirt would get it in his head to do next.

"Okay. Here's the deal. I'm going to get the fans out of my truck and you'll need to let them run for a day or two. Then, I'm going to go under the house and see where the water is running. But before that, why don't we start vacuuming up as much as we can and pump it outside, okay?"

"Okay." Heather sighed a huge whoosh of relief. "When we're done, I need to run get some milk for Robbie's dinner. Would you mind if we did that while you check the crawl-space? I hear there's a storm coming and I don't want to be out in it."

"No problem. If I'd have known you were out of milk," Danny was looking at Robbie now and talking in a silly voice, "I'd have brought you a cow!"

"Moo!" Robbie shouted.

"He's a sharp kid." Danny tousled the boy's hair and then ran out to get the fans.

She watched him muscle his equipment out of the back of his truck with no little envy. Even in air so thick and close, he was such a hard worker for other people. Heather may have been able to get pregnant at the drop of a hat, but Jen Strohacker was the lucky one.

5:55 p.m.

Yielding to Isuzu's innate fashion sense, Abigail ran upstairs and changed into some business-like slacks and a blouse before she left to meet the guy who was building the food cart. Just for kicks—and because she had a little time to kill—she also restyled her hair and touched up her lipstick. It would be intimidating enough if this guy was even half as good-looking as everyone claimed. Since she'd been such a shrew on the phone, she really wanted to look her best when she groveled and begged his forgiveness. She even grabbed an umbrella on her way out the door, but she'd never admit that to Isuzu. Zuzu was bossy enough.

Danny's hardware and lumberyard was over a mile east of Old Town so Abigail opted not to walk. A Quick In Go convenience store at the strip mall across the street from Danny's had a parking spot right in front. Perfect. The grocery list she'd written that morning was tucked into her purse so after her meeting, she could just pop into the QIG and pick up a package of batteries and some milk for breakfast tomorrow.

As she got out of the car, the blustery weather grabbed her carefully styled hair and used it to give her face a good slapping. Oh, she was having some fun now. A glance at her watch told her she was late. Her sigh of frustration felt as if it had been sucked out of her lungs by the stiff breezes. So much for the good impression she'd intended. As she trotted across Homestead Avenue, another gust of wind whipped her umbrella inside out and nearly tugged her off her feet. Why had she brought this useless umbrella? The wind was nearly strong enough to turn her into Mary Poppins.

"From now on, I'm ignoring you, Zuzu," she muttered under her breath, as she trudged down the sidewalk, across Danny's parking lot and to the entrance of the hardware store. Once there, she struggled to get her umbrella turned right-side out and closed so that she could pass through the front doors. Maybe the predictions about a storm being on the way were right for once, she thought as she was blown inside.

Abigail was grateful for the sudden sense of calm the store afforded as she adjusted her clothes. A quick glance around told her that there was nobody behind the desk. He had said six, hadn't he? She checked her watch. Surely he'd wait five minutes for her?

"Hello?" she called out. She knew Danny was taking Jen to get an ultrasound and that Handsome-guy . . . wait . . . she dug his business card out of her purse . . . Justin Girard was manning the desk for him. She sighed and dropped her umbrella on the counter. Behind her, a display of lady's tools with flowers on them caught her eye. Might as well kill some time shopping while she waited. Oh, how cute! Didn't she need a tiny hammer with flowers on it? She was comparing all the color options when she heard someone come into the store from the lumberyard.

"Wheew," a masculine voice muttered from the door that led out to the lumber area. "That is some seriously fierce wind."

Her heart went into a freefall as she looked up, then glanced quickly away and spun around. Oh, good grief! *It was him! The guy she'd danced with last night! And her hair!* Tiny hammer still in hand, Abigail reached up to finger comb some of the damage the wind had done. Ducking behind a tall display of carpet samples, she fished her compact out of her purse and checked her lipstick. It was mostly still there.

"Can I help you?"

Abigail spun around again, startled. Suddenly he was standing right behind her.

His expression slowly morphed from business to surprise to pleasure. "Well, hi there! Hey, I didn't think I'd . . . you know . . . see you so soon."

"Yeah, I know! Me neither!" Her heart pulled out of its nosedive and soared. He was every bit as handsome as she'd remembered. And then some. In this light, his eyes were even bluer than they'd seemed last night.

"You're looking for a hammer?" Arms over his chest, legs spread wide, he tilted his head and grinned at her.

"A hammer? Oh!" She glanced at the silly tool she still clutched. "No! No. I was just . . . you know . . . looking."

"Ah. Because you know, we have a matching screwdriver. And a tape measure. I could get you outfitted with a tool belt, too, if you want?" He had perfect teeth and the best creases at the corners of his mouth.

Abigail laughed, her cheeks growing as pink as the brilliant clouds that streaked the horizon. "No, really, that's sweet but I'm not all that . . . handy."

Propping his elbow on a stack of boxes, he settled in for a conversation. "So how come you're not out line dancing on a Saturday night?"

"Me? Oh, that was just a one-time thing."

"Really?" There was approval in the question.

"It was a bachelorette party. I don't—" some nervous twitters augmented her babblings, "—you know, generally hang out at bars . . . and stuff, like a lot of single people do." It felt as if fire ants were racing up her neck. "Not that I'm saying *you* do! I mean, because I guess you do . . . Sometimes? For burgers with friends? Not that that's b-bad or anything, I . . . should shut up now."

"No! I . . . no. Don't. I . . ." He palmed the back of his neck and seemed to be searching the ceiling for words. "I gotta be honest with you. I wasn't going to go back to dance with you on Friday."

"Oh." Lips stretched into a bright smile she chirped, "me neither." Oh, she wanted to curl up and die. The tips of her ears flamed and her stomach lurched.

His smile was relieved. "Really? Because I—"

"No, no." She laughed breezily. "No need to explain. I get it. Trust me. I get it." *What? What did she get? She didn't get it. Not at all. Change the subject! Change it now.* "So! You work here?"

"No, not really. But listen, I just want to explain about the other night—"

"You don't work here?" She did not want to hear about the other night. She was in no mood to be dumped by a guy she'd never even dated.

His brows furrowed at her abrupt change of subject. "I, uh . . . I have an office in the back. Danny and I work together on a lot of small building projects and handyman gigs locally." He shrugged, "But, right now, I'm meeting some uptight booster club member about some awnings for a food cart charity deal. You?"

Abigail's jaw sagged. *Him?* He was the guy she'd chewed out on the phone? *Ack! No!* "I'm—" she winced and her eyes slid closed, "—your uptight booster." Could this day *get* any worse?

"Oh?" Confusion further diminished his smile as he processed. "You? You're the one I talked to on the phone?" She nodded guiltily. Off in the distance a storm siren began to wail. She wanted to join in. His gaze flitted from her face and out the window.

"Doesn't that sound mean we need to run for cover now? Last time it went off, Danny had us go across the street to the strip mall to get his wife . . ." his voice trailed off as he peered up into a sky that was beginning to look seriously angry.

"Actually, no. We get those all spring in Rawston. If you ran for cover every time one went off you'd be hiding in your bathtub for three solid months. Trust me. They'll turn it off. They always do." She didn't want to be distracted by the stupid siren. She needed to make amends and then get out of here and never lay eyes on him again. No problem. She had a job offer in LA. She'd just go home and pack. Tonight.

"Yeah, but I heard the weatherman talking about a storm warning and they said—"

"I know. They say that every day." The need to correct his bad impression of her was as urgent as the siren's shrill howl. "Anyway, before we get started on this awning business, I really feel like I need to apologize. For the phone thing. And, you know, explain. It's just that I've never been good with bureaucracy. I guess I just had to jump through too many hoops to get my puny little hair salon off the ground," she said and smiled at him. Gracious. Tall, dark, and handsome. "Anyway, city hall wanted a new storefront. Then they wanted a cutesy porch. The chamber of commerce wanted flowers and special paint and all this charm and who got to pay for it?"

"You?"

Abigail could tell he was only listening with half an ear. The blasted, confounded, cursed siren was ruining everything. Unflappable, she told herself and took a deep breath. Project an attitude of being unflapped. Normal. "Yeah. Me." Though she only had his partial attention, she plunged ahead. "So, when they go and slap this ridiculous permit thing on us," she shot him a chummy glance, "and you *know* it's going to cost a fortune in fees . . . I just freaked. Do you think you can forgive me?"

"Sure, sure," he said, clearly agitated by the debris now blowing by and hitting the cars and trees. A recycling bin had tipped over and a blizzard of cans was tumbling and scraping across the parking lot. Newspapers blew past and lodged for a moment in trees and bushes before they broke free.

The siren had totally distracted him. "Sounds like you're under a lot of pressure," he muttered. "You're sure we shouldn't head to a shelter somewhere or something?"

The sound of a second siren joined the first, frustrating Abigail to no end. It was time to cut her losses and leave him with the impression that she was just the uptight booster he thought she was. "You know, you're right. I really should get going. I'll see you later, okay?" She tried to sound breezy. Unperturbed.

"No, wait." He swung to look at her, his jaw muscles jumping. "I don't feel good about you going out there. The sky is really looking like it's getting ready to hurl some cats and dogs at the very least. Why don't you wait here?"

"Oh, that's really thoughtful and everything, but I've got to run. We can finish this up another time, when it's not so . . . loud." Or never.

Justin transferred his gaze back out the window, his expression pensive.

She jumped as a massive flash of lightning illuminated his profile. The entire room lit up and the building vibrated from the ensuing crash of thunder.

"Just another day here in paradise?" Justin turned and quirked a brow at her as it began to rain. Big, fat plops spattering the ground.

"Okay." Abigail licked her lips and turned to look out the window with him. The sky had grown unnaturally dark. "That was a little radical. Yeah. I need to head home."

"About that . . . . I don't . . ." He scratched his head and seemed to lose his thread as the sky opened up and rain fell sideways.

Abigail watched with dismay as the windows grew foggy. This was going to soak her to the skin. The sirens were giving her a headache.

"I'm beginning to think this isn't your garden-variety tornado watch. Or is this," he inclined his head at the row of trees that bowed like Japanese soldiers before a battle, "normal for you Rawstonians?"

"We do get the wind and thunderstorms out here and this is the fifth, maybe sixth, tornado watch in less than a month," Abigail said and sighed. "Anyway, real quick before I let you get to a shelter, about the food cart? The red tape of the permits on the awning situation seems insurmountable to achieve by the Quilt Fair. So, just forget it, okay? I'm going to figure something else out. There is no money left to pay the food cart mafia for their ridiculous permits. I'll just rent a couple of those tent canopy things, whatever you call them. One of those outdoor things . . . you know . . ." her laughter was stilted. "No problem. Maybe if I hurry, I can do it now. Problem solved, ta-da!"

As Abigail triggered the automatic doors, she could see the sun, low on the horizon, peeking through the clouds. The storm seemed to have passed. Time to bolt.

"Seriously. I don't think you should go out there."

"I know. And I thank you for your concern. But trust me. I grew up here. I'll be fine. Thanks. Okay, bye-bye."

Leaving her ridiculous umbrella on the counter where she'd left it, and before he could respond, she rushed outside. The wind and the rain felt wonderfully cool on her blazing cheeks as she darted across the parking lot to the street corner and beat on the walk button with her fist. Her car was just across the street. She'd never been so eager to climb inside and lock the doors. And have a good cry.

7

Fingers entwined, Brooke Nakamura and Nick Gleason stepped out of the blast furnace that was the RHS gymnasium and into the cooler air near the propped-open back doors. The temperature was changing quickly outside, and Brooke reveled in the fresh air that dried her neck and face. The music was alive and pumping and jumped outside after them, giving Brooke the blissful feeling that she and Nick were still at the party, but alone, too.

Across the parking lot, the high school's tennis courts and batting cages loomed in the distance. Scoreboards towered at both ends of the football field, proclaiming this land to be the Home of the Rawston Raiders. Next week, a handful of food carts would be set up on the fifty-yard line, as the area would be transformed for the Rawston Taste portion of the Quilt Fair. Brook knew her dad, mom, and Aunt Zuzu would work their tails off to make a ton of sushi to donate to the school's fundraiser. It would be fun.

Brooke breathed deeply. Life was good, here in Rawston. Beautiful. The sun was setting and the sky was moody and glorious; swirling and billowing with excitement, just like her dress. The wind felt good after the stuffiness of the crowded gym. It was wall-to-wall people in there.

"Can you hear me?" Nick shouted at her and she laughed at his dopey expression.

"No! Can you hear me?" she hollered back. The bass had throbbed so long and so loud that her ears were ringing.

"No!" His grin mischievous, Nick tugged her past the doors and around the corner into the shadows of the basketball shed. The covered area was little more than a tall lean-to, jutting from the gym. It was mainly used for one-on-one and intramural games when the gym was occupied. He leaned against the brick wall, and held her so they stood facing each other. She tucked the netting of her skirt between her legs, to keep the wind from whipping it and snagging it on the bricks.

"Having fun?" he shouted.

"Yes." Brooke nodded and wrapped both of her hands around his forearms and could see her nails twinkling in the waning sunlight. She felt beautiful when she was with Nick. Abigail had done amazing things with her hair, and her dress was perfect. This night was perfect. Nick was perfect. "It's magic."

"Yeah. It is." The song changed and the tempo slowed and thrummed pleasantly in Brooke's chest. Nick pulled her arms up, around his neck and he locked his hands at the small of her back. Leaning in, he brought his mouth to her ear. "Dance?"

"Out here? Just the two of us? Now? "

His nod was broad and playful. "Yes! Why? *Can't hear the music?*"

"*What?*" she hollered back and rested her head against his shoulder as they began to sway to the beat. This was so fantastic. To be young and free and wrapped in the arms of someone who was not her brother and not yelling at her for missing a cue. Tyler, in fact, was still in the gym, tearing up the dance floor with at least a dozen different partners. Hopefully, he wasn't trying to spin or toss them or chastise them for not hitting their mark. She grinned at the images that flitted through her head. All the girls wanted a turn with the Olympic hopeful, and Tyler basked in the attention.

"You look awesome tonight, Brooke. Beautiful." Nick's words were like helium. They made her so giddy she clutched him tighter, just so she wouldn't float away. "And you are the best dancer out there."

"No, you are!" She protested, giggling.

"Bull. Your brother is ten times better than me."

"No way. Besides, he's my brother, which means he'll never be as good a partner as you." She could feel him inhale, his chest expanding against hers.

"Brooke . . . I've wanted to talk to you about something for a really long time, but," he said and laughed, "I guess I haven't had the nerve." His face was pressed against the side of her head now and his voice tickled her ear.

She nodded because the way he was holding her, she got the feeling he didn't want her staring at him as he spoke.

"I know we've been best friends for a couple of years . . . but . . . I . . . I think it's more than just . . . you know . . . friendship now, Brooke."

She knew. And she agreed. Bubbles, like those in a freshly poured goblet of sparkling water rose in her belly and crowded her throat. She pulled back just enough so that he could hear her. "Me, too!"

His arms tightened around her waist, and she responded by locking her fingers more firmly at the nape of his neck. Above the beat of the music and the pounding of their own hearts, neither of them could hear the hail begin to drum on the shed's roof.

Nor could they hear the sirens screaming back in town.

6:26 p.m.

Just as the light finally changed to walk and Abigail stepped onto Homestead Avenue, it began to hail in earnest. But this was not the innocent marble-sized hail that would build up like so much slush and then quickly melt away. Oh, no. This was snowball-sized hail and looked as if it had been packed together from marble-sized hail. By monster fists. And hurled by those same fists in some macabre game of dodgeball. Behind her—and over the wail of yet another storm siren—she could hear it bouncing off the few cars that were still parked at Danny's Hardware. It slammed her shoulders and back, and it hurt worse than paintballs shot point-blank.

Head down, purse up, she wobbled and slid toward the Quick In Go. Luckily, she favored large purses because hers was now pulling double duty as a hard hat. What had seemed like such a brilliant parking plan at the time was a major inconvenience now. It was nearly impossible to walk on these slippery golf- and grapefruit-sized balls of ice. And dodging them was even trickier. The mere block to her car seemed suddenly endless. And merciless.

Just as she was considering diving into a hedgerow and hoping for the best, she heard a pickup truck pull up beside her and a familiar voice shout, "Get in!" The driver's side door swung open and Justin reached for her arm. Abigail felt herself being propelled over his lap and into the safety of the seat beside him. He turned his flashers on as all around them they were suddenly assaulted by icy shrapnel. The drumming on the roof and windows was ear splitting and terrifying.

"Good grief," Abigail cried, clutching her purse to her chest and squinting at the onslaught. "This is insane! All this ice? In all this heat? What on earth? "

"You've never seen anything like this before?" Justin asked.

Eyes wide, she blinked at him. "Not like this, no way."

83

"Where are you parked?" His mouth was set in a grim line.

Abigail pointed across the street to the next driveway. "At the Quick In Go." The noise on his roof sounded like the drums Abigail had heard at the Samoan dance showcase at last year's Quilt Fair. Bongos. Tattooing out some sort of crazed anti-rhythm.

"I'll drive you to your car, but I really think we'd be better off inside somewhere. I don't know how long a windshield can stand up to this kind of battering." Slowly, Justin accelerated, slipping a bit before he gained traction and began to move.

"Thank you." Gnawing her lower lip, Abigail peered up at the black clouds that were circling like buzzards over a carcass. "This is not normal."

"This huge hail?"

"And that. Up there. What is happening in the sky," she explained and pointed to a swirling mass of black thunderclouds.

"Whoa. Looks like the mother ship is trying to land."

"Yeah," she breathed. It really did. "Oh, you missed the turnoff."

"Sorry. I'll turn around up here in the factory lot." The hail had turned the parking area white in a bizarre hailstorm that had steam rising from the hot asphalt. In the rearview mirror, she could see that the truck's tires left a huge black circle in their wake.

Abigail's gaze jerked back to the awesome activity in the sky. The atmosphere had an almost otherworldly feel. Blessedly, the hail had slowed and finally stopped, but the rain started again. And this time, the downpour was even more torrential than the last. Justin had the one windshield wiper that still worked—his, thankfully—on high speed.

As he pulled back into the street he frowned, staring straight ahead. "What's . . . that?" There was something in his voice. Something that made her blood run cold.

"Where?"

He tapped the windshield, but Abigail could tell that he was looking into the horizon. "Over Walterville way."

Since the hail had broken the windshield wiper on her side, she scooted over, next to him and peered into the twilight. Vision was dodgy because of the rain and the streaks the wiper left, but when a bolt of lightning lit the sky, it illuminated two distinct, boiling, heart-stopping, black masses of air that seemed to be on a collision course.

Abigail watched as the clouds collided in a spectacular burst of lightning. Then, three funnels, one after the other, like the long, bony fingers of the grim reaper, dropped out of this unholy union and beckoned them just before they touched the earth and began a ghoulish dance.

Justin snapped the radio on.

"...*twenty minutes ago! In fact, three individual tornados converged into what we believe to be an EF4, possibly EF5 tornado coming Rawston's way, and it's one of several spawned by a supercell that has been growing and wreaking havoc for miles. Reports are coming in from the Walterville area now that indicate large-scale devastation of the northeastern quadrant of that town. The number of fatalities continues to grow from the already unthinkable dozens, and wind speeds reach between two and three hundred miles per hour. If you can hear this broadcast and live in the Rawston area, take cover now! We are getting reports of debris in the air! It's already leveled much of Walterville and shows no signs of letting up as it travels toward the Rawston, Southshire areas. Again, if you are just joining us, an extremely dangerous and deadly tornado touched down in Broadacre twenty minutes ago, traveled through Walterville, and is heading toward Rawston. If you have a basement or crawlspace, get down there and take cover immediately! If not, go to the room in the center-most windowless section of your house, bathroom, closet, under the stairs! If you can cover yourself with a mattress, do it!*

6:52 p.m.

Someone was screaming. More than one someone. Bob Ray groaned and shot an irritated glance at the ceiling. A brawl? Now? This was going to ruin his fun. He pushed off the spot where he'd been lounging against the bar and enjoying a very deep, very sexy conversation with his new friend, Renee. On tiptoe, he backed up and looked around.

Finally, he located the source of the noise and frowned. It was a couple. Looked like they were dressed in motorcycle leathers. They looked pretty bedraggled. Reaching into a cabinet on the wall behind the bar, he turned off the sound systems and everyone stopped talking at once. As Bob Ray came out front to where Renee stood, he could finally understand what these two were screaming.

"Tornado on the ground! And it's headed right at us!" the man shrieked as he barreled into the center of the room. "We're in its path and there is no time to escape!"

The woman who hurried along at his side was trembling and clutching his arm and crying. "It's *huge!*"

"Probably a mile wide! Maybe more. It's got to be a killer! Take cover! *Now!* We're outta time!" Panic ensued. Women screamed, men shouted and cursed, and dozens dove under the pool tables. Other people began to unload one of the two supply closets. Renee's eyes were huge with terror as she turned them on Bob Ray.

"Do something!" she shrieked, her fear bordering on hysteria. She clawed at his arms with her nails, both pushing and pulling him into action. *"Help me!"* Her feet were as leaden as his and they both stood—the frozen core of a frenzied mob.

Bob Ray's heart was pounding so hard he was scared it was going to explode. Thousands of thoughts rushed through his brain, just like they used to out on the football field when a giant linebacker would come soaring through the air at him, and he had to get rid of the ball. Fast. As he tried to locate and gather his senses, people jostled and thrashed and shoved him out of the way. Some even ran outside. Maybe to see how close the twister was. Maybe to try and out run it in their cars. Should he be doing that, too? Immediately, the single and multi-occupant restrooms were filled and locked. The first closet was crowded and the door pulled shut and blockaded.

Finally springing into action after what seemed like a lifetime of indecision, Bob Ray and a couple of men who hadn't yet taken cover feverishly tossed equipment out of the second closet. Renee stood by, pupils dilated, and screamed along with the thunder just beyond the ceiling. While Bob Ray was pushing several heavy boxes out of the way, the men jumped inside and pulled the hysterical Renee in with them. The building was vibrating now, and the wind was shrieking like a teakettle boiling over. Before Bob Ray could get back across the room, Renee had slammed the door shut. He jiggled the handle, his heart choking him with fear. *"Open up!"* he shrieked, and swore and beat on the door. "I'm still out here!"

Renee screamed at the men who cowered inside with her. "No! There is no time left! Don't open it! *Don't!*"

Fury had him savagely kicking the door. Inside, Renee screamed curses at him, and the men hiding with her held the knob tight and shouted for him to stop. Something huge crashed into the side of the building, and Bob Ray finally accepted the fact that they had no intention of taking a chance to save his sorry hide.

On instinct now, he sprinted back behind the bar. Yanking open the industrial, half-sized refrigerator that was built into its underbelly, he flung out jars of maraschino cherries, lemon and lime wedges and everything else they kept in there. This refrigerator had been special order—made to handle a thriving business, yet stay compact and out of the way. Had to be at least a cubic yard of space in there, probably more. He'd fit. Barely. He ripped out the racks, squeezed inside, and using the little shelves on the door as a handle, pulled it shut.

It was pitch black and—except for the roar of blood pulsing like water through a fire hose in his ears—quiet in there. So. Were these the last minutes of his life? Was this all there was? Was he going to die in a refrigerator, under a bar? Was that his destiny?

Bile rose in his throat as he remembered Heather. How were Heather and Robbie doing? Were they in the tornado's path? A terror he'd never known gripped him as he imagined them in that trailer as a twister bore down. Tears were wetting his cheeks as he began to bargain with God. *"God!* I know I'm a loser! But please, don't take it out on my kid and Heather. They're good, God. Please. *Please*, take me if you have to, but let them live. And if you let me live, I promise I'll be a better man—a better father and a better husband. Please, God, *please."*

Head wedged between his knees, Bob Ray cried like a baby. The woman he'd been ready to throw his marriage vows out the window for had just sentenced him to death. Heather never would have done that. Never.

She was good and kind and sweet to him even when he treated her like dirt. Though she'd been just as young and scared as he'd been before the wedding, she'd done the right thing. And, even though it had to be grueling, being stuck in a broken-down dump of a trailer all day with a baby, she was a good mom to Robbie. Always buckled him in his carseat and played with him and prayed for him and treated him like he was a blessing. Unlike him. He couldn't remember the last time he'd even touched the kid. And the weird thing was, he loved that little boy. More than anything. Robbie was his *son*. Just a baby. So sweet.

Bob Ray's jagged sighs were filled with self-loathing and regret.

It was hell, just sitting here waiting. And waiting. Everything seemed to be happening in slow motion now. Then, just as he was beginning to wonder if this whole storm thing was maybe some kind of monster con-job by the two people who'd come screaming through the front door, his ears popped and the air seemed to whoosh from the tiny refrigerator as if it had been vacuum sealed.

Suddenly, Bob Ray was certain that if the tornado didn't kill him, a complete lack of oxygen would.

8

6:53 p.m.

Robbie was screaming in her ear as Heather frantically yanked down the red velvet curtains that hung over the Rawston Christian Church's baptistery and flung them into the water tank. Thankfully, it had been drained after the last round of baptisms. As carefully as she could, she climbed inside and, once she had herself and Robbie well padded, she pulled the wooden cover over their heads. Settling into the darkness, she turned them both on their sides. As much as possible, without hurting him, Heather tried to cover her baby with her body and the yards of fabric.

"Shhh, Robbie, baby. Mommy's right here," she whispered, her voice shaking both from exertion and emotion. "We're just going to play the hiding game right now, okay? Like we do with Daddy sometimes?"

Robbie's shrieks quieted some as he listened to her muffled voice. "Da-da?"

"Yes, Daddy is coming to find us so you have to be really quiet while we hide, okay?"

Robbie's little body shuddered and he sighed. Heather drew him infinitesimally closer into her embrace. Just before she'd torn the curtains down, she'd stuffed a shivering Robbie under her T-shirt and zipped her sweatshirt up over them both. Then, she locked her arms around his tiny, chilled body and began to murmur her prayers in his ears. She prayed that the arched timbers over the baptismal would hold. She prayed that the baptismal would stay put. She prayed for Robbie. She prayed for herself. And she prayed for Bob Ray, wherever he was.

When she was done praying for her guys, she started on everyone else she could think of who was perched, like so many dust bunnies, in the path of this giant vacuum cleaner.

After that, she asked for forgiveness for kicking in the church's kitchen window. But the building had been locked, and she hadn't known what else to do. In a frenzy, she'd beaten the remaining shards out with a rock, and then dragged a wailing Robbie in after her. Panting, gasping, wheezing, she'd surveyed the building, her eyes searching, searching, searching, her mind spinning.

Safe. Safe, God, what would be the safest place? It was then, she saw the cross, suspended above the pulpit, and its vertical beam seemed to be pointing to the baptistery. "Thank you, Jesus," she'd breathed and dashed, with Robbie hollering under her right arm, up the steps to the back room's entrance. She'd set Robbie down and muscled the cover back to see a deep, well-supported space, just perfect for the two of them.

While she hunkered down over Robbie, Heather also asked forgiveness for everything else she could think of, including bringing Robbie into a teenaged marriage and messing up her and Bob Ray's lives with the stupid, selfish choices she'd made. And, when she felt that she'd done all she could and whispered her final "amen," she kissed her son's cheeks and told him how precious he was. And that he was a good boy and a blessing, no matter what anybody else might ever say to him. His cheeks were so plump and soft and his hair still just tufts of peach fuzz. She inhaled his sweet Cheerios and diaper

powder babyness and tried not to let him know she was crying. Because it wouldn't be long now.

She hoped that when the devil she'd seen earlier touched
down to do battle with God's house, that she and Robbie could
stay together. Robbie's head grew heavy on her arm and his
breathing slow and regular. The little stinker had fallen sound
asleep. She smiled as a peace—the kind that passed all understanding, she guessed—began to calm the terror in her heart.

6:54 p.m.

Abigail clutched Justin's arm as they stood inside the Quick
In Go and watched the grim reports coming in on the Weather
Channel. Wind whistled through the gap in the glass entrance
doors and customers milled, nerves strung tight, wringing
their hands. As they paced, they wondered what would
happen and what, if anything, they should do to protect themselves. Several were on cell phones with friends and family,
getting and giving updates. They found Jen Strohacker standing in the back with the store's manager, anxiously watching
the TV. She must have come in from her tanning shop two
doors down in this same strip mall. When she saw Justin, she
rushed to him, her eyes round with worry. "You haven't seen
Danny, have you?"

"No. I thought he'd be with you."

"No. No. My ultrasound appointment was canceled. He ran
over to Bob Ray and Heather's to help with a flooding problem.
He's not answering his cell phone . . ." Her voice rose and her
hands shook.

"Jen," Justin pulled her hands into his and said, "I think
phone service might be sketchy at this point. He's probably
already home."

Sucking in a huge breath, she bobbed her head. "You're probably right. I'm just on edge because of the baby and everything."

Abigail glanced back and forth between them, sensing how much they both wanted to believe, seeing the worry, palpable, vibrating and pulling them all to the brink. She had no profound words of wisdom or comfort. Nothing but feelings of inadequacy and terror. She reached out and took Jen's hand, as much to comfort her, as to comfort herself.

The bearded man who sported a turban and a nametag that read *Desh Pradesh, QIG Manager* rushed out from behind the register and addressed the dozen or so people who were seeking shelter in his store. "May I have everyone's attention, please? People, I believe the storm will no doubt be causing us some damage within a few moments. First, I ask that you all try to stay calm. I have had some emergency preparedness training." He'd located several flashlights and held them up. "Why don't some of you take these and make sure the batteries work? If not, the new batteries are at the end of that aisle. Also, the first aid kit is here with me." He held it up.

"I hope we will not be needing it. Extra fresh water is stored in the back. Help yourselves to anything you need to make your stay more comfortable. And I mean anything. Except the till." Everyone chuckled nervously. "And ma'am? The one who is expecting a blessing, I have a chair here for you, if you wish. My wife also is expecting soon, and I know standing at this stage can be tiring."

With a grateful smile, Jen's knees buckled as she sank into the chair he offered.

"Is there anyone you need to call?" Justin whispered in Abigail's ear.

She licked her dry lips. "I should call my aunt," she whispered back, but wondered if her shaking fingers would be able to dial.

"Good. I want to check in with my grandparents." Standing arm in arm, they found their phones and called their families. Justin's grandparents were safe and heading to a shelter in Southshire with some neighbors. Abigail couldn't reach Aunt Selma or Guadalupe at the quilt shop, so she could only hope that they'd gone to Aunt Selma's together. Aunt Selma had a full basement with a storm shelter built in.

"They're saying it looks like the storm might miss Southshire, so I guess my family is okay." Justin pulled her close and rubbed her shoulder. His voice was just as compelling as it had been last night, but now it carried the timbre of comfort. And strength. She was so glad he'd come after her. Going through this without him would be unthinkable.

"What do you—" she began, but was interrupted by a young woman with small children in tow as she came bursting into the store.

"Don't go out there!" she shrieked, her breath coming in ragged gasps as she herded her kids deep into the room and away from the windows. "It's heading straight at us! And . . ." she was sobbing now, "it's enormous!" Her kids, one on her hip and two preschoolers were blubbering along with her. Behind her, the entire sky was roiling and black now, lit only by sudden flashes of lightning. The flying debris was getting bigger now, sheets of metal roofing flipping and whipping across the parking lot, as rain battered the Quick In Go's front windows. In the distance, sirens were wailing like Irish banshees, forecasting certain death.

Tension had them all gripped in its clutches as everyone turned their attention back to the TV. The Weather channel now showed the tornado barreling down on Old Town.

"... once again, the tornado has crossed Fisher's Mill Highway and has reached the outskirts of Rawston, and we are watching it here in the studio as Doppler Radar tracks its progress. This weather system is producing violent winds and debris; if you are outside, take cover immediately ... we are getting a report right now that the tornado is heading directly toward Old Town Rawston ... we've got video ... you can see that it is a very powerful tornado, and its base is estimated to be at least a half-mile in width, maybe twice that ..."

The funnel was massive. Abigail's eyes slid shut and sorrow spilled down her cheeks. *No. Please. No.* Not her beautiful shop. She battled back a wave of nausea as she looped her arms around Justin's waist and pushed her face into the comforting softness of his flannel shirt. Alternately, he rubbed and patted her back, and crooned some calming nonsense in her ear. Oh, how far they'd come in less than twenty-four hours.

The sound of the front doors slamming open had them spinning around. Chaz came flying in, shouting into his cell phone. Tripoli Cleaners was in the other arm of this U-shaped mall, directly across the parking lot. "Get out of your apartment! Take your mama and aunt down to the basement, Kaylee! Hide in the middle, in that furnace room! The one with no windows, hear me? Now! No! Don't take anything. Just run! Run! Go, go, go! Now! Yes, yes, baby. I love you, too. I'm fine. And I'm praying for you, baby. I love you ... You're breaking up. I'm losing you, baby. Are you there? Kaylee?" His head dropped back on his shoulders, and he squeezed his eyes shut. "Jesus, please. Please, keep them safe." A heavy sigh rushed out in a groan and his shoulders flagged.

Abigail's breathing came in rapid gasps, and her heart was racing. Panic had her feeling as if she was going to fall. "*Kaylee*," she whispered.

"You okay?" Justin asked.

She whimpered. She knew she probably had to be cutting off his circulation by this point, but couldn't seem to unclench her grip on his arm.

Chaz stepped over to them and dragged a hand across his face. "Kaylee says the tornado has come as far as Fisher's Mill Highway." Chaz glanced at Abigail and added, "That place you ladies held her party last night is out there."

Abigail swallowed and nodded.

"It's nearly at Old Town now," Chaz said. They all sighed, at a loss for words. "I'm not sure that this is the best place for us to be . . ."

Justin glanced around. "I know. But we don't really have time to move now."

Desh covered the mouthpiece of his phone and said, "The QIG main office is requesting a head count from each of our local stores. Can everyone please come gather here, at the counter?" The three people, two men and a woman, who stood watching TV, turned to comply, as did the young woman and her children. Abigail guessed that the man who wore a white shirt and tie was some kind of businessman, just getting off work. The woman was middle-aged and her basket was loaded with batteries and canned goods. The second man was older, and looked as if he hadn't bathed in several weeks. Homeless, Abigail deduced.

Desh was getting a headcount when the power went out. Silence fell and they were plunged into darkness for a second before lightning illuminated a man standing in the doorway. People squealed at the ghostly apparition and one of the children began to shriek. Haruo Nakamura, normally a very reserved and quiet-spoken man, stood, his hair blowing in the wind, his arms beckoning and shouting at the top of his lungs. "Come on! I have big walk-in refrigerator, no window! Reinforced steel! There is still time!"

"No!" the young mother cried and gathered her babies to her knees. *"Don't go!"*

"Ma'am," Justin said, and strode toward her, Chaz on his heels. "We don't have time to argue. If what you say is true, you're better off with us. Let's go." He picked up one of her wailing kids and Chaz went for the other. *"Now!"* he shouted over his shoulder and she jumped to follow. Abigail helped Jen to her feet and they, too, plunged into the storm.

6:55 p.m.

Selma Louise Tully had lived through one of these monsters before. Barely. But, she'd learned a few things about preparedness. Unfortunately, she'd become complacent in the last four or five decades. She'd begun to ignore the siren's warnings. Forgotten a lot of the terror. Birthed and raised a family and gotten old and a little addled. And so, *she* was prepared, because Clyde had insisted, after the last big one back in '66.

And, Guadalupe was with her; so that made one more body safe and sound.

But Abigail and Elsa and many of her other friends and neighbors were God only knew where, right now. Like Clyde had with her, she should have insisted that they hide here in the special shelter he'd built for this very day. Her next-door neighbors had all been so cavalier only a short time ago, turning down Selma's urgent invitations to join her and Guadalupe in the basement shelter with amused thanks, but not really believing the storm would amount to much. Selma sent up prayers over them all now.

Because they'd lost everything in the Topeka, Kansas, tornado of '66, her husband had become obsessed with beating the weather at its sometimes murderous game. He'd moved his family to another state. He'd studied European bomb shelters. He'd designed and redesigned the perfect family shelter for the perfect storm. And he'd labored, long and hard, a modern-day Noah, building the edifice that would one day see his family through whatever nature might get in its head to hurl at them.

The corned beef hash had finally burst out of the cans after twenty or thirty years of disuse, and most of the candles and other emergency supplies such as flashlights, had been pilfered by the kids for backyard campouts and sleepovers. Every couple of years or so, Selma would head down to the shelter beneath the basement and restock a few supplies in order to honor Clyde's wishes, but largely . . . she'd forgotten about the place.

Nearly fifty years was a long time to outfit and maintain a tool that was so rarely needed. And yet, if the news was even half as bad as was being forecasted on the Weather Channel right now, the time for Clyde's shelter had finally come. Two decades after the man himself, had passed.

"Jesus, have mercy on us. We're in the valley of the shadow, here," Selma whispered into the gnarled knuckles of her folded hands as she and Guadalupe stood on the threshold of her wrap-around porch to better view the ominous funnel in the distance.

Guadalupe's head was bowed as she prayed over her daughter, Elsa, who was in the high school gym at prom, but even so, Selma could tell she was crying. She dug a tissue out of her pocket and tucked it in Guadalupe's hand. "Elsa will be alright, honey," she murmured. "I've been praying for that kid since the day she was born, you know."

Guadalupe sniffed, her laughter, jerky. She blew her nose and blotted her eyes. "I know, my dear friend."

From where the two women were standing together at Selma's front door they could see that the twister over on the Walterville side looked to be barreling up Fisher's Mill Road. Selma lived ten minutes north and west of there. Over the years, people had tried to get her to move closer into town. Save time and gas, they said. But because Clyde had slaved over this place for so many years, building a safe, comfortable haven for her and the kids, she just couldn't make herself move.

The wind was really tearing up the street now. "Shall we head down to the shelter?" Selma asked and tugged on Guadalupe's sleeve. "Looks like it's still south of us. But it could surprise us and turn."

"I hope not," Guadalupe said and stepped inside after Selma. They bolted the doors and closed the windows, praying all the while. One last glance out the front window . . . and then the strangest thing happened.

A Ford Mustang, its turn signal flashing, horn blaring and doors flapping—like a winged Pegasus heading south for the winter—made a perfect four point landing on the neighbor's roof. It didn't take a full minute for the two women to make it down to the basement and into the storm shelter.

PART TWO

THE EYE OF THE STORM

*When we sail in Christ's company, we may not make
sure of fair weather, for great storms may toss the
vessel which carries the Lord Himself, and we must
not expect to find the sea less boisterous around our
little boat.*

—C. H. Spurgeon

9

It was five very difficult yards to traverse between the Quick In Go and the Sakura Gardens in the buffeting wind, especially with such horrendous debris flashing by, but they all made it into the restaurant. Haruo locked the doors behind them and began to herd everyone with his arms, the way he might a flock of geese. "Go to the back! To the kitchen. This way!"

All of the food had been unloaded from the large, walk-in refrigerator and was sitting in metal roller carts around the kitchen. Isuzu and Mieko held the door open and shouted for everyone to hurry. Abigail grabbed Isuzu in a quick hug. "I forgot you were here tonight," she cried, relieved to have Isuzu near.

"And I did not know you were at Quick In Go!" Something crashed into the roof directly above. "Start praying," Isuzu ordered and pushed her inside the walk-in with the others. The sound of shattering glass had everyone crying out and squeezing inside.

The power was off and the darkness was complete once the big door was shut and tied and blockaded. The children shrieked and wailed. Some adults made nervous noises. The absolute lack of vision made all other senses pop with clarity.

Bodies, hands, hair, the dank aroma of fish and ginger, the chilled air, feral winds, and crashing debris had them all in the throes of terror.

"Please, people," Desh's disembodied voice filled the void until he found his flashlight and illuminated his chin. "Carefully, find a place to sit down. If you can, lie down flat and as close together as possible. Gentlemen, shield the women and children," he instructed. Everyone fumbled to comply. "Lock your arms around each other. Hands gripped tightly at the elbows or wrists."

Abigail heard Chaz taking Jen under his wing. "I've gotcha, Jenny girl. You just don't tell Kaylee about the way I'm hugging you, now, you hear?"

Jen's game reply was muffled by his shoulder.

The beam from Desh's flashlight found Jen, and Abigail could see that Chaz was wrapped around her like a tortilla. "Danny's not gonna kill me, now, is he?" Chaz joked, trying to lighten the mood. "Nobody take pictures, okay?"

Handing Justin the flashlight, Desh climbed in on Jen's other side and tried to shield as much of her body as he could. "I will not tell a soul," he promised Chaz, "because I know this woman's husband. He is a fine man who would do the same to shield my own pregnant wife."

Using the flashlight's beam, Justin located the young mother who'd arrived with her three children. His voice was compassionate, but firm. "You can't hold them all."

Sobbing, she nodded as Justin lifted one of the howling preschoolers and passed him to Haruo and Mieko. He took the other in his arms. "I promise to do everything I can to keep her safe."

Again, she nodded and burrowed, with her baby, into the arms of the homeless man.

"I had a little boy like you, once upon a time," the vagrant crooned to her baby. To the mother he vowed, "Ma'am, don't you worry one bit now. That storm is gonna hafta come through me to get your little guy." She wept into his filthy shirt.

Justin handed the wailing girl to Abigail. She was probably only about three, all rounded belly and sticky cheeks topped by a mop of bright red curls.

"Shhh, honey," Abigail soothed, though her voice was tight and strained with fear. "Your mama is right over there, okay, sweetheart? We're just going to keep you safe. Hush now. It's okay . . ." The kid kicked and flailed, but Abigail held her tight.

Justin settled down next to them and to Abigail, he said, "Lay down, on your side, facing me." When she'd done that, he mirrored her and, pushing the child between them, wrapped them both tightly in his arms. "Don't let go," he cautioned as she looped her arms around his neck and drew his face against hers. His arms were locked at her waist and he settled a leg over her hip. "Tell me if I am hurting you by holding you too tight."

"You can't hold me tight enough," she whispered, her voice clogged with emotion. She tried not to cry, but it was hard and she could feel a tear roll into her ear.

"Shhh," he murmured and then began to pray. Her eyes slid closed as she listened to his low voice begin to comfort her. "Jesus, Lord, have mercy on us now, please. And wherever Danny and the rest of our families are, be with them. Lord, of heaven and earth, Your will be done. Give us peace, Father God."

Abigail was nodding and murmuring in agreement, and the child in their arms grew quiet and still as she listened to the soothing cadence of his voice. All around them, people murmured reassurances to each other that they were all present and accounted for and that everything would be okay. *Stay calm. Don't panic. Hold on tight. I love you.*

I love you, too.

Outside, the polar express that everyone always claimed delivered a twister came barreling at them with an incredible roar rarely heard on this earth. And then, in the restaurant's dining room, Abigail could hear glass shattering as the violent winds blew the windows out. All at once, she felt her ears pop, the way they did when she crested a mountain pass in her car, only far, far more painfully. The babe in her arms shrieked.

Justin's grip tightened at her waist and he used his leg to pull her and the child ever closer. If possible, the noise increased as out in the dining room, all hell broke loose. In the freezer, everyone was yelling and screaming now.

"God in heaven, save us!" someone, probably Isuzu, shouted. *"God! Please, God! Can You hear me? Jesus, please be with us. Father, God! Have mercy on us!"*

The babies were screaming and wailing. Beyond the walk-in's walls, debris crashed and thudded, and the air grew thin and hard to catch.

"It's okay! Don't panic! Stay where you are!" Desh cried. "It will leave us in a minute! It is almost over!"

"Hold on tight!" Justin curled Abigail into a ball over the shrieking child and covered her head with his shoulder. The glass that shattered now was just beyond the fridge's heavy door in the kitchen, and consisted of dishes and glassware most likely. The clanking of flying pots and pans, the crashing of spinning furniture, and screams, the kind usually heard on a roller coaster, rang out all around. Again, Abigail felt sudden, sharp pain in her eardrums—as though she was descending way too fast in a plane.

"Jesus! Jesus! Jesus! Please be with us! Stay with us! Father God, have mercy! Don't let even one of us die! Save us, save us, save us!"

The shouts from Isuzu and Jen to God swirled all around and Abigail began to echo them.

"Jesus, Jesus, please listen! Please . . . please . . . hear us . . . please forgive me . . ."

The wind was roaring in the room with them now, and the walls were huffing, like breathing bellows. Out in the parking lot, it sounded as if the Boeing factory had fired up several hundred test models and was gunning jet engines to see if they could break the sound barrier. And then, just when the sound was at its apex, the roof took off.

The walls taxied across the parking lot in hot pursuit.

The spinning wind ripped the refrigerator door out of Bob Ray's hands and flung it up and over the top of the bar as if it were the useless wrapping paper on a birthday gift. His legs were sucked out of the confined space first, and then he felt himself being pulled onto his back and then up and out.

This is it. I'm dead. The thought was surprisingly clear as he clawed at the sides of the refrigerator and slowly lost his grip. *"God, oh, God! Help me!"* he shouted. He was levitating. Flying with all the other debris, clawing, gasping, grabbing for all he was worth at anything that wasn't airborne. Dirt and mud sprayed his face and filled his eyes and mouth. He was choking. Something hard, could have been a pool ball, or five, hit him in the side and back, knocking the little wind that was left, clean out of him. Arms flailing he found the padded armrest of the bar and grabbed it and held on.

Once, a long time ago, when he was eleven, or maybe twelve, Bob Ray's uncle had flown him out to California for the summer to give his mother a break. One of the things Bob Ray had loved most about his trip was body surfing at the beach.

He spent every day that he could, riding the waves, until . . . one day.

One day, Bob Ray was caught by the undertow. That current picked him up like he was a ragdoll and smacked him face first into the beach. He'd seen stars. Couldn't breathe. His nose bled, and he'd learned a healthy respect for the forces of nature more powerful than his body. Luckily, that day, the ocean had grown tired of slamming Bob Ray around like a dog with a chew toy and spit him out on the beach to contemplate the idea that there were some times in this life when he was simply out of control.

This was one of those times.

—⁂—

Time suspended for Abigail, as she lay coiled in a ball and wrapped in Justin's arms. Her heart was thrashing so hard her temples throbbed. She tried to think rationally, but she'd never been so terrified or so sure that her life was over. And even if she wasn't killed, life as she knew it—the life she'd so carefully constructed—was certainly over forever. Lacing her fingers together with Justin's, she pressed their hands over her mouth to shelter it from the sucking current enough to catch a breath. She was desperate to cry, but the wind was a cruel thief, stealing her tears, her sobs, and robbing her of self-pity and even the ability to breathe.

Shoulder forward, she hunched over the child's head, hoping to provide a pocket of air, and a little refuge from the battering they were taking. At one point she'd managed to pry her eyes open long enough to see a blizzard of mud and missiles, no doubt made of everything from kitchen utensils to car parts, which meant there was a hole in the walk-in. Which also meant that the funnel could reach in and grab them and turn them into so much shrapnel. Justin was still there. Clutching her. Protecting her. Taking the brunt of the assault. Abigail had heard it said somewhere that in times of unbelievable stress, a person's true personality came to the forefront. If that was true, Justin was a wonderful man. When all this was over, if she ever had the chance, she was going to tell him. Thank him. Guys like Justin were rare. Especially in her life.

When Abigail considered her own father in that micro-cosm of time, her biggest regret was that she had not accepted his apology. Humbly, he'd come to her, hat in hand, to mend fences. And when he'd told her of his sorrow over choices made and told her how dearly he loved her and carried the weight of terrible guilt over not being there for her as she grew up, she'd rebuffed him and closed her door in his face. The moment of satisfaction she'd enjoyed, watching him shuffle, shoulders stooped, out to his car where he sat for several ago-nizing minutes before driving back out of her life, had been fleeting.

That had been five years ago. Yet, even now, Abigail would still wake in the middle of the night in a cold sweat, wres-tling with the issues of her relationship with her father. How she still tended to be ultra-defensive with men. How she was inclined to view her Father in heaven through the imperfect lens of her father on earth. How she rejected God because of her father's human frailty. How she distrusted men in general. How she distrusted God, specifically.

If she made it out of here alive, she had some serious stuff to figure out.

Justin figured it had to be that wartime syndrome that caused men and women who barely knew each other to get married right before they shipped out to active duty happening to him right now. Because at this moment, nothing on this earth, not even his own life, was as important to him as keeping the woman he held in his arms alive and safe. He couldn't explain it, but as they lay, praying together, he knew there was more to this woman than he'd first thought. Enough, in fact, that if they lived through this storm, he might finally be able to consider the Midwest as more than just a temporary stopgap on his way back to the East Coast and to home. Not that dinner and *Wheel of Fortune* with his grandparents wasn't a hoot, and he was glad he could help them out when they needed their gutters cleaned or their furniture rearranged.

But he'd longed for the simple, familiar things he'd left behind. Fireflies at twilight. Sand between his toes when he played football with his buddies at the beach. A seagull's cry and the smell of the ocean. Rolling, tree-covered hills, a white church steeple in sharp contrast to autumn's brilliant leaves, friends and family. All this, he'd taken for granted. Here in Rawston, Danny was the only thing that had kept him from losing his marbles. But even Danny's stellar friendship could never make up for the companionship of a good woman. As he cradled Abigail's head beneath his shoulder, he prayed that God would spare them both so he could ask her out on a date and hopefully discover who she really was.

10

After what felt to Abigail like infinity and beyond, the storm finally retreated in search of a new battlefield to conquer. The quiet was almost as loud as the wind it seemed, for the ringing in her ears was deafening. Everyone must have been suffering because it was at least a minute before they all trusted that the twister was really gone and attempted to sit up. Carefully, they disengaged from each other's grip, shook off the rubble, and began to assess the damage.

"Are you okay?" Justin asked as he slowly released her from the tight hold he'd had on her and the child.

Abigail pulled back a fraction, reluctant to move. "Yes. You?"

She could feel him nod. "So far so good. A few bumps and bruises but nothing that a little time won't cure."

The child between them squirmed. Her cries of protest were muffled by their bodies. Slowly and gently, Justin rolled off them and helped the sobbing child to sit up. "*Shh, sh, sh.* It's okay now. Mama is right over there," he comforted the child as she squalled in fear and indignation. "She's fine," Justin called out, thinking of the mother's worry.

"I'm here, Elizabeth! I'm here, Eric!" The young mother was weeping with joy over the healthy cries of her children.

"Is everyone all right?" Haruo asked and dragged himself to a quasi-standing position in the battered and squashed refrigerator. It was still too dark to see much, but it was obvious the damage was severe. It suddenly dawned on Abigail that she was shivering. Could have been trauma. Could have been the fact that they were, after all, hiding in a refrigerator. The chilled air was mostly gone but the floor still felt icy and now, slick with something that smelled fishy.

"How are you, Jen?" Abigail was worried about her friend and the unborn baby.

"Thanks to Chaz and Desh, so far, so good," Jen called. "Although I think I might be off sushi for a while."

In spite of everything, Abigail managed a smile as she asked, "Zuzu?"

"I got wings," Isuzu grunted.

Abigail sat close enough to feel Justin's chuckle. "*It's a Wonderful Life*?" he asked.

"Yes," Abigail said, referring to Zuzu's line from the movie.

"Who *are* you people?" Chaz asked. But there was a smile in his voice, too. Some laughter twittered in the darkness and suddenly, there was a lot of excited discussion as everybody took stock of the situation. Thanks to Haruo's quick thinking, they were all alive. Miraculously, but for some minor injuries, the entire group had come through the nightmare relatively unscathed.

"Nobody move just yet, okay?" Desh instructed. "It will be better not to stand until there is sufficient light. Much of this debris is probably very dangerous."

Desh and Haruo were the first to find their feet. She couldn't be sure in the faint light, but it almost seemed as if the refrigerator was half as tall as it had been when they entered. It took a few minutes of shifting objects around in the dark, and the sounds of metal scraping against metal, but eventually, Haruo was able to force the walk-in refrigerator's door open. A shaft of light had Abigail squinting and she ducked her head to give her eyes a moment to adjust. After Justin had the wailing toddler standing and balanced, he helped Abigail stand up next to him. When she could focus, her gaze traveled first to Justin and then to the child at his knee. Like Justin's head, the toddler's beautiful red curls were mud spattered and matted.

Abigail shifted her gaze out the door. Where there had once been ceiling, sky now filled the vista. The reality of what they'd just endured was slow to sink in.

Hard to believe. Almost . . . dreamlike.

Dully, Abigail's gaze drifted back to Justin. "Do I look as alien as you?" she asked, touching first the layer of mud on her face and then, the toddler's curls.

Squinting, he studied her. With the back of his finger, he reached up and stroked her jaw and up over her cheek. Then, he plucked some straw out of her hair. "Wow." He glanced around. "Wow."

She followed the path of his gaze with her own. "Yeah, wow," she breathed. It was as if a colossal sledgehammer had attacked the restaurant and flattened everything but the reinforced refrigerator.

Haruo was the first one to venture out the door. It seemed as if he had to climb through a maze that was something akin to a child's fast-food restaurant jungle-gym, before he finally called back that he was standing on solid ground. After a full minute, he returned and peered back into the refrigerator. "You will want to be extremely careful when you come out. It is not—" there was a catch in his voice, "—it is not . . . the same."

Desh decided it would be prudent for him to go next. That way, Chaz and Justin could help the women and children from behind, and he and Haruo could assist from outside. Jen made it out first. Then, one at a time, everyone else traversed the twisted exit, only to emerge gasping at the sight that met their eyes. Abigail waited for Justin and they came out together. Their entire group stood in silhouette against the setting sun, a bedraggled collection of shock and awe, taking in their first glimpses of the holocaust.

Abigail fumbled for Justin's arm, which he slipped around her waist, correctly sensing that she could use the support.

"Gone," she gasped, and stared agog at the ruin that evoked images of Hiroshima.

"Yeah." Slowly, they turned in a full circle and were stunned to discover that they'd stepped out of a time machine and onto another planet. For there, as far as the eye could see, was nothing but a flat, sprawling field strewn with rubble.

"Look," she whimpered and pointed and then pressed her face into Justin's chest.

The Quick In Go was gone.

Not flattened. Not in tatters.

Gone.

Only the concrete pad remained. If Haruo hadn't come for them, they'd all have certainly perished. Abigail could feel Justin's Adam's apple bob as he swallowed. "Thank God," he breathed into her hair and held her ever tighter.

The rest of the Rawston Market strip mall's shops were in various stages of carnage. The refrigerator was all that was left of the Sakura Gardens. Tantastic had a partial interior wall left standing. Across the parking lot, the front wall and roof of the Tripoli Cleaners was missing, but Chaz said his brother had decided not to come in to work, because of the storm, so for that, he was praising God. The Pump was a pile of rubble.

Not one car that had been in the parking lot was drivable. Most were upside down or on their sides. Some were just plain gone. Storm sirens were still sounding and security systems and car horns blared, waiting for their wires to be cut or their batteries to die, whichever came first. The smells of splintered lumber and broken gas lines were the most powerful. Twisted metal, shattered glass, mud and slime everywhere. Whole buildings looked as if they'd been put through a wood chipper.

It completely short-circuited Abigail's brain. Her ability to think a rational thought was gone, rendering her capable of uttering only squeaks and gasps and guttural sobs as she clutched Justin's shirt and attempted to remain vertical. Her knees felt like rotting tomatoes, and even blinking had become a chore. Eyes glassy with shock, she stared at pieces of what had once amounted to someone's life. The hours and energy it took to build—shattered in a matter of moments.

She felt . . . violated. As if she'd been robbed of the padding between life and death. Now, there was simply a razor's edge, it seemed, between her . . . and this.

What was the point? Build and work and study and for what? For this?

The tornado may have gone, and the sky may have cleared, but it left its darkness behind and took her confidence with it.

Dazed, Abigail bent down and pulled a scrap of tattered white lace from where it was caught on a shard of metal and absently wondered if it had come from the cleaners. Could it be a piece of Kaylee's dress? The beadwork was beautiful. An hour ago, it had been something that someone cherished. And now? Now it was a picture of their lives.

Shredded hopes. Shattered dreams. Something once bright and shiny and full of promise. She swallowed at the lump in her throat that was leavened and rising with depression. Over here was the scrap of a red and gold silk curtain from the Sakura Garden. She plucked it up and ran her fingers over the dragon pattern. Over there was a baby's blanket. Where could that have come from?

Everywhere, tatters of the fabric of life fluttered. Drawn to them, Abigail gathered and grieved. To whom had they belonged? What had become of their lives? How would they begin to recover? To replace? To rebuild? It all seemed so utterly hopeless.

She tucked the scraps into her pockets and tried to calm the panic that swirled in her stomach with deep, measured breaths. Justin moved to her side and instinctively rubbed the knotted muscles in her neck. She leaned into his hands, thankful for the strength and warmth. Thankfully, the rain had stopped, and the wind had died. And to add to the surreality, a bright, double rainbow arced against the huge black cloud that had packed up and headed east.

❦

Kaylee was relieved to discover the Rawston Common's apartment complex basement stood the test of time, and everyone who had taken shelter there would live to deal with the massive clean-up. Mama and Aunt Lydia had been amazing, singing gospel tunes in their beautiful two-part harmonies to boost the morale of Kaylee's neighbors just before the storm hit. And, when the storm arrived, they'd clung to Kaylee and prayed over her and all the good folks who were weathering this tempest down there with them.

Kaylee had never been so glad to be in her mama's arms as she had when she'd heard the twister slam into the building. As it was, she was in great shape, unless she counted getting smacked in the side by a slab of slate on her way across the parking lot. Her arm hurt like the dickens, and Mama was certain it was broken, possibly in several places.

Everyone had insisted that the laundry room was the best place to weather the storm. But, miraculously, the fact that her landlord hadn't gotten around to fixing a leaky washing machine had probably saved their lives. The floor in the laundry room had been wet for several weeks and begun to smell seriously rank, like a pile of damp towels that had been left in a wad for a week. It was because of the smell and inconvenient dampness more than anything that all fifty-three units' worth of tenants who'd been home at the time had chosen the opposite end of the basement to gather and huddle. Chaz had been right. The windowless furnace room had been the only safe spot. And, though they'd been clobbered with the ceiling tiles and insulation, the floor above had not caved in.

Not the way it had in the laundry room.

———

When the wind had finally let go of Bob Ray, it dropped him like a bowling ball, and he'd scrambled back under the bar to avoid being pummeled by debris. There, he'd crouched while the storm completed its demolition and moved on down the road. After a brief inventory he decided that—aside from a pretty intense headache and some serious scrapes and cuts— he was good. Physically, anyway. Over the ringing in his ears, he could hear water rushing. And then, someone crying out for help. Somehow, a pool table had ended up on its side and boxed him in. It had probably protected him from the mirrored walls that had been the Low Places's trademark.

Sitting up against the bar and using his legs, he leveraged the pool table away. Bits of dirt and broken glass, like glitter, rained down on his head. "Can anybody hear me?" he shouted. His heart was still hammering and his breathing was as labored as if he'd run a marathon. On his hands and knees now, he crawled out of the tiny space that had saved his life and, using what was left of the pool table for balance, managed to stand. At the shocking sight that met his eyes, his jaw fell slack, and he swore under his breath.

As if it had been in a four-lane car crash, the building was totaled. Beyond repair. No, make that beyond recognition. Slowly, Bob Ray turned in a circle, trying to take in the unbelievable devastation. Rubble was the only word he could think of to describe what had become of Low Places. Everywhere he looked there were piles of splintered wood and broken bricks.

His gaze flitted from one unrecognizable pile to the next until something had him doing a double take. Knees buckling, Bob Ray stumbled back, recoiling and gasping as his heart clawed its way into his throat. *A body. A* dead *body*.

He knew this guy was deceased. Didn't take a rocket coroner to figure that one out. Still, he forced himself to venture forth to feel for a pulse. He'd been right. Dead. When he stepped back, he saw another body. And then another.

Tears coursed down his cheeks. He knew these guys. Played pool with them mere hours ago. Scoped out the women with them. It could have been him. It should have been him. Why wasn't it . . . him?

A cry sounded from somewhere amid the rubble. Bob Ray was afraid to move for fear he'd step on somebody. "Is anybody else in here?" he shouted.

"Here!" The muffled cries of several men sounded from where the bathroom used to be. "Here! Over here! We're under here!"

Bob Ray was glad that the sun was still high enough to give him a little light. Driven by terror, he was able to muscle far more weight than he'd have thought himself capable of, even on a good day. He tossed aside several heavy timbers and more than a little brick. Beneath the wreckage was a pocket, supported by toilet stalls. Huddled inside, there were at least four men and two women crouching in various stages of shock.

Bob Ray reached in and pulled a woman out first, and soon they were all upright and had staunched the blood flowing from various wounds. The folks that were able began an organized rescue effort and were soon frantically helping Bob Ray search the debris for more of the lucky ones. The second restroom yielded another half dozen survivors, several of whom needed to be transferred to the hospital as soon as possible. One man quickly cleaned out an area for triage, and the badly wounded were able to lie down while being tended to by those more fortunate.

Eventually, working together, the men were able to lift a ceiling beam and dig out the closet that Bob Ray had been beating on and begging Renee to let him enter. Once the door was removed, the men who'd arrived reached in to begin pulling people out. One at a time, bodies emerged until all three were laid out side by side.

"They're all gone," one rescuer pronounced. "Dead. Beam got 'em." He gestured to the huge timber they'd pulled off the closet.

Trembling, Bob Ray stared at the ghoulish scene. If the redhead who lay staring sightlessly up at him had had a heart, Bob Ray wouldn't be standing there right now. Turning, he braced his hands on his knees and wretched until his stomach was empty.

───

Using her head, as well as her arms, Heather pushed back the lid of the baptismal and peered out into the sanctuary. The first thing she noticed was that the beautiful stained glass windows were gone. Such a pity. But, beyond some corner roof damage, the old stone building seemed to be amazingly solid.

Gently pulling her T-shirt over Robbie's head, she unzipped him and left him asleep where he lay. Then, Heather climbed out of the baptistery and moved to the gaping arch where a beautiful stained-glass rainbow, dove and olive-branch pattern window had once been the building's crowning glory. Ironically, a real rainbow had taken its place, off in the distance. As near as she could figure, her single-wide mobile home lay somewhere in that unrecognizable pile of rubble.

Her heart clutched as she wondered . . . what had happened to Danny?

The last time Selma had ridden out a tornado, their house had spun off like a scene out of the *Wizard of Oz*. So, she didn't have very high expectations when she and Guadalupe ventured up out of the storm shelter that Clyde had labored over so many years ago. Weeks later, she'd tell people that the only word that would cover her reaction now was *shock*.

For not only was the house still standing, but the electricity was on. The stack of magazines she'd left on the table was still arranged in a tidy pile. Every drop of her chamomile tea was still waiting for her in the delicate, bone china cup. Beyond the front window, aside from the car parked on her neighbor's roof, her entire block seemed to have been largely spared.

"Dios mío," Guadalupe murmured, lapsing into her native language, "Gracias, gracias, gracias." Together, the women moved to the porch to join the neighbors already congregating in the streets and comparing storm notes.

"They're saying on the radio," said the woman who owned the new rooftop garage, "that Old Town is gone."

"No!" Selma pressed a fist to her chest. She didn't want to believe it, but knew it must be true. Her precious quilt shop

120

was her livelihood. *No. No. Forgive me, Father. You are my liveli-hood.* The quilt shop was just a hobby.

"The high school?" Guadalupe demanded. "Was the high school damaged?"

The neighbor nodded. "News is still coming in on the casualties."

"Madre, madre mía . . ."

Selma reached to steady Guadalupe, who rocked on her feet. "Now, Guadalupe," she said, matter-of-factly, "let's not borrow trouble. Instead, you start praying, and I'll get the Olds and drive us down there."

"Uh . . . Abby?" Jen's voice had an odd quality that had Abigail and Justin turning around. She'd walked away from the group and was standing by herself.

"Jen? Are you okay?"

"Well . . . I'm not sure, being that I'm new to all this and everything, but I'm thinking my water just broke."

11

7:34 p.m.

Jaw slack, Abigail glanced first to Jen, then to Justin, and then back at Jen.

"You are kidding, right?"

"Well," Jen admitted with a sheepish grimace, "I was definitely scared enough to wet my pants, but I'm reasonably sure I didn't."

For Jen to have to endure labor pains, out here in the dark and the dirt and the danger and this . . . this . . . she brushed her hands on her pants . . . *stuff*, was unthinkable. There would only be enough light for another hour at the very most. The batteries in their flashlights wouldn't last all night long either.

"We gotta find Danny," Justin muttered and glanced at his watch.

Over in the parking lot, the homeless guy had spotted a lawn chair perched on top of—or at the bottom of, depending on the viewpoint—a rolled minivan. Seemingly without a thought for his personal safety, he climbed the wobbly rig, slip-sliding as he fumbled his way to the top. There, he doggedly worked the lawn chair loose from a tangle of wire and tree limbs. When he returned, he planted it on solid ground a good distance away from the rest of the group, where worries about loved ones and personal property were being hashed out, and small children fretted and cried.

"My lady? Your throne awaits." He stepped back with a flourish and bowed.

As she hobbled over to take a seat, Jen played along with him and asked, "What is your name, good sir?"

"Bernard, ma'am. But you can call me Bernie."

"Thank you very much, Bernie."

"Anytime, Missus." He held his arms out. "The world is my castle. So, you just sit and take a load off. That's what I always do after a long day." It was clear he was trying hard to cheer her up.

Jen reached out and clasped his filthy hand. "You're a real blessing to me, Bernie." Her sweet words took Bernie aback. Chin quivering, his smile revealed a number of missing teeth.

"Well now, don't that beat all? And here I was, a-thinkin' that 'bout you."

There was a lump in Abigail's throat as she smiled over at Justin. Expression soft, he winked at her as the old guy shuffled off, no doubt to unearth more treasure.

Justin reached for Abigail's hand. "Can I have a quick word with you?" He smiled down at Jen. "You relax while we try to figure out what to do now." Jen nodded as they walked over to join Desh, Haruo and Chaz, who were deep in a conversation about safety issues and where they should all go from here. So far, the chances of getting help right away seemed pretty grim.

"Jen is in labor," Justin told them.

The men all exchanged worried glances.

"Isuzu and Mieko have been dialing 911 nonstop and can't get through on any of our phones," Chaz said and rubbed his jaw. "The storm must have taken a cell tower down, because I can't seem to get a hold of anybody about getting Jen out of here. I don't know what else to do. The streets are filled with trees and cars and . . ." he gestured off to the street, "and . . . buildings . . ."

Desh cast a worried glance out to where Chaz pointed and said, "Since we've been standing here, not one vehicle of any kind has passed. Perhaps this is because all the roads around here are backed up with debris."

"I'm sure you're right," Justin agreed and absently ran a hand over his chest. "My truck is missing, but even if it was here and worked, we'd still have to wait for the heavy equipment to come and clear the roads before we could actually go anywhere."

"How long do you think that will take?" Chaz asked.

"No telling. And, even if we could get through to 911, I don't know how they'd get an ambulance to us, or even land a medevac helicopter in the middle of all this stuff. I have a sinking feeling we're going to be here for several hours . . . maybe longer. I'm no expert on tornados, but you can just tell . . ." His gaze slowly traversed the landscape. "We're not the only ones who will need an ambulance."

"True." Chaz nodded. "We're lucky, too. Rawston Market was pretty much deserted except for us. The gym, Jen's place, and our business all decided to close early for the storm. I'm pretty sure that everybody who was in the mall at the time made it into the restaurant with us." Haruo and Desh agreed.

"There was nobody left at the lumberyard, either," Justin said. "Everyone was out on deliveries or out on a jobsite, working up estimates today and Danny was with Heather and Robbie before we lost contact with him."

"So," Abigail said, clearing her throat and trying to keep the terrible worry out of her voice. "We're all alone out here?"

"For now, yeah," Justin said. "Most places out here close early on Saturday. The factory is closed on weekends, so are the banks and most of the businesses down here."

"So, we're probably going to be low on the priority list." Her shoulders flagged.

"If the most populated areas are top priority, then . . . yeah."

A short while later, after tossing around a number of different plans of attack, a fledgling scheme was formed. Before it got any darker, a now frantic Haruo and Mieko had decided to strike out on foot and try to get to Brooke and Tyler over at the high school. Since the young mother and her three children lived over in the neighborhood behind the high school, they'd take her with them. The businessman offered to carry one of the kids. Desh was also extremely worried about the safety of his own pregnant wife and decided to set out with the middle-aged woman, because they both lived in the same general neighborhood.

Because her water had broken, everyone agreed that Jen should stay put and wait for a ride to the hospital. Walking any distance in the dark, in her present condition, would be too dangerous. Everyone else would stay with Jen.

En route, the ones who'd left would all search for someone to come and pick up Jen just as soon as possible. It was the only logical plan. Then, as if they were all long-lost friends, everyone hugged each other good-bye and shed a few emotional tears. They thanked Haruo for his wisdom and generosity and vowed to stay in touch.

They also took two of Desh's three flashlights.

That left only one flashlight and a crew of Isuzu, Chaz, Justin, and Abigail to care for Jen. And, of course, Bernie. If he was even still around. Abigail's stomach lurched with anxiety as she wondered what the next hours would bring.

7:58 p.m.

First responders from Southshire and Fisher's Mill began to arrive in Rawston almost immediately, sirens screaming, flashing red and blue lights, visible in the waning daylight. Selma eased over to the side of the road to let several emergency vehicles roar by. She and Guadalupe had been in the car for half an hour now and had only been able to travel a mile, maybe two, down the Southshire Highway. They were listening to the radio reports and growing more anxious by the moment.

". . . and authorities are warning people to find adequate shelter before dark. Right now, we can tell you that the Salvation Army, the Red Cross, and the National Guard are mobilizing and preparing to set up command posts and triage centers throughout Rawston and hope to begin offering shelter, first aid, fresh water, coffee, and myriad types of emergency assistance within the hour.

Right now, the death toll has already reached into the dozens, with hundreds injured, and more missing. Southshire hospital is accepting all life-threatening injuries now and sending less serious cases over to Westfield and Lost Lake . . .

We're getting reports here at K-RAW now of places hardest hit, starting with the areas first struck on Fisher's Mill Road . . ."

The road that had been barely passable was becoming steadily clogged with traffic as folks flooded into the tornado's path, eager to offer assistance and to find loved ones. Impatiently, Selma ground her gears, searching for reverse. "Guadalupe, I'm going to do something a little bit unorthodox, and so I'm going to ask you to tighten your seat belt."

"Why?"

"Because I'm in the mood for a little off-road action," Selma grunted and, cranking the wheel, punched the accelerator till the tires squealed.

Guadalupe reached for the dashboard and braced herself. "And you think your car is up to the task?"

"It's been forty years and she hasn't failed me yet."

"Then via con Dios, mi Amiga," Guadalupe said, just before she was thrown back against her seat as they dove into a newly sprouted spring wheat field.

8:00 p.m.

While there was still some light left to navigate, Justin hiked down the street a ways in search of help. While he was gone, Abigail, Isuzu, and Chaz decided to scout around for any supplies that could come in handy while they waited for Justin to return. Isuzu went to look for bottled water, while Chaz headed off to the Cleaners to dig up some warm clothing before the temperature fell.

Abigail figured they'd all eventually need to sit down and went off in search of seating. She hadn't traveled too far when she happened upon a pile of stuff that the storm had savaged from a pet shop. Even in the fading twilight, she could see that the plastic wrapped bundle of dog beds had been cute. Doggy paw prints on fabric made for loyal friends. . . She stared at the tags on one of the tattered dog beds. PetSmart.

The closest PetSmart was at least ten miles from here. Ten long miles. A sudden rush of goose bumps crawled up her spine, and she found herself battling a panic attack.

Oh, God, she wondered, *how could You let something as horrific as this happen? How can you say You're a loving God and let puppies suffer like this? Why?*

She was too numb to cry now, which was a good thing because she had a feeling that once she started, she wouldn't be able to stop for a long time. Abigail shook the debris off two beds for large dogs the best she could and hauled them back to where Jen waited and settled them next to Jen's chair.

"How are you doing, mama?" She hoped she sounded upbeat as she rejoined Jen. Positive. Sanguine in the face of this nightmare. She dropped down and made herself as comfortable as possible. Could Jen tell she was shaking? Assuming a relaxed pose, she crossed her feet at the ankles to still the tremor in her legs.

Jen's normally beautiful face was bathed in sweat and the crease between her brows stood out white against the layer of mud. "I don't feel so hot. Back in the refrigerator, something fell on Chaz and it hit me pretty hard, too, so my back aches."

"Oh." Tough to find a positive spin for that one. Abigail licked her lips and groped for something encouraging. "Try not to worry. Justin is getting help." Nervously, she tugged a scrap of loose fabric off the dog's bed. Twisting the strip into a long rope, she tied her hair up with it and then leaned back, hoping she exuded a lot more confidence and peace than she felt. "He'll be here any second now." As if on cue, Justin returned. "See?" Abigail leapt to her feet and rushed out to meet him. "Did you find anyone to come take Jen to the hospital?" she asked quietly.

With a glance back at Jen, Justin kept his voice low. "No. I found some other folks about a block up the street. One has lost a lot of blood, two are suffering from broken bones and concussions, and some are okay. Like us, they're waiting for help to arrive, too. The good news is that one of them talked to someone who heard on a car radio that the first responders are starting to arrive from Southshire and Fisher's Mill. They said that Rawston EMTs have just transported the first, most seriously injured.

"This storm . . ." he swallowed and looked up at Abigail, ". . . this storm was huge. They're saying EF5."

"No," she breathed out the word in a whoosh. They stood, not speaking for a minute as they digested the magnitude of what they'd just lived through. Finally, Abigail broke the silence. "So, hey, uh . . . that whole awning permit thing?" She squinted up as the first stars began to emerge in the night sky. "No hurry, huh?"

A grin nudged his lips up, and he laughed that warm, wonderful laugh she remembered from last night. "That's good, because I have a feeling the commissioners have bigger fish to fry now."

They smiled at each other for a long moment. "I am sorry," Abigail said. "My behavior this morning was inexcusable. Especially looking back at it from this angle."

"Funny. That all seems like a lifetime ago, huh?" He grinned. "I'll forgive you if . . . you'll forgive me."

"What for?"

"I have a policy. And I violated it. For you." At her raised brow, he shrugged. "I don't date women I meet in bars. Mainly because I don't go to bars. Unless charbroiled beef is involved. And even then, it's just to eat and not to pick up women. But you . . ."

Abigail smiled. "I get it."

"Oh, good." Justin's shoulders sagged and his grin was comically sheepish. "Earlier, when you said you don't normally hang out there, I was relieved and wanted you to know that I don't either. But it came out wrong. I'm sorry."

Abigail nodded and allowed herself a second to forget the horror and simply bask in his smile. "It's okay," she whispered. Something fluttered in her stomach. He really was nice. Really and truly . . . nice. She couldn't imagine any of the men she'd dated in the past ever being as heroic as Justin had been through this ordeal. She held his gaze with her own and wondered exactly what it was that made him tick. And if he was this good looking, why wasn't he already attached? First chance she got, she'd ask Danny.

Bob Ray had hitched a ride to the edge of town with one of the guys from Low Places who'd not only survived but still had a functioning vehicle. The going had been slow and frustrating, and they'd had to stop more than once to drag stuff out of the way. Finally, when the road could take them no closer to Rawston because of wrecked cars and fallen trees, he got out, thanked his benefactor, and struck out on foot. With every step, he begged God to let Heather and his son be okay.

"Please, please, please," he chanted as he rounded the corner of Fisher's Mill Highway and turned onto Sycamore Drive, the street that led to his alma mater. Good old Rawston High School was all lit up. But not the way it used to be, back when he was playing football. This looked more like emergency lights being run by a generator. And the flashing red and blues of cop cars. And ambulances. And fire trucks.

A siren squawked as an ambulance backed up and then turned and nosed out onto the road that lead to Southshire. Gravel shot from beneath the tires as it picked up speed and turned the siren on full blast.

Bob Ray quickened his pace. What had been going on at the school? Should have been empty, this time of night. It wasn't a game night . . . He'd broken a sweat by the time he reached the football field. Everywhere he looked there were traumatized kids, standing around dressed in formal wear, clutching their parents and each other and crying. Bob Ray blinked. *Prom? Was that tonight? Ah, man.* He slowed as he came into the light and sucked in a huge breath.

The gym had collapsed. There were kids on gurneys and lying out on the brick rubble as EMTs set up I.V.s and bandaged wounds. A lot of kids were covered in blood and two kids were covered all the way, with sheets. Fingers of fear closed around Bob Ray's windpipe, and his breathing came in shallow puffs. *Death.* It was here, too.

But these kids . . . they weren't like Renee. They were just . . . kids. Innocent. Young. They had their whole lives ahead of them. Just like Heather. And Robbie. Looking into their tear-streaked faces, Bob Ray felt about a hundred years old. Their parents were frantic and sobbing. Just like he'd be, if Robbie had been in there.

For the first time in his life, Bob Ray could understand parental fear.

9:00 p.m.

Justin jumped down off the top of an upended car and headed back to "camp." They'd been sitting in a circle around the flashlight, Chaz and Isuzu on one 3x3 dog bed, Abigail and Justin on the other and Jen in her lawn chair. They'd created a makeshift three-sided shelter out of some broken crates and sheet metal for Jen, just in case the now clear sky clouded up and it started to rain again. The temperature had lowered considerably, and they were huddling together to conserve a little warmth.

"Looks like they're inching their way toward us," Justin said. "I can see the lights flashing on the police cars about three-quarters of a mile from here. It won't be long."

He was wearing a men's suit jacket, as was Chaz. For the women, Chaz had selected an assortment of wool and mohair sweaters. He even managed to dig up a Pendleton blanket for Jen's lap. The world as they knew it might have ended, but at least they were stylin'. Well, except for the mud and the holes.

Hands on his hips, Justin turned his attention to Jen. "How are you feeling?" he asked. "Any contractions yet?"

"Don't you sound like you know what you're talkin' bout?" Chaz laughed up at him. "He even kind of looks like a doctor now, wouldn't you say?"

"I say he is Handsome-guy," Isuzu deadpanned with a glance at Abigail.

Abigail nudged her. "Shut up," she mouthed.

"Actually, my sister-in-law is a midwife," Justin explained, pushing his jacket aside and planting his hands on his hips, "so, that makes me an expert-in-law. Plus, my brothers have six kids between them, and their wives aren't exactly shy about discussing childbirth over dinner. I tell ya, I know a lot more about breastfeeding than I ever wanted to, that's for sure," he muttered.

Abigail smiled at his pained expression.

"Contractions?" Jen asked, and shook her head. "No. But my back is killing me."

"Is it a steady ache, or does it come and go?"

Jen's brows gathered in a pensive frown. "It was hurting pretty bad about five minutes ago, but then it was better. But it's really bugging me again."

"Back labor."

At Chaz's amused snort, Justin said, "Hey, I can't help it if my brothers' wives are the queens of TMI."

"You should have been a doctor, man," Chaz said, still ribbing Justin. "Then she could be paying you for this house call."

"Don't give him any ideas," Jen said and grunted at the pain gripping her back.

Justin knelt down next to Abigail and shined the flashlight at his watch. "I have 9:02. Five minutes ago would have been 8:57. Next time it starts to ache, let me know, and we'll try to figure out how far apart the contractions are."

"This can't be happening," Jen said.

Justin gave her shoulder a reassuring pat. "Relax as much as you can, okay? I hear first babies are notorious for taking forever to arrive. My nephew took forty-eight hours."

"*Ohhh.*"

"I'm not helping, am I?" Justin lifted his baseball cap and scratched his head.

"No, no. You are. It's just that I want Danny."

"Of course you do." Abigail shot Justin a helpless look. "I don't suppose, now that the police are probably less than a mile away that, you know, maybe we should all try to walk Jen down there?"

They all pondered the idea and discussed the ins and outs. "It's dangerous. There is glass and sharp stuff everywhere," Justin said.

"But is having a baby out in the middle of it all such a good idea?" Abigail asked.

Justin lifted a shoulder. "No, but then falling down when you are in labor isn't such a hot idea, either."

"*Auugh.* I can't believe we live in this day and age and we are sitting out here without water or electricity or any way to communicate and get help. I didn't think this kind of thing was even possible," Abigail said.

"I say we pray," Isuzu said, and grabbing Chaz and Jen's hands, began to pray. In Japanese. For a long, long time. When she was finally finished, everyone sighed and echoed her amen, certain that she'd covered all the bases.

"I have sushi." A disembodied voice came from beyond their small circle of light.

"Bernard?"

"Yes, my lady. At your service. I also found several bottles of fresh water."

Prayerfully, Isuzu looked up to the heavens. "Thank you! That was quick."

Abigail's jaw dropped as Bernard set a Tupperware container of Sakura Garden sushi before them and added two bottles of water. "Eat!" he encouraged and then turned a five gallon plastic bucket upside down and took a seat. "I have dessert, too. But that's for later." He patted the cloth grocery sack at his side.

No one wasted a minute arguing. Justin pried the vacuum-sealed lid off and passed the sushi around.

"Oh, this is so good," Abigail said around a huge mouthful.

Isuzu nodded. "I make this one. I know because I make the California Rolls."

"Some day, you are going to have to teach me how to make this stuff."

"Sure. Just as soon as restaurant is built."

"Oh. Yeah. Well, I can wait."

Jen's nostrils pinched as she inhaled sharply. Her words hissed out like a leaky balloon. "What time is it?"

"Why?" Abigail asked, afraid of the answer.

"*Baaack* pain."

"Uh-oh." Abigail clutched Justin's arm in alarm.

"I've got 9:07." Justin rubbed the back of his neck. "Five minutes apart."

Abigail gnawed her lip and glanced uneasily at Jen. "What does that mean?"

Justin exhaled. "Shoot, I don't know. I tried to tune out everything the midwife-in-law said after the part about the water breaking."

"Some doctor you turned out to be," Chaz griped. "Anybody here know anything about childbirth, you know, just in case?"

"I see good episode of *House* last month. Very informative," Isuzu said.

"I saw that!" Chaz said. "But I don't think the mother lived on that one, did she?"

"When my nephew was born, I was at a Knicks game," Justin said.

"When I was a kid, our dog had puppies . . ." Abigail offered. "Not the same, though, huh?"

"No." They all agreed, it wasn't the same.

"Five minutes between contractions is generally the time a woman should head to the hospital," Bernard offered. "It's usually best to deliver within 24 hours of the water breaking. To avoid infection."

Mouths agog, everyone turned to stare at Bernard.

12

Bernie," Abigail said and peered through the diffused light into the strange old man's face, "why do I get the feeling there is more to you than meets the eye?" They'd aimed the flashlight straight up and topped it with the sushi container to create a makeshift lamp.

He chuckled. "I reckon you could say that about most folks, huh?"

"But how do you know so much about labor?" Justin asked aloud what the rest were thinking.

"Long story." He shrugged. "I don't like to talk about it all that much. It's your garden-variety sob story."

"Ah." Abigail picked a stick up and began poking around in the rubble. She pulled out a child's T-shirt, shook it off, and smoothed it over her knee. It had a fuzzy giraffe on the front. It was so small. And soft. She wondered who it had belonged to. And if they were all right. Justin reached up to trace the giraffe's soft neck.

"Anyway," Bernie continued, seeming unable to resist his captive audience, "I used to be a doctor. OBG in fact."

Justin gave Abigail's hand an imperceptible nudge with his finger. It was a message. He wasn't sure if he should believe Bernie. Abigail nudged him back. She wasn't either.

Bernie propped his forearms on his thighs and squinted at the flashlight. "Used to be a respectable kind of guy. The kind of guy you'd call a workaholic. Got married. Had a couple of kids. Nice house, nice cars. The whole ball of wax. But I was so busy working to get all that stuff, I didn't have any time to maintain it. So, the wife ran off with the guy who taught her self-defense class; the kids hated me because they didn't know me; the house and most everything else went to them in the divorce settlement; and because I couldn't stop working long enough to deal with the pain, I hit the bottle."

Chaz made an empathetic sound in his throat, and Isuzu reached over and patted his shoe. The fact that he was wearing two different shoes had Abigail wincing.

Bernie's wheezy laughter was mirthless. "Got so dependent on booze I couldn't function at work." There was a definite catch in his gravelly voice when he could finally continue. "Lost a young mother during what should have been a routine C-section. It . . . it was . . ." He dragged a sleeve over his face and struggled to compose himself. "Vowed to never deliver another baby as long as I lived."

Abigail glanced at Jen for her reaction, but as usual, Jen didn't appear disgusted or appalled. Just sympathetic. And sad for Bernie.

"Malpractice accusations, lawsuits, criminal trial, a little prison time, and here I am. Ruined, shameful, lost, unable to cope, you name it. Just . . . taking each day as it comes until I can check out. Thought maybe today was my ticket to hell, but I didn't have the guts to stay outside." Again, he fell silent, and no one had anything to add.

Selma had amazing night vision. Ever since her second cataract surgery, it was like a miracle. She could read without glasses and see fine print better than she could when she was half her age. So, when it came to navigating a debris strewn wheat field at warp speeds, she was a regular Dale Earnhardt, Jr.

Luckily, the tornado's swath did not include long stretches of Route 66, and Selma made good time over to Exit 5 and onto Fisher's Mill Highway. Eventually, they had to stop shy of Sycamore Drive and the high school, but they were light years closer than they had been before Selma decided to 4-wheel-it in a rear-wheel drive. Jerking the Olds to a stop behind a smashed up school bus, she and Guadalupe threw open their doors and hit the ground running. Ahead, the gymnasium area was brightly lit, and it was obvious that the paramedics had been hard at work for a while.

"No," Guadalupe whimpered, bracing herself for the worst. "No, *no, no.*" She pressed her knuckles to her lips.

"It's okay, honey. Try not to panic," Selma said, panting, trotting, and trying to keep up. It was easy enough to say, but she'd been in Guadalupe's shoes before—in fact the circumstances were eerily similar—and knew that staying calm was next to impossible.

"*Elsa!*" Guadalupe began shouting from a block away as she rushed toward the school. "*Elsa! Elsa, donde esta?*" She was crying now and making no effort to hide her growing hysteria.

"*Mama!*" Elsa screamed from the parking lot, and charged toward her mother and flung herself into Guadalupe's waiting arms. Her eyes were puffy and her nose was red and she was jerking from the kind of body-wracking hiccups that come with hard crying. "It was s . . . so *horrible! So terrifying!* I c . . . can't believe . . . I'm *alive*."

"Elsa, Elsa, oh, thank God you are all right!"

Elsa's beautiful prom dress was dirty and torn, but she was—except for an odd bruise here and there, and some serious emotional trauma—injury-free.

"What is it, *hija?*" Guadalupe peered into Elsa's eyes as the child was crying so hard her guttural babblings were now impossible to understand.

Elsa tried to speak, but had to stop twice to pull herself together. "Two . . . of the kids are *dead*, mama," she cried, her voice guttural with horror. "And, others are missing and so many are hurt."

"*Muerto?*" Guadalupe gasped. "No!"

"Yes, mama. But they are not telling us who, until their parents arrive. But I think I know, Mama . . . I think . . . I *know*."

Selma hung her head and began to pray. Because if anyone would know exactly how they felt, it was Selma Louise Tully.

Everyone was on edge. And not just because they'd just barely escaped with their lives from a history-making tornado. And, not just because of the terrible stench of manure that had blown in from a local dairy or the occasional startling collapses of now rickety buildings. No, at the moment, everyone was feeling the stress because Jen had begun labor in earnest. She was a true champion, clearly in terrible pain, but handling it with a strength and grace that was amazing, given the situation. Luckily, the battery in the flashlight was still going strong, and the emergency crews were gaining ground in their direction. Everyone had hope that it wouldn't be long now. But that didn't relieve the torment that plagued Jen every sixty seconds.

"Bernard," Abigail asked, agitated, "Isn't there something we can do to help her with the pain?"

"No," he said with a grunt. "Not without an anesthesiologist on hand. Just keep breathing like you're doing," he said to Jen. "Pick something to focus on."

"Here," Abigail said and spread the tiny shirt with the little giraffe on Jen's knees. "Look at this and—"

"*Hee, hee, hoo,*" Jen breathed.

"Atta girl," Bernard praised. "You're doing fine."

"It hurts so bad, Bernie," Jen gasped between contractions.

"You do seem to be progressing pretty fast. How many weeks along are you?"

"Almost thirty-eight."

"Hmm. Could be worse." Bernie bent down and dug through his grocery bag.

"Found this in the same place I found the sushi. Can't believe it didn't break." He held up a bottle of sake.

Bernard handed the bottle to Chaz. "I was gonna tip it later, but I think we oughta bust it open now."

"I'm not sure now is the time to party, my man," Chaz said, staring at the bottle he suddenly found in his hands.

"Not to drink. To scrub."

"No, thank you." Chaz tossed the bottle to Justin.

Justin lifted his hand and caught the bottle with a thwack against his palm. "What are you trying to say, Bernie?"

"Just that you might want to have sterile hands. In case you have to deliver the baby."

Selma was driving Elsa and Guadalupe back to her place when she spotted a young man walking down one of the back roads that was reasonably debris free. Slowing the Olds to a crawl, she peered at his face as he squinted over his shoulder and into her headlights. She rolled her window down and poked her head out. "Bob Ray? Bob Ray Lathrop? It that you, honey?"

"Ms. Tully?" He held a hand up over his eyes to shield them from the glare until he came around to her side of the car.

"Sure is, sweetheart. Do you need a ride home?"

Bob Ray sighed up at the sky. "Ms. Tully, I'm not sure I even have a home anymore."

"Get in and we'll go see. If you don't have a place to stay, I'll take you and your family home with me."

Weary to the bone, Bob Ray didn't argue. He came around the other side of the car and got into the front seat. "Hi." He turned around and gave a little wave to Guadalupe and Elsa who were snuggled together in the back seat.

"Hi, Bob Ray," Guadalupe said.

"How are you doing, sweetheart?" Selma asked. "And where is that wife and baby of yours?"

He choked back a spate of tears. "I—I don't have any idea. I was at work. I think they were at home when the tornado hit."

"Oh, honey." Selma reached out and gave his thigh a thumping with her free hand. "That's gotta be scary."

For the first time in his life, Bob Ray Lathrop felt the need to get real. His father and Ms. Tully's son, Paul, had been close friends, and Bob Ray had grown up knowing he was special to Selma. "I'm terrified. I have just been to hell and back and am not sure what is—or is not—waiting at home. And, because of that, I have probably never been better."

Selma's brows disappeared under her short bangs. "Now that is not what I expected to hear tonight, of all nights."

"Not how I expected to answer, ma'am. But tonight I think I finally learned a terrible but invaluable lesson at the School of Hard Knocks. I finally figured out exactly what is important to me. And I'm just praying that my wake-up call didn't come too late."

"Sometimes, it takes everything turning upside down to show you what is right-side up. I have had similar epiphanies in my day."

"I know, ma'am. I remember."

13

"Atta girl. That's right," Bernie said, as he coached Jen from over Justin and Abigail's shoulders. "One more and you're done. Justin, get ready."

Try as she might to wait for the professionals, after midnight, Jen finally had to give in to her urges to push. And scream. They'd all scrambled to assemble a bed of sorts from the PetSmart pile and Chaz had run back to the cleaners for another load of battered, but still usable, dry cleaning. Abigail was holding the flashlight, and Justin was supporting her baby's head.

Jen tensed, her entire body bunching. Then, with one amazing shriek, she pushed her son into Justin's hands.

"I got him! I got him!" Justin was laughing and his smile was huge. "He's a slippery cuss. What should I do now, Bernie?" Arms waving in the sudden lack of confinement, the baby was squirming and bleating like a lamb.

"Put him up on mama's tummy and let's get his nose and mouth cleared out and get him covered up. Chaz? Get that blouse you got from the cleaners?" Bernie pointed to the plastic-wrapped garments Chaz had brought over earlier. "That cotton blouse oughta do the trick. Zuzu? Wipe him down real good with that. Do his nose, like I showed you. Chaz, let's get something we can wrap him in when she's done. Abigail, hold the light up a little higher, that's right. Good."

"Oh my goodness!" Abigail stared at the baby, suddenly overcome with emotion. "Oh, Jen!" she breathed. "He's so . . . *beautiful!*" She laughed and cried and tried not to drop the flashlight as she moved the beam to the baby's face. Abigail glanced around and could see that everyone was brimming with happy relief, just as she was. Mother and baby were alive! It was a miracle. "Do we need to cut the cord?" Abigail asked Bernie.

"No hurry on that. Let him get used to breathing on his own first."

"How is he?" Jen asked, peering down at the top of her baby's head. She was exhausted, but smiling.

Bernie leaned forward. "Looks like he's pinking up real nice. Good job, team. You're all quick studies." He slapped his thighs with the palms of his dirty hands. "Looks like you got a healthy, strapping boy, far as I can tell. Hard to perform an Apgar out here, but I don't think you have anything to worry about with him being a preemie. He's gotta be a six- or seven-pounder, easy. Chaz, bunch up some of that laundry, will ya? Put it behind mama's head so she can get a look at her boy. Justin, grab that blanket and put it over mama and the baby now."

As everyone quickly and efficiently did their job, long-awaited help finally emerged from the shadows. A policeman led two EMTs through the rubble and over to their group, his radio crackling with cross traffic. "We got some reports of screams coming from this area and—" The officer stopped talking when he saw the baby and laughed. "Well, if this isn't a pleasant surprise after everything else I've seen tonight. Come on, guys! Over here."

All smiles, the EMTs got to work checking Jen and the baby and getting her ready to transport. Heavy equipment must have been clearing the area while they were all otherwise occupied, because Abigail was amazed to discover there was now a maneuverable path down the middle of Homestead Avenue for the ambulance.

When had that happened?

Behind the front loader tractor, a siren squawked and another EMT backed in as close as possible and parked. The back doors of the ambulance were thrown open and a gurney was pulled out and carried over to Jen.

"Besides mother and baby, it's just you four?" The police officer asked, indicating Justin, Abigail, Chaz, and Isuzu.

"Actually, it's—" Hands on his hips, Justin paused and glanced around for Bernie.

Puzzled, Abigail's gaze followed his gaze with her own. Funny. Bernie was here just a minute ago, but he seemed to have vanished. Squinting into the darkness, they both took several quick turns around the area where they'd delivered the baby, but Bernie—also known as Dr. Bernard Blumenfeld— was gone. Clearly, that's how he wanted it.

"Yes," Justin said and cast a knowing glance at Abigail. "Everyone else walked out earlier and as far as we know, the businesses were all closed and locked and there were no other people in the mall."

"Good." The officer radioed his findings in and then said, "Right now, the Red Cross has set up an area in the hospital parking lot for people to go and sign a survivors' list to help everyone check on loved ones. They tried that out up in Dakota during a nasty flood, and it worked really well. Their voluntary sign-in list is really helpful and it's growing. If you'd like, I can give you all a ride to the hospital."

"Yes, please," Abigail said. Justin took her arm and they paused to talk to Jen for a moment before she was lifted into the ambulance. She reached out for Abigail's hand.

"Thank you, all," Jen said. "So much."

"I don't think any of us will ever forget your baby's birthday, huh?" Abigail said with a smile.

"Where are you taking her?" Justin asked the paramedic.

"Rawston Legacy is southwest of the high school and—amazingly—it was just this side of the tornado's path. Even though she's not an emergency, they can take her in the maternity ward." Turning to Jen, he asked, "Ma'am, is there anyone you need to notify about the baby?"

"Yes! My husband. Please. If you can, have him meet me at the hospital. His name is Danny Strohacker and his cell phone isn't working."

"We've been hearing a lot of that tonight. Cell phone reception is intermittent at best," the policeman said. "Could I get his name again?" The officer relayed a message to be on the lookout for Danny and to have him meet Jen and his son at the hospital.

"His son." Jen lay back and smiled at the baby. "He's gonna love that."

<hr />

After stopping a number of times to assist people in need and to help clear debris from the road, Selma, Bob Ray, Guadalupe and Elsa finally made it to Hollingsworth Boulevard, the four-lane thoroughfare that ran by Barnaby Estates. As they slowly wove down the street, they were all shocked at the horrendous wreckage over here in Bob Ray's neck of the woods. Upended and tossed on their tops and sides, single- and double-wide mobile homes were strewn about like the cars of a hobbyist's Lionel model train wreck.

"How am I even going to find my place?" Bob Ray stared in disbelief, his nose pressed up against the glass. Aside from the full moon, there was only a little diffused light coming from his neighbors' Coleman lanterns and auto headlights as they worked through their rubble.

"Are you sure you want to go in there? I see that there are paramedics in there with your neighbors now," Selma said. They all knew she was thinking that finding Heather and Robbie's bodies would undo Bob Ray. "Yes, ma'am. My family may need me, and I have to try to get to them before any more time passes."

"Of course." Selma parked over at the side of the boulevard, and Bob Ray jerked the door open before she'd come to a complete stop.

"I'm in a corner lot, the first street on the left," he called over his shoulder before he turned and sprinted into the night, frantically shouting Heather's and Robbie's names. When the women finally caught up to him, Bob Ray was standing, his shoulders hunched, his hands cradling his temples. "I don't even know where to *begin*." There was a terrible panic in his voice, coupled with helpless confusion and grief. The mountain of refuse that had been his home was broken in two piles. One half was over in Mrs. Carmichael's yard. The other was strewn all over the neighborhood. Their clothing, towels, and bedding were shredded and fluttering in the remaining branches of stripped down and toppled trees.

"How . . ." he faltered as tears overwhelmed him. "How could *anything* survive?"

His closest neighbor, Mrs. Carmichael limped over to their group to talk about his place being mostly over in her place now. "Don't worry, honey," she told Bob Ray in her raspy voice, and pointed out to the road with her cigarette. "They wasn't home when the storm hit. I seen 'em leave, so if you're lookin' for 'em here, you won't find them."

Relief had Bob Ray's head roll back on his shoulders as he exhaled thanksgiving at the sky. "Did Heather say where they were going?"

"Yeah, she was outta milk. So I'm guessing she went over to Safeway, cuz she had the baby in his stroller. I gave her a few bucks to buy me a lottery ticket and one of those barbecued chicken pizzas in the black box I like so much. I had a coupon. Said I'd share it with her and her visitor, since you had to work."

"She had a visitor?"

"Yeah, some guy in a pickup truck came by. Can't say I know him. Big guy. Silver crew cut. Came to fix your toilet and tub. By the way, they're over at my place, if ya want 'em back." She coughed up some reedy cackles.

Bob Ray sighed. "Nah. Thanks though. Did the guy say his name was Danny?"

"Could be. My memory ain't what it used to be."

"Thanks, Mrs. Carmichael. How are the neighbors?" he asked, running his hands through his hair and turning to survey his street.

"Totaled. The whole park. Pretty much totaled. Everybody made it to the big shelter down on Morton Street though, as far as we know. Lotta folks weren't home."

Selma and Guadalupe moved through the wreckage and began to gather some clothing for him and Heather and their baby. When Guadalupe's purse was stuffed to its oversized gills, they loaded Selma's.

"Look at this," Selma said as she pulled a rag off a pointed limb and aimed her tiny key light at the scrap. She held it up for Guadalupe to examine. "Isn't this . . ."

"Mm-hum," Guadalupe said. "Danny's Bible cover. This is the one Jen was showing to us at the store this afternoon, I'm sure."

"So he was the visitor. Probably left in a hurry once the storm started up. No doubt wanted to be with that baby of his. Though . . . it's odd for him to leave this behind." Brows knit, Selma studied the tattered scrap. "I'll give this back when I see him again."

Elsa took the fabric and pressed it to her damp cheeks. Selma slipped an arm around her waist. "How are you doing, honey? Do I need to get you back to my house so that you can get to bed?"

Giving her head an emphatic shake, Elsa adjusted her slipping tiara. Her words were halting as she said, "I don't think I could sleep. Maybe not ever again."

Selma nodded. "Good enough. I feel just the same way. You and me? We can stay up all night and play cards and watch movies and do facials. What do you say?"

Elsa sniffed. "Sounds real good."

"Okay, but, if you're going to hang with me, I can't chance having you fall. Hold still now." Selma bent down and grabbed the torn hem of Elsa's skirt and yanked it off. She tucked the remnant into her purse.

Bob Ray stepped back to make room for Selma and Elsa. "Mrs. Carmichael was just telling me that they're saying the Red Cross has set up an information booth in the hospital parking lot. They might know something about my wife and baby."

Selma liked that. *His* wife and baby. That was a good sign. "Come on, girls! Let's go. We're off to the hospital."

14

2:00 a.m.

Abigail was wedged between Isuzu and Justin in the back seat of the police cruiser on the way to the hospital. Chaz rode shotgun while one at a time, the policeman answered their questions.

"I'm really sorry it took so long to get out to you all tonight, but we just don't have enough help yet. I've been transporting folks all evening long. We didn't expect an EF5. Mowed right through the middle of Rawston like Gulliver's lawnmower. Took neighborhoods and businesses alike. I'm talking *gone*. So many places . . . just," he choked up as he spoke, "gone. People are wandering down the streets, shell-shocked. I saw some of the same stuff back when I was in Iraq. It's just like a war zone here. Not to be indelicate ladies, but there are body parts and cadavers and injured people everywhere, so brace yourselves."

Abigail stared with horror at Justin and Isuzu.

"We've got medical teams from other states arriving with supplies. The hospital was not hit too badly. Regular citizens have been coming in from Fisher's Mill and Southshire and even as far away as Antonito and Midpoint to transport people and help folks dig the injured and dead out of the rubble.

Everybody's pitching in to help each other out. It brings tears to your eyes, know what I mean?"

"This has to have been the weirdest day of my life," Abigail whispered to Justin.

He glanced first at her, then at Zuzu, then back at her with a weary smile. "And just think. I was a big part of it."

Abigail lifted her eyes and their exhausted gazes caught. "Can you believe you delivered a baby tonight?"

Justin snorted. "No. But I can tell you that for once I'm going to hog the conversation at Christmas this year."

Abigail smiled. "Your sister-in-law is going to be impressed, I'll bet."

"Oh, yeah. I'm sure she's never delivered a baby in the middle of a tornado-ravaged parking lot before."

"You were brave. My hands were shaking and all I had to do was hold the light."

"If I was brave, it's only because Bernie was there and Isuzu was praying like a foghorn in my ear."

"Bernie. Was he for real?" Abigail mused aloud. "I wonder where he went. And why do you think he didn't want to get help?"

Justin lifted and dropped a shoulder. "Probably thinks he doesn't deserve it. Plus, he's used to living outside."

"That's so sad."

As they pulled up to the Rawston Legacy Hospital, the first thing Abigail noticed was the stunned and bloodied crowd milling around the debris-strewn parking lot. Children and adults alike cried and looked to each other for solace for their pain and grief. Others frantically searched for loved ones and pets. Some simply sat eyes glassy, in wordless shock. A large truck, generally used to haul furniture, had a big sign attached to the side: *MORGUE UNIT*. Just outside the truck's back doors, gurneys were lined up, loaded with bodies draped in sheets.

Abigail gasped, and Justin shot her an empathetic glance.

A generator had been set up and bright lights on tall poles illuminated storm victims by the dozens. They stood around drinking coffee, or sat on the curb, or gathered on blankets and in groups of folding chairs. The Salvation Army was already ministering to the walking-wounded and displaced masses, and the Southshire Red Cross had a table set up as an impromptu information center on local shelters for the newly homeless.

The police officer drove them down to a temporary off-loading zone. "Here we are," he announced and twisted around in his seat. "Check the lists here for your friend, Danny. If he hasn't voluntarily signed in here, he could be at a hospital in Southshire or Fisher's Mill or even farther away. Due to the family privacy laws, you might find yourself frustrated. But don't worry. A lot of people will turn up in the morning, when the sun's up."

"Thank you," Abigail said, heartened by his encouraging words. With a gentle nudge to wake Isuzu, the weary foursome climbed out of the police car and stepped into the crowd. A flat screen TV was perched on a card table under a portable awning, and people crowded around to watch the latest on the traumatic storm.

So many good and innocent people had been hurt or killed. It made no sense. Where was the justice? Heart heavy, Abigail plodded along behind her friends, staring into the grieving faces of young and old alike. And these? These were the lucky ones.

Abigail tracked the aroma of fresh coffee until she spotted silver urns and platters of cookies. Her belly was hollow, and she had a feeling some sugar and caffeine would no doubt give her sagging spirits enough of a boost to see her through the next few hours at least.

"Haruo!" Isuzu found her brother standing next to his son, Tyler, who was in a wheelchair. She tugged Abigail's blouse and pointed to the sidewalk. "I'll be there."

Abigail nodded and gave her a quick hug.

"And I'll catch up with you all later, too," Chaz said, holding up his cell phone. "I just got about ten seconds of cell service, but it was enough to find out that Kaylee is on her way here with a broken arm and some bruised ribs. Everyone else is fine." Though the worry shimmered in his eyes, it was clear that just hearing her voice was a huge relief. With a quick hug for Abigail and a clap on the back for Justin, Chaz left their group, his eyes already darting from face to face as he scanned the crowd for Kaylee.

"You're stuck with me, I guess." Abigail sighed as she handed Justin a cookie.

"No hardship there," he said.

Amusement did wonderful things to his face, and she felt her cheeks grow warm. Tentatively touching her hair, she could only imagine how she must look. "Do you see Danny anywhere?" she asked as she selected a cookie for dinner. Or breakfast.

"Not yet."

Abigail poured them each a steaming cup of coffee. Between the warm drink and the food, she was beginning to catch her second wind. "There's Jen," she said, and pointed with her half-eaten cookie at the ambulance under the ER portico, vying with battered cars and trucks for a spot to offload patients. They were still a ways away when the back doors were opened, and mother and baby were unloaded and wheeled through the throng and up to the wall of sliding glass doors. Danny still wasn't with her, but then, how would he know where to find her right now?

As he had done so often that evening, Justin spoke her thoughts aloud. "Let's go see if we can find Danny and tell him where Jen and the baby are."

Coffee in hand, Abigail slowly meandered with Justin through the parking lot, looking for Danny and gathering bits of information here and there. The high school gymnasium had collapsed. Kids were still being transported to the hospital. Two of them, to the morgue. Names were pending family notification. Old Town had been demolished. Her home was gone. Many of Rawston's oldest neighborhoods were gone. The numbers being transported to the morgue were rising steadily. Walterville had been hit hard. The damage to Rawston was the worst so far. Hospitals were overflowing. Southshire had only minimal damage.

Justin looked at her with concern as she reacted to each bit of news. "Are you all right?"

Tears welled and stung her eyes, but she pinched them back and gave her head a quick shake. "I can't process it all right now. As much as I'll miss my building, I can't believe how many people were killed. It's just . . ." she lifted and dropped her free hand, ". . . so surreal." Her face and throat ached with the effort it took to stem the emotional flood. The arm Justin draped around her shoulder was supportive in several ways, and she appreciated it more than he would ever know. Though she tried to block it out, the depressing reality had her feeling nauseated. All that work. Building a clientele. Building her home and shop. And for what?

The point of life on this stupid planet suddenly eluded her, and she swallowed back a surge of bitter bile that threatened to make her sick. As they searched the crowd for Danny, odd thoughts flashed through her mind. Random thoughts. Rogue ideas mixed with raw emotion.

This would be the perfect opportunity to move out to California. She could live with her mother in her mom's little bungalow in Beverly Hills. They never got tornados out there. Her new friend DJ had made her an offer to work in a high-end celebrity salon that only a fool would pass on. Think of the amazing people she would meet—the fast track life she would live. DJ's client list and social circle were regularly featured on the covers of the magazines at the check-out stand. DJ himself pulled seven figures, and his house had been written up in Architectural Digest. The fact that she hadn't jumped at his offer before now seemed ridiculous, especially in light of tonight's disaster. There was so much there, and so little to keep her here.

Then again . . .

She had dear friends and of course, her precious Aunt Selma. And . . . her father and his family, if she could ever screw up the nerve to face him again. The homesickness would be horrendous. She'd lived her whole life, right here in Rawston.. But wouldn't it be prudent to cut her losses and leave now before the feelings that were germinating for Justin took root? Everything in her mind pointed to this logic. How could she have only known him for twenty-four hours? Would he stay here or go back east?

Her head was spinning. There was just so much to consider. Abigail had never believed in love at first sight. Love, Aunt Selma always said, was something that grew over time. Anything else was just so much lust. And lust didn't last.

So, what exactly was she thinking when it came to Justin?

Taking a deep, heartening breath, she considered him as they stepped into the long line at the Red Cross information table. He was muddy and rumpled and in need of a shower and a shave, but still he was the handsomest man in the parking lot. In Rawston. Make that the entire state. So, yeah. The physical thing was a lot of it. But she'd had really handsome boyfriends in the past. And, after the second or third date, they made their expectations clear, and if she didn't put out, they generally drifted away. Sooner rather than later, most times.

But if she took Justin's looks out of the equation . . . there was so much more. His face when he'd held Jen's baby? Just thinking about his joyful expression had her eyes swimming. And, what about the way he'd risked his own personal safety to protect her, a virtual stranger, during the storm? And that young mother and her small children? He'd taken charge and remained levelheaded when the woman had fought to stay in the store with her kids.

She sighed. Hopefully, things would be clearer in the light of day.

When they finally reached the head of the line, the woman in charge of the admission lists did not have Danny's name recorded as one who'd voluntarily signed her public release list, or been listed by immediate family as one who'd been admitted to Rawston Legacy. Or Southshire's Good Samaritan Hospital. Or Fisher's Mill's Emanuel.

"But," she'd said with a tired sigh, "that doesn't necessarily mean diddlysquat. Not every family is willing or able to sign for their injured. Not everyone who is injured can speak for themselves. Not everyone had ID on them when the storm hit. Not everyone has been transported yet. Information will be coming in for days. You'd be amazed at the number of people who turn up unscathed. Good luck," she said, her kind eyes filled with compassion.

Though he'd nodded at all of the volunteer's assurances, it was obvious Justin had doubts about her optimism. Conflicting emotions had his jaw muscles jumping and the worry kindling in his eyes. He pushed back his hat and scratched his head, a gesture that was becoming endearingly familiar to Abigail. "Thank you, ma'am."

"Certainly. And, if you would, please sign your name here, and that way I can assure others who might be worried about you, that you are alive and well."

Taking up a pen, Justin signed his name, jotted his cell number and then handed the pen to Abigail.

"Would you have a Selma Louise Tully on any of your lists?" Abigail asked after she'd scanned the page she'd signed.

A quick perusal of several lists in her computer had the volunteer shaking her head. "I'm sorry, no. But no news is good news, as they say."

"Thank you." Abigail sighed, as disheartened as Justin. When they stepped out of line, Isuzu joined them. "Have you seen Danny?" Abigail asked, hopeful that she'd spotted him.

"Not yet," Isuzu said and Abigail noticed that her eyes and nose all red and puffy. It was obvious she'd been crying for a while now.

Scared, Abigail touched her arm. "What's wrong?"

Isuzu shook her head and the tears that spiked her lashes began to spill. "Tyler has broken leg. Many fracture. Brooke is in surgery . . . doctor not sure if she will walk again."

The hospital parking lot was so crowded, Selma had to circle the entire thing several times before a spot came open. To Bob Ray, the tension in his gut felt as if he'd swallowed a couple of burning coals. He repressed the awful need to scream and swear and slam his fists on Ms. Tully's dashboard. Not knowing where Heather and Robbie were was driving him mad. Ms. Tully was a godly woman. She probably wouldn't appreciate a crazed outburst like that, but he wanted to give vent something awful.

In the back seat, Elsa had finally lost her battle to stay awake and had fallen fast asleep on her mother's lap. Smiling with maternal love, Guadalupe stroked her daughter's hair and whispered to Selma and Bob Ray that she'd decided to stay in the car. "Take your time," she whispered. "We will be comfortable and sleeping."

Selma walked with Bob Ray toward the information line and waved him off. "Honey, you go look for your bride. I'll save you a place. If I get to the front before you come back, I'll ask after Heather and Robbie. I have some other folks, my niece Abigail, and such that I want to check on, too."

"Thank you!" Bob Ray kissed Ms. Tully's soft, paper-thin cheek and jumped into the crowd. His head whipping left and right, eyes flashing, he pushed past people and ran, his heart thudding with both dread and anticipation.

Heather? Where was Heather? Please, please be here.

"Hey! Watch it!" a woman snapped as he barreled past and bumped her arm.

"Sorry," he called over his shoulder but didn't stop. He was a man with a mission.

"Bob Ray?"

He skidded to a stop at the sound of his name and spun around. "Heather?" He hollered. Heads turned to stare, but he didn't care.

"Bob Ray! Over here!"

Jumping up, he spotted her standing next to a grouping of chairs on the hospital's front lawn area. Robbie was fast asleep, bundled safely in a giant red blanket. His heart caught in his throat. *Heather!* Tears were streaming down his face now. *Heather, beautiful, beautiful Heather.* His best friend. The girl who'd given him a healthy son.

Getting to her was like trying to make an end run against an opposing team on the football field. He had to weave and dodge and push, but he finally made it to his family. She gasped as he swept her into his arms and spun her in a circle. Then, in front of God and everybody, Bob Ray kissed his wife. Hungrily. Eagerly. Passionately.

It was a kiss filled with gratitude and apology and most importantly, love. They were both in tears by the time he was done. Clasping her face between his palms, he pushed his nose against hers and kissed her lips, her chin, her jaw and her eyes. "I was so scared," he confessed. "So scared that I'd lost you. Tell me," he begged, and threaded his hands through her hair. "Tell me I still have you."

Eyes shining, Heather laughed like the girl he'd first seriously courted in high school. "You have me," she breathed against his mouth. "You have always had me."

The inferno in his belly began to ease and in its place the feeling of becoming a real husband and father took residence.

"Oh, Zuzu. No." As Abigail drew her friend into her arms for a hug, no one voiced what they were all thinking. A brilliant Olympic career? Over. Years of hard work? Haruo and Mieko had to be heartbroken. "I'm so, so sorry," she said around a lump of sympathy.

"Thank you," Isuzu said and sniffed, her smile, watery. "They are alive. This, I am so thankful to Jesus for. And He is working out everything, I trust. Just hard to see."

Impossible, Abigail thought, but only nodded. She didn't share Isuzu's generous opinion. "How are your brother and sister-in-law holding up?"

"They are thankful both kids are alive, but very scared for Brooke."

"What about her boyfriend? What was his name again?"

"Nick. The kids were outside when tornado hit," Isuzu haltingly explained. "When they find Brook she is . . . unconscious. She have serious spinal injury."

Abigail swallowed and blinked. "And Nick?"

"No one see Nick."

❧

Heather finally understood the need of the father to barbecue the fatted calf for the prodigal son's return. Bob Ray was home. She settled in next to the boy she remembered from her childhood. It was that Bob Ray who lit his eyes now. It was that Bob Ray in his touch. In his voice. He drew his foot up over his knee and propped their sleeping toddler in his lap before he turned to face her. For several long seconds, he sat in silence.

Heather could see the thoughts, like logs in a jam, struggling to organize themselves and flow out. She waited, fearing what she would hear, but resigned herself to wait. Her husband was back, but God knew he wasn't perfect.

"I was so scared," he began, his eyes welling. "I thought God was punishing me with this storm for the stuff I've been thinking about . . . about . . . what I was missing out on. Here I was, married to a beautiful girl and blessed with a healthy son and I wanted . . . something more."

Heather nodded. She knew.

Shame had his eyes sliding closed and his chin dropping to his chest. "I thought maybe I'd lost you and the baby and

160

that I'd have to live with that . . ." He had to stop, for the sobs closed off his throat and had his shoulders heaving. "Heather, I swear I never cheated on you. But I was thinking about . . . doing it. I . . . I . . . wanted to. I was just so sick of the responsibility. I just wanted . . ." his head dropped back and he peered into the night sky, "I wanted to play football again, you know? And party with the guys and stuff. Stupid. Stupid. Idiot. I was partying tonight, working, but really? Party time. And, when the hammer came down," he paused and wiped his face on the baptismal curtain, "everything I thought I wanted? It wasn't *real*. And it could never, ever compare to what I already have with you." His sigh was ragged and he clutched her hands in his, rubbing his thumbs over her knuckles.

Heather stared at her hands, encased in his. The words he spoke cut her to the bone, but . . . hadn't she had similar feelings? More than once she'd fantasized about disappearing and living a life without Bob Ray's misery. Thought about meeting someone new and starting over again. How could she be angry with him for sharing the same thoughts? Clearly, it took a lot of nerve to confess. Maybe he really had matured in the middle of the storm. Stranger things had happened.

"I don't blame you if you don't believe me. I know I've been a total jerk." His face was so wet, Heather closed her fingers over the cuff of her sleeve and dabbed at his cheeks, nose, and eyes with her cloth-covered palm. Tears welled all over again and spiked his lashes. "T . . . t . . . tonight I learned that . . . one second you're here, a selfish jerk, and the next minute . . ." his sigh was ragged and consumed with emotion, " . . . you're *dead*. I know this is going to sound stupid, but I think *God* is trying to tell me something. Have you ever had that feeling where you know that He wants your attention. And you can run, but you can't hide?"

Heather grinned. "Yes. I have been praying for us. For you. For so long."

Bob Ray swallowed hard. "I don't deserve it, but I want to try again. To start over. To go to church and to be a good husband and a . . ." For a moment, he was overcome again. "And, a father to Robbie. The kind of dad I always wished for."

Bob Ray hadn't spoken so earnestly in years. For him to be talking to her this way now was unbelievable. It had to be an answer to her prayers.

"I want that, too, Bob Ray," she whispered and heads together, they cried.

"I found my parents!" Chaz told Abigail, Justin, and Isuzu, his smile huge with relief. "My brother and his family are all good, too. They're at church right now, finding shelter for people who don't have anywhere to go."

"I may need to go visit them," Abigail said and exhaled a heavy sigh.

Chaz stepped behind her and rubbed her shoulders. "Relax, girl. You are just a pile of knots. Listen, you're gonna be fine. My parents live over by your Aunt Selma. That whole area was pretty much untouched."

"Have you seen Kaylee?"

Giving his watch an impatient glance, he patted her neck and said, "She's only a few minutes away. My phone is working fine now."

Abigail exhaled tension and breathed in relief. Digging through her purse, she found her phone and saw that she had a frantic text message from her mother in California and several from friends in other states. There were also a number of text messages from local friends and family, concerned about her safety. Quickly, she sent out a mass text, letting everyone know that she was fine and at Rawston Legacy Hospital look-ing for a friend.

Justin was also able to let his family know that he was okay. "My grandparents are leaving the shelter and heading home. Southshire was lucky. There was some wind damage, but noth-ing big," he told her as soon as he'd hung up.

"Oh, I'm so glad—" she was interrupted by giddy squeals as Kaylee and her mother and her aunt found Chaz. In spite of a broken arm, Kaylee was jumping up and down and franti-cally exchanging notes with Chaz about everything that hap-pened over the last hours, whenever Chaz wasn't shutting her up with a kiss.

—————

"Our place is completely wrecked," Bob Ray told Heather. "Seriously. Looks like someone drove our trailer in a demoli-tion derby and lost. Big time." They'd been talking nonstop since he arrived. And, even though the news was terrible, he'd never felt more at peace. More convicted about what a lousy husband and father he'd been. More willing and eager to make amends and some serious changes in his life. And Heather. Beautiful, sweet Heather. Her forgiveness was a total gift that he in no way deserved. He'd spend the rest of his life working hard to make her happy.

"I know," Heather said and shivered. "When I got here, I saw on the news that the tornado had plowed straight down Hollingsworth Boulevard."

Head dipped to kiss his son, he murmured, "Luckily, Mrs. Carmichael is okay, but the place is totaled. Half of it's in our yard. Half's in hers."

"What about Danny?" Heather asked as she remembered she'd left him there, when she and Robbie had headed off to the store for milk.

"Wasn't there. Neither was his truck. Mrs. Carmichael said she thinks he left before the storm hit."

Heather's relief was audible. "Thank heavens. I was so worried. When I left, he was . . ." She swallowed, obviously emotional at the thoughts spinning through her head, she tried again, ". . . when I left he was under the house, looking to see if our insulation was soaked and hoping to find where the water was coming out."

Bob Ray pushed back a stab of worry. Danny was from around here. He knew when to take shelter. He was a smart, strong man. He had to be safe. He had to be.

"I'm sorry I wasn't there when the storm hit, Heather. That will never happen again. I promise you, I'll be there whenever you need me in the future."

"I know."

Those two simple words sent a powerful rush of healing through his body, and he loved her more, if possible, than any person or thing he'd ever loved before.

"I guess it's lucky we don't own anything worth sweating over, huh?" He smiled at her, drinking in her sweet face and unselfish love for him and Robbie.

She shrugged. "Unless you count your football trophies and—"

"Heather? *Heather?*"

Both Heather and Bob Ray turned at the sound of her name filtering through the crowd and growing closer.

15

As Heather's parents emerged from the milling, misplaced throng, a surge of adrenaline had Bob Ray tensing with the fight or flight syndrome. Rising to his feet, he shielded his son in his arms as he stepped between his in-laws and his wife, at their frantic, take-charge approach. Though he was tempted to stalk away and leave Heather to deal with her intimidating father, he stood his ground.

Huffing and harried, Mike and Denise were urgent with fear and when they saw their daughter, their relief was extreme. Palpable.

Bob Ray couldn't help but wonder why they thought this disaster in their daughter's life was more worthy of their attention than the last. As usual, her parents were dressed impeccably for a post-tornado meeting, their Tommy Bahama togs perfectly coordinated, their hair well-groomed and stylish. Both were still tan from their annual spring fling in Fiji. How he used to admire their style and wealth. Tonight, it seemed as vain and useless as the gold pinky ring on Mike's finger.

Heather's mother, Denise, reached them first. "Heather, oh, thank God! Mike! Over here!" She gestured for Heather's father to hurry and join them. "Oh, we've been worried *sick* about you! And the baby! Living in that horrible trailer park during a *tornado* . . . why anything could have happened!"

The muscles in Bob Ray's jaw jumped with resentment, and he was glad when Heather stood and tucked her hand into the crook of his elbow. Robbie was still fast asleep in his arms, blissfully unaware of the day's traumas.

"We've been watching the news and saw that the storm hit that whole area." Denise's gaze strayed with longing at Robbie as she spoke to Heather. "How are you, sweetheart?"

"I'm fine, Mom." Heather darted a quick glance at her stony-faced father.

Bob Ray could see how awkward she felt with them after so much estrangement. Irritatingly, there was no warmth for him in either of their expressions. In their minds, Bob Ray was a loser. An undercurrent of so many angry memories shimmered between them and her parents.

Mike's being there right now had to be Denise's idea. This was the first time Heather's father had seen her since the wedding. Clearly something was up. Bob Ray caught Mike staring at his angel-faced, curly-haired grandson. Emotions too numerous to count flickered across Mike's face, giving the older man a vulnerability that almost had Bob Ray feeling sorry for him. Robbie was his first grandchild, and this was the first time he'd laid eyes on the kid.

"Honey," Denise pressed Heather, emboldened by the horrendous trauma of the situation and no doubt counting on it to distract from the deeper issues. "Your father and I have talked it over. And we want you and little Robbie to come home with us."

Bob Ray went stiff. His narrow gaze settled on Denise's face, and their eyes clashed. So, he wasn't included in this magnanimous invitation. He'd never admit it, but it stung.

Oblivious to her son-in-law's feelings, or simply not caring, Denise continued. "The storm didn't do much damage out in Lakewood. We can take care of you both until you can get on your feet again. In fact—"

Bob Ray shook his head. "No." He turned to focus on Mike as he spoke. "Thank you, so much. But, no. As much as I know Heather appreciates your generous offer, I seem to recall you telling Heather she was my responsibility several years ago. So, with all due respect, I'll provide shelter for my wife and son."

Behind him, he felt Heather squeezing his arm, and he exchanged a quick, encouraging glance with her. Superman was reflected in her shining eyes, and it looked as if she was biting back a whoop of pride.

"What are *you* offering her?" Derision filled Mike's hard voice. "Another trailer?"

Denise was exasperated, as well. "How are you going to support her, Bob Ray? That low-life bar is gone now."

"I know," he said, keeping his voice firm and steady. "I've already found a place for us to live and a job to get us by for now." Selma had offered them room and board in exchange for some much needed work around her house—though he didn't feel the need to share this information with them. "So, as much as I appreciate your belated concern for my wife and son, they'll be coming home with me tonight."

When Abigail finally spotted Selma near the Red Cross table, they ran toward each other with open arms, shouting with joy and hugging and kissing and hugging some more.

"I've been so worried about you, honey," Selma pulled Abigail's damp face down and ran her arthritic thumbs over her streaming cheeks.

"Me, too. Oh, Selma, they're saying Old Town was hit hard. Were you at home when the storm touched down?"

"Thankfully, yes, honey, I was. Guadalupe and I were in my dear Clyde's shelter, praise the good Lord, because we later learned that Guadalupe's home is ruined. But my house is just fine. Don't worry about your place. It can all be replaced. Believe me, I know. You'll come home with me tonight and stay just as long as you want. Forever is just fine with me."

"Auntie Sel," Abigail swiped the tears from her cheek with the edge of her palm. Her lips were quivering as she tried to form the words around her sudden wracking sobs. "Oh, Selma . . . our buildings . . . our sweet little shops are *gone*. I'm homeless." Funny, what that word used to mean to her before tonight. Before Bernie.

Before she lost everything in the blink of an eye.

"No, no, no. Never, honey. Your home is with me."

"Is this a dream?" Abigail asked plaintively, desperate for Selma to help her understand. "I keep thinking we're going to wake up in the morning and all of this will be a horrible nightmare. It's not real. How could anything this . . . this terrible be real?"

"I know. I had those same thoughts back in '66. I know, honey. I know." Selma clutched Abigail as the younger woman sobbed.

Abigail had never suffered such conflicting emotions. So much terrible loss of property, and yet so much precious gain in human life spared. Anger at the storm, gratitude for her aunt. Sorrow over the death, joy over the life. Fury over being a victim, relief over being spared.

Distrust of God warring with total dependence on Him.

"Now, you listen to me, honey. You are going to be just fine. Better than ever, in fact." At Abigail's whimper of protest she said, "*Shh*. It's okay. Don't you worry about any of this now. It will all sort itself out. In the meantime, you know how I love a full house. We'll take a little time and get all of this mess squared away. And when we're not so exhausted, we'll make some decisions for the future. Abigail, honey, please, listen. I know. Shhh, now. Listen. I have invited others who have lost everything to come and stay with me as well. It will be wonderful. All suffering, all celebrating, all together, helping each other through. You know I'll be glad not to be rattling around all alone in that big old house. Sweetie, it's for times just like this that Clyde built it."

Abigail clung to Selma's firm voice and adamant expression. What would she do without her? And Justin. The surge of panic began to ebb a little.

"I have a new friend with me, Auntie Sel," Abigail finally pulled herself together enough to haltingly explain about Justin and how he wasn't sure yet, but it looked like he might need a place to stay for a while, too. "He's a good friend of Danny Strohacker's."

"Danny Strohacker, you say? Really? That's wonderful. The more the merrier, you know I always say that. I have a car full to take home, now. I want to get Bob Ray Lathrop—you know him?—no? Well, you will—and his wife and their little boy and Guadalupe and Elsa back to my place and into bed. Why don't you find out what you can about Old Town, and I'll come back for you both as soon as I can, okay?"

Abigail knew that it would be at least an hour or two before Selma returned. She also knew Justin was anxious to check on his house. She glanced around. "Justin lives out in your direction . . . he's somewhere around here now. Oh, and Aunt Selma, he delivered Jen's baby tonight! It's a boy! A beautiful, healthy boy."

Selma beamed. "Well, I'll be! What a lovely light in all this darkness!"

Spotting Justin, Abigail waved him over. After a quick round of introductions, Selma leaned back, adjusted her glasses and peered up at Justin with a huge smile on her face. "How nice to make your acquaintance, Justin." She chuckled. "Any friend of Daniel's is a friend of mine and that is the truth, plain and simple. If you need a place to stay, you are welcome to bunk with the rest of us."

Justin embraced her and kissed her weathered cheek. "Thank you, ma'am. I might just have to take you up on your kind offer. You know, you look really familiar to me . . ."

"Now honey, that's the oldest line in the book. I'm old enough to be your big sister."

Justin laughed at the merry twinkle in Selma's eye. "You attend first service at Rawston Christian, right?"

"Busted!" Selma crowed.

Abigail watched the two, in awe at how trauma created such instant friendships. When a breach finally came in their steady conversation, Abigail jumped in with both feet. "Aunt Selma, Justin and I were talking about walking for a while and maybe helping out where we could, as we go through Old Town to see my place and then on to Justin's house. Would it be easier for you to meet us up closer to your neighborhood? That way you don't have to try to drive through town again? "

Selma's snow white head bobbed enthusiastically as she listened. "I know there is a great need for rescuers everywhere. If you two feel strong enough, then—" she placed an age-spotted hand on each of their arms, "—God bless you. Oh! And I've got a flashlight in the glove box. Come on with me."

⸻

As Abigail and Justin walked away from the parking lot and toward Old Town, they met people streaming through the devastation back toward the hospital by the dozens. Survivors were walking zombies as they carried their children or small dogs or maybe some small personal items they'd managed to salvage. If their eyes weren't vacant, they were filled with grief and confusion. He admired the way Abigail would stop and offer encouragement or share directions along the way. Her gentle warmth came out in myriad little ways—a touch, a hug, a sympathetic nod—and she always seemed to know just what to say or do to pull a smile out of someone or plant a seed of hope in their heart.

Everywhere, people asked them both if they had seen their missing family members. In turn, Justin would ask after Danny. No one had seen him, but Justin supposed, that was because everyone was busy looking for their own Dannys.

Giant Xs were being spray-painted on houses and cars that had been checked for survivors. Roman numerals beneath each X indicated how many deceased had been found inside. In the eerie quiet, a voice would shout out a name once or twice then wait for an answer. If none came, they'd try again. A dog barked and a baby cried. The smell of gas from broken pipes permeated the air, sap from broken trees, smoke from gas fires and worst of all, death. Every kind of creature had suffered equally.

At one point, a man came rushing up to Justin, eyes wild, and begged him to help him pry his car open. He'd come home from work to discover that his wife wasn't home yet from a soccer game with their sons. After walking for miles and searching everywhere, he just found their car. On its top with his wife and boys still trapped inside.

"*I can't reach them!*" he shrieked, grappling with and straining at the door, clawing and kicking at the metal. Justin and two other men who'd stopped to help sprinted over and, using everything they could find as a tool, finally managed to pry the doors open.

But it was too late. The damage too brutal.

The young husband and father sent up a spine-chilling, mournful wail that pierced the darkness, then fell against Justin's chest before he slid to the ground in a heap and sobbed, head in his hands. Out of the shadows, strangers came and comforted the stricken man along with a devastated Justin and Abigail. Gathered in the desolate shadows, they sat with him and prayed and comforted him until he found a ride to his parents' home.

Once he'd gone, heart heavy, Justin stood and held his arms open to Abigail. Sharing his grief, she slipped naturally into his embrace. Pressing his cheek against the top of her head, they held each other and mourned the stranger's wife and boys.

Every now and then, a car or truck would rattle and limp by on a bent frame or ruptured tires. Lumber stuck—like tooth-picks in a sandwich—from the grills and doors. The wind-shields and windows were broken, the auto bodies dented and twisted and looking as if they should be impossible to drive. More than once they were offered a ride and, though they turned them down, Justin was struck by the generous, compassionate hearts of the good folks of Rawston.

A dog came limping up to them at one point, whining, his tail wagging, body wriggling. When Abigail tried to pet him, the dog skittered away, then looked back at her and whimpered.

"Come here, honey," Abigail crooned to the dog. To Justin, she said, "I think he might be hurt. He doesn't want me to touch him, poor thing." As she spoke gentle words of comfort, the dog continued to repeat the pattern.

"You know . . ." Justin cocked his head and regarded the dog, "I think he's trying to get us to follow him." He scratched his chin. "Come on. Let's see what he wants." The dog bounded off, barking, then stopping and wriggling and waiting as they picked their way through the rubble after him. Then, off he'd go again, sniffing and pausing to yip until he stopped and started barking loud and insistently. Though his paws were sore and bleeding, he scratched at the ruins and then ducked his head, poking it into the rubble.

He was licking someone's face. Justin and Abigail helped each other to the dog with anxious steps and joined the animal in its frenzied digging. Bit by bit, they worked together, pulling lumber and sheetrock and metal off the pile until they eventually exposed the bodies of an elderly woman and what must have been her husband. The dog licked their faces, whining and then looking back and forth at Justin and Abigail. Justin reached in and touched the woman first, and then the man.

"Gone," he whispered.

Stricken, they stood and attempted to get the dog to follow them away from the bodies. But the animal hunkered down against the woman and his tail-wagging slowed and then stopped as he watched them walk away. Again, tears poured down Abigail's cheeks, and Justin welled up as they moved on through the chaos.

That night, they helped dig a family out of a basement, prayed with a terrified mother over her missing children, loaded a badly wounded man onto a battered pickup truck, carried two small children for parents already loaded down with twin toddlers, administered crude first aid when and wherever it was needed, and did their best to bolster spirits. They kept an eye out for Danny but hoped that the fact that they hadn't seen him yet meant he was already at the hospital with Jen.

The hours flew by. The horror mounted. And their bond grew.

Once Selma arrived home and had Robbie settled, she rushed off to get Elsa into bed. Heather watched the elderly woman in awe. She had more energy than a nuclear power plant. Heather had tried to lend a hand, only to be told, "I haven't had the pleasure of putting a baby to bed for ages. You go sit a spell. Git, git git!" Heather had only lived a quarter of Selma's years but felt as if she could drop into bed and sleep for a month.

While Bob Ray and Guadalupe gathered towels and sheets, Heather wandered through the house, looking at framed pictures of Selma's family that spanned at least five decades displayed on the top of the piano and hanging on the walls.

Would she and Bob Ray ever leave such a beautiful legacy? Tonight, they'd made a good start. As her gaze roved the generations, she had to wonder where all these people were now. She was pretty sure her husband, Clyde, had died, but the rest of them? Where were they tonight? Were they safe? Were they worried about their mother?

Bob Ray and Selma's voices drifted up the stairs and Heather met them in the living room. ". . . back when we lived in Topeka. That was in 1966. This storm reminds me a lot of that one. Hello, honey," she said to Heather. "I was just telling your hubby about the Topeka tornado of '66. We were all hiding in the bathroom. All eight of us, if you can imagine that. My junior-high-aged kids were crammed in the tub, the high-school kids in the shower, and Clyde and me were wedged between the toilet and the vanity. And just like that scene in the *Wizard of Oz*, the tornado tore the house off the foundation, all but the bathroom, and sent it spinning two miles east. Aside from being showered with toilet water and a lot of glass and mud and debris, we all crawled out just fine.

So, that's why we have such a great shelter now. Clyde felt that no Midwestern American family should be without some place to hide when *El Diablo*—that's Spanish for the devil—hit."

"Where are your children now, Selma?" Heather asked, curiously.

Fingers shaking with a palsy born of old age, Selma pointed out each of her children to Heather. "Julie is a widow in Montana. She'll be a great-grandma any day now. Called to check up on me already. Mary is also a grandma in upstate New York, nursing her disabled hubby. I'll call her later today. Cathy is in Thailand, where she and her husband are missionaries. She probably doesn't know about the storm yet. Lorna is in an Oregon nursing home with Parkinson's disease, and her children are nearby. And Tommy is a bush pilot in Alaska. And my Paul . . . passed away nearly two decades ago. They all moved away from the Midwest for various reasons. They are all grandparents now and in their sixties. They will all call— as will their children—and try to convince me to move later today." Pride and love for each image shone in her eyes, and she lovingly dusted the frames with her fingertips.

"They're beautiful."

"Thank you, honey. And I don't think it's a sin to agree."

They'd made it to the hallway and Selma pressed a load of towels into her arms. "These are for you guys, sweetie. Your bed is made up and there are plenty of pillows. Guadalupe is making sandwiches if you are hungry, so stop by the kitchen and pick up a plate on your way by.

"Thank you so much, Mrs. Tully." Heather smiled, her voice choked with gratitude. "Your home is just perfect."

"Call me Selma, darling girl. Everyone does. And thank you. I was just telling Bob Ray here that Clyde designed it for our family himself."

"He did an awesome job." Heather's eyes swept the wonderful, lived-in, cozy home with envy. She'd grown up in designer mausoleums, but this cheerful, comfy nest filled with the history of happiness was what Heather dreamed of for her family.

"Thank you, honey. It's a regular bunker. The bedrooms are all in the basement where it's safe, if the storm comes back, so sleep tight. If the storm kicks up again, there is a trap door in the laundry room, that goes down an additional 8 feet for a 10x10 storm shelter, stocked with canned food, a first aid kit, lanterns, sleeping bags, water, and a safe that holds some of the more important stuff. If Clyde could see us all here now, he'd be so proud and happy. I'm just thrilled to have you here with me. Stay. Stay just as long as you need, forever is okay with me."

Bob Ray laughed and while they chatted for another few minutes, his gaze traveled to the pictures on the wall. "Selma? Isn't that my dad?"

Selma adjusted her glasses. "Yes. That's him. Standing there with Paul. They were never apart. In life," she said and sighed, "and in death."

Bob Ray nodded. Heather wondered exactly what they were talking about, but would ask tomorrow, when she'd be awake enough to understand.

"I have collected a bunch of bathrobes over the years," Selma said as she turned back to the bathroom linen closet. She pulled out two, one for her and one for Bob Ray. "I got a ten-pack of toothbrushes at the dollar store so pick your favorite colors. The toothpaste and deodorant and lotions and stuff are in the med cabinet. Toss your dirty clothes in the bathroom hamper, and I'll get a load going while you clean up."

The backs of Heather's eyes burned with love as she watched her big muscular husband hug and kiss the tiny Selma on the cheek. "Thank you," he said his voice raw with emotion. "You have always been there for me."

"Oh, honey. I'm glad to do it. Your dad was special and a big part of my life."

"I know." Bob Ray sniffed and swiped at his eyes. "Everyone tells me I missed out on knowing him."

"You're a lot like him, Bob Ray. He was a wonderful man. He'd have been a real good daddy to you, if he'd had the chance."

"Yes, ma'am."

"I have a TV dish, if you want to catch the news, up here in the living room and down in your rooms. I always keep plenty of food in the house during storm season, so eat up. There's milk in the refrigerator for Robbie and cereal in the pantry. I'm headed back out now to pick up my niece and her new friend. I'll be back in two shakes of a lamb's tail."

⸻

Rawston's crown jewel, her charming Old Town, as rumored, had been leveled, breaking what was left of Abigail's heart. It was a disaster. So much so that, without street signs and buildings to guide her as landmarks, Abigail wasn't sure where her home even was. When they finally came upon what they decided must be her building, she and Justin could only stand in the moonlight and stare. The entire second story of her salon had sailed away, as had her apartment, her furniture, all of the personal belongings she'd amassed over the last half-dozen years. The first floor had pretty much exploded and only the innermost bathroom was upright. Her staircase listed dangerously and led nowhere.

Beauty supplies were strewn everywhere and her chairs and shampoo bowls and the lobby furniture she'd so lovingly refinished had been shredded. In the lobby now was a Toyota Corolla, its lights on high beam, illuminating the mess. Abigail clutched Justin's arm with one hand and her heart with the other, trying to register, to comprehend the fact that her business and home were really, truly gone. All that work. Scattered. Shattered.

"Oh, man," Justin breathed as he took it all in at her side. "Unbelievable."

"I know," Abigail murmured, dazed. She had never felt so completely violated. She had nothing now. Not even a piece of ID to say who she was. After several minutes spent soaking it all in, she found a plastic bag in the rubble and began to load a few intact things from the salon. A bottle of shampoo that hadn't broken, a brush, some soap and other supplies, her beloved shears, a piece of the material she'd made her curtains from.

"Don't go any farther in," Justin warned as she rooted among her broken shelving units to see what the storm had spared. "All of the support beams for the second floor are gone, and your remaining walls aren't looking too sturdy."

As if to drive his point home, a wall crashed with a ka-*whomp*, sending dust and debris scattering. Abigail quickly backed away from the building and sighed in defeat. "I guess we can go now."

Selma's Quilty Pleasures had fared no better. When they arrived, there was some movement coming from inside the quilt shop debris. Had someone been in there and become trapped? Clutching her plastic bag, Abigail ran after Justin to see if she could help. When she got to his side, he held up a finger, silently cautioning her to be quiet as he picked up a broken 2x4 that was lying in the street.

"Looters," he whispered, "probably looking for cash." As they stood and listened to their hushed conversation, it became clear that Justin was right.

"No, not that. Only grab small stuff we can hock on eBay. Look for the cash register."

Stealthily moving toward the thieves, Justin finally made it close enough to confront them face-to-face. There were two men and a woman. They jumped at the sound of his voice. "Hi, there. Can I help you?" Justin asked, shouldering the board.

Guiltily, they backed away. "We . . . we . . . we're looking for survivors?"

"Really? Awesome! Thank heavens for good citizens like you guys, but don't worry now, the store was closed when the storm hit so no one trapped here. Me? I'm looking for *looters*. Can you believe that anyone would stoop low enough to *steal* from a little old lady who just lost her store in a storm? The very idea makes me *crazy!*" The wood whistled through the air as he wielded the 2x4 like Babe Ruth swinging for a home run. The three stumbled backwards in the darkness then whirled around, and ran.

For the first time since they'd left the hospital, Abigail laughed.

—∞∞—

As they neared Justin's house, he stopped and pulled a piece of an American flag off the broken branch of a tree. "Here's another souvenir for you," he said, and tucked it into Abigail's bag. He'd already contributed a man's suit tie that he'd found wrapped around a barber pole and joked that along with the tattered scrap of wedding dress, she'd already gathered something old, something new, something borrowed, and something blue. "You're all set for when you find Mr. Right." His smile was guileless and his humor, light. But there was something in his voice that had her heart thudding.

179

"Thank you," she'd replied, furiously blushing as she plucked an embroidered doily out of a heap of debris that clung to the grill of an overturned car.

They began to make a game of it. Who could find the weirdest souvenir scrap. Justin found a Sponge Bob pillowcase and Abigail, a child's ballet tutu. He found a pair of Christmas-themed boxer shorts—which she made him drop—and she found a T-shirt that said I'm with Stupid. Her bag began to bulge with the pieces of people's lives. She held up the bag at one point and commented, "This bag contains all my worldly goods."

"I guess that's why we're supposed to store our treasure in heaven, huh?"

Abigail didn't answer right away, mulling the faces of death she'd just seen. "Justin?"

"Hmm?" He reached for her hand and helped her around a battered sports car that lay on its side in the middle of the street.

"Do you ever get the feeling that your prayers are just bouncing off the ceiling?"

"Sometimes. But Danny says we're the ones who drift away. Not Him."

"But don't you ever wonder how a God who is supposed to be so merciful could clobber Rawston this way?" Though she'd been raised to believe in God, she was seriously wrestling with the idea that God could allow such devastation.

"You know who you should ask? Danny. Whenever I have a question like that, he has the answer. And it always makes sense."

Abigail fell silent. Pondering. Wondering. Treading water in a sea of confusion. As soon as she could, she would ask Danny her questions.

They crossed over the Balady River Bridge to the northwest neighborhood side of town. It took a while, but they finally made it to Justin's house. Rather, what was left of Justin's house. Abigail could see that he'd been doing a wonderful job upgrading an older home. It was an Arts and Crafts style and, at one time, his rockwork had been beautiful. Now, much of it lay in ruins. The landscaping had been plowed up like a fallow field, ready for planting. Gaping holes in the roof had rendered it unlivable. The place was still there, yes, but it was a mess.

"I'm so sorry," Abigail whispered as they stood in the middle of his street, peering at the house lightened only by the flashlight's beam and the moon's glow.

For long moments, they drank in the destruction, their hearts breaking, their minds processing, their souls crying out for justice. In a low voice, he pointed out the plans he'd had for the home; to give the worst house on the block a face-lift, flip it, and put the money toward his retirement and another investment. All that hard, after-hours work, lifted into the air and tossed into the trash. Windows were blown out and the sound of water running told the only story they needed to know about where Justin would be staying tonight. This week. Indefinitely.

As they worked their way toward the front lawn, a dark missile came streaking out of the ruins and had Abigail squealing and her heart speeding.

The growling shadow stopped at Justin's voice, just short of attacking. "Rawhide?"

It was a dog? Abigail peered down at the now leaping mass of muscle.

"Down, boy!" The dog had no intention of obeying and leapt into Justin's arms and bathed his face in a slew of frenzied kisses. Justin's laughter rang out. "Easy there, buddy." Rawhide whimpered and wriggled and groaned long, deep-throated cries that spoke of the trauma he'd just endured. His tail, like Indiana Jones's whip, flailed, beating both Justin and Abigail in unmitigated joy.

While man and dog held a scratching, wagging, licking, crooning love fest, Abigail dug out her phone and called Selma. As luck would have it, she was already in the neighborhood, and if Abigail looked north and west, she'd probably see her headlights.

Within minutes of hanging up, Selma was able to park at the end of the block and shout for them to come on home. They answered her with relieved shouts of their own and started walking. As if he spoke English, Rawhide bolted toward the sound of Selma's voice and leaped into her car. "Why, hello there, Mr. Dog." They could hear Selma's chirpy laughter echo down the street. Rawhide scrambled into the front seat and perched his front paws on the steering wheel, clearly eager to be on his way.

"How does it look, honey?" Selma asked at their approach.

"The house is still standing," Abigail told her, "but it's uninhabitable."

Selma tsked. "That's okay. Justin, I have a futon in my den with your name on it. I love dogs, so your guy here will be a welcome addition to the party. Get in, you two. It's time to go home."

PART THREE

BEYOND THE STORM

*The groans of earth shall be surpassed by the songs of
heaven, and the woes of time
shall be swallowed up in the hallelujahs of eternity.*

—C. H. Spurgeon

16

Abigail slept fitfully and woke to the beginnings of daylight peeking in through the high basement bedroom windows. She blinked around the room and tried to orient herself as she surfaced. Why . . . was she at Selma's? Oh. Right. Because she was homeless. The heaviness that sleep had temporarily lifted came crashing back. Normally, daylight was welcome in her room, nudging her eyes open and chasing shadows away. But today, it brought with it dread. How would she cope with what she saw in the unforgiving light of day?

Rolling on her side, she could see the alarm clock. 5:50 a.m. After last night's hot shower, she'd had two-and-a-half hours of sleep. She needed many hours more, but there was still so much adrenaline zinging through her system, she knew it would be futile to lie here, trying to doze off.

Upstairs, she could hear the sounds of footsteps and muffled voices. A toilet flushed and the water rushed through the pipes. The faint smell of bacon and coffee wafted into her room.

Selma's kitchen had been mustard and avocado for so long the color scheme was nearly back in vogue. Her appliances were all the same ones Clyde had installed when he'd built the place—Westinghouse, harvest gold. And though the refrigerator would abruptly growl to life like a ravenous lion, roaring and groaning every half hour, nobody could convince Selma to replace it. She harbored a similar affection for the thrashing, clanking dishwasher and the buzz saw of a disposal.

The plank floors were warped and worn and squeaked here and there, and the cabinets were much the same. Clyde had built the large open room to feature an oak table that would seat his entire brood when all the leaves were in. It was a room that invited one to come and linger over a cookie and a cup of tea. It was a room that harbored laughter and tears and more than a few secrets whispered between siblings. And it was a room where people could come and be fed, both body and soul.

There were people seated at the kitchen table as Abigail rounded the corner into the room. Guadalupe, she recognized. And her teenaged daughter, Elsa. And . . . what on earth? Her eyes widened in surprise. The stripper from Kaylee's bachelorette party?

"Coffee?" Selma held up a pot.

"Yes, please." Abigail shuffled over to the table and dropped into a chair.

"You haven't met Bob Ray Lathrop yet, honey. Bob Ray, this is my niece, Abigail. Abigail, Bob Ray."

Ah. Up close and in person. "Hi," Abigail took the mug from Selma and grinned at Bob Ray's sheepish expression. Clearly, he remembered her from the other night. "How do you know my aunt?"

Bob Ray cleared his throat. "Her son and my dad were best friends." A pretty young woman toting a toddler on her hip came into the room as he was talking and kissed him on the cheek. He looked at her with adoration and lifted his arms to take the little boy. So. Bob Ray Lathrop was a family man? How . . . strange. She smiled at Heather as Selma made introductions.

"So you and Selma have known each other for a long time." Abigail looked back to Bob Ray.

"All my life."

"Which of Selma's sons was your dad's friend?"

"Paul."

"Oh."

Heather looked back and forth between them, clearly trying to decipher the meaning behind the loaded "Oh." Before Abigail could explain, Justin stumbled into the room, wrapped in one of Selma's crazy bathrobes, his hair standing on end, his jaw dark with stubble. He was adorable. Just the sight of him lifted her mood and had an involuntary grin tugging at her lips.

"Coffee," he croaked and dropped into a chair next to Abigail. She slid her mug into his hand and he drank deeply. "More." Grin blooming, Abigail stood and grabbed the pot and another mug for herself.

Guadalupe and Selma began loading the table with plates of bacon and scrambled eggs. A platter of buttered toast had stayed warm in the oven and there were pots of jam on the table. Hash browns laced with red onion and a bottle of ketchup followed.

Selma urged everyone to hold hands. Abigail took Bob Ray's and Justin's hands, and they all bowed their heads. "Father God, how we thank You for sparing us and this home. Thank you for bringing us all together this morning. Thank you for Your tender mercies. You are sovereign, Lord. You are wonderful. We love You and trust You. Please, Lord, be with those who are suffering today. Give them peace and let even the horror and the pain of this situation be used to further Your kingdom and point eyes and hearts toward Your majesty. In Your name we pray, Jesus, Amen."

All around the table amens were murmured, but Abigail could not bring herself to echo the sentiment. How could Selma even say something like that? Asking God to use the horror to point hearts to him? What kind of a God would do that? Allow that? All her life, she'd gone to Sunday school, but that was always the one thing she could never seem to accept without question. A so-called God of love who would allow such pain and suffering. As she blinked at her eggs, she could feel Justin's eyes on her in her peripheral vision. She glanced up at him and offered a tight smile. As if he could read her mind, his hand went to the back of her neck and worked at the knot of muscles he found there. Oh, the pressure of his strong fingers was wonderful, and she gave herself up to the healing power of his touch with a vocal sigh. Eyes closed, she listened to the conversation flowing around the table.

CNN was on. The reports were horrific. Dismal. The number of dead approached two hundred. Hundreds were still missing. Help poured in from other states. The governor had declared a state of emergency. The President of the United States was on his way. Condolences and offers of aid came in from other countries. Shelters had filled up fast, and hospitals were overflowing. People were searching for loved ones. Facebook sites had been created to assist folks in locating each other. FEMA's Region VII was on the move.

And there were the pictures.

They all watched, mesmerized by the idea that anyone could possibly survive such a disaster. Houses and cars were gone, yes, but even great chunks of concrete and asphalt had been sucked off the earth's surface and tossed into piles that exploded and leveled whatever they landed on. An entire fence built of giant boulders had been snatched up the way a child would grasp a pile of marbles and hurl them across the yard. Several high-rises had been reduced to single-story dwellings, affording a clear, unobstructed view of damage for as far as the eye could see. It was the apocalypse, now, and for over an hour they watched and murmured among themselves. When the stories began to repeat themselves, they all headed off to shower and face the day.

—⊗⊗⊗—

While Abigail waited for her turn in the bathroom, she returned a call to her mother. Karen had been up watching the news all night and was beside herself with anxiety. "Get out of there, honey! Come to California! I can get you a ticket today."

"Oh, Mom," Abigail pressed the phone to her ear and heard her sigh crackle across the miles. "I want to, really. But I have to stay and get everything sorted out with insurance before I can go anywhere. Besides, there is so much to do here."

They haggled, Karen insistent, Abigail wavering, neither giving in. "Abigail, I love you, honey. I was so scared I would never be able to say that to you again." Karen's angst pierced Abigail's heart, and they cried together and told each other so many things they'd left unsaid over the years. Abigail promised to get out for a visit to house hunt as soon as she could. That satisfied Karen for the time being, and they hung up after Abigail promised to kiss Selma for her mom.

When she'd finished with her family, she started calling friends. Isuzu told her that Brooke had come out of surgery and was expected to recover eventually. The doctors did not expect her to skate again and feared some lasting handicaps. However, she was out of the coma and asking for her parents and brother. And Nick.

189

"Our house is gone. So we stay in lobby at hospital for now. Nice couch here and many blankets. Pastor come to visit and bring things we need. God will give us new house when His time come."

Abigail marveled at her faith. Her niece and nephew's golden skating careers had just gone up in flames, their houses and restaurant were totaled. They had no material possessions other than some blankets and stuff the pastor brought. Why wasn't Isuzu throwing a fit? Screaming and railing over the unfairness of it all. After they rang off, Abigail sat at the edge of her bed and stared at the wall and pondered until her phone vibrated in her hand. *Kaylee*.

She'd called to say she and Chaz had moved into their new house along with her mother and aunt, and his parents and brother. They'd stayed up all night and, after a lengthy discussion, had decided to go ahead with the wedding. "I know a lot of folks might think we're being selfish, what with so much heartache all around. We are worried about that, and to tell the truth, we have a lot of survivor's guilt. But we also see our wedding as a beginning. We're starting fresh. We have hope, and with God's grace, we'll recover and move on. We want our wedding to be a symbol of hope to our friends and family."

Tears welled in Abigail's eyes. "Oh, honey, I'm so happy for you. I wouldn't miss it. Is it okay with you if I bring a few friends?"

"I was just going to ask!" Kaylee's enthusiasm was contagious. "We'll have plenty of food! The caterer is from Springfield, and they are all good. It's going to be pretty casual now. The church suffered some damage, but the electricity and water are on, so we should be fine. Come as you are at 6:30 Saturday night and bring your appetite."

The carnage was even worse, if possible, in the daylight. The tiny details such as torn family photos, a broken locket, a child's dollhouse, were what struck Abigail as she and Justin entered Old Town Rawston that morning.

The entire Old Town area: all of the cute buildings, the flowers, benches, the quaint signage, the meticulous landscaping, the historical statues and other charming landmarks, fountains, the cobblestone streets, the centuries-old trees, the Old Town Square Park with its charming gazebo—all of it reduced to a landfill in less time than it took to order a latte at Mr. Bean.

Everything in her shop had been destroyed, but it was the little things that shoved a lump into her throat. The blue vase that she'd splurged on just last month crunched beneath her booted feet as she hiked and picked her way through the refuse. The desk she'd spent a month sanding. The curtains she'd laboriously sewn with Selma's help.

Up and down the street, other business owners were also scavenging for whatever they might be able to salvage. There were some tears, but surprisingly, there was also humor. Some of it dark. Some of it silly. But all of it welcome. Most of the business owners and apartment owners, such as Abigail, were simply glad to be alive. And to find each other in the same condition. The Toyota was still sitting inside her shop. Its battery had finally died and the headlights that had illuminated the interior last night were off.

"Justin!"

"What?" He stopped sifting through her rubble and stood and stretched.

"This! It's my dresser!" It was lying on its back in the middle of the street.

Justin stepped to her side and helped her drag it to the sidewalk and set it upright. Opening a drawer, she squealed.

"Everything is still here!" A surge of joy she'd never known before at the simple act of opening a dresser drawer had her mood suddenly soaring. Justin watched indulgently as she opened each drawer and sighed with satisfaction at clothing still miraculously folded in tidy stacks. Selma had loaned them each a backpack and she stuffed hers as full as she dared with fresh underwear, and jeans, some tops and socks.

"We can come back later for the rest," Justin assured her as she nearly toppled over from the weight of her backpack. He took a half dozen pairs of jeans out of her pack and loaded them into his. "Come on, my little fashion plate. C'mon, Rawhide." The dog jumped to follow at the sound of his name.

Abigail's giddy mood lasted only until they got to Quilty Pleasure. All of Selma's beautiful quilts. Tattered and torn and caked with mud. "Poor Selma," she groaned.

"Ah, man." Justin twisted his cap back and forth on his head.

Bolts of fabric and scraps were strewn everywhere. Abigail picked a package of quilting squares out of a flower basket and pressed them to her cheek. These were some of the Noah's ark pattern that Jen loved. She'd save these. She grabbed a few other bits and pieces and tucked them into Justin's pack. She had no idea why. More souvenirs to commemorate the occasion, she guessed.

At Justin's suggestion, they headed back to Selma's to unload their packs, have some lunch, and then hit his place for a load of his clothes. Side-by-side they walked, neither acknowledging how much they appreciated the contact. Now and then, they would have to stop and try to figure out where they were. It was frustrating. Though she'd grown up in this town, the vista was so completely changed, she had no real idea where she was standing half of the time. Every landmark that she'd ever known was missing. The buildings were flat, the street signs, gone. Even the sky was gray and ugly. Rawston was now just a huge landfill out in the middle of the prairie.

Someone's pet dog was lying in the street, dead. It seemed like every time she spotted a bit of silver lining, reality would rear up and smack her in the face. Already Justin could read her moods. "Are you okay?" he asked gently.

"Yeah. Fine. I just . . ." She lifted and dropped her arms. "I'm stunned. Everything I worked for my whole life is . . . broken."

"Not this." He held up a framed copy of her North American Hair Stylist of the Year award. Unbelievably, the glass had not broken and the frame was in perfect condition. "I was going to clean it up and give it to you later."

Abigail exhaled a smile. He was so sweet. So thoughtful. She took it from his hand and explained as they walked. "When I won this, I met a guy named DJ in LA who does hair for celebrities at his shop and at some of the movie studios. He offered me a job. I told him I had to think it over, because I had a lot going on here and I didn't want to . . . to . . . rush into anything . . . you know . . ." A quavering smile tugged at her lips.

Justin swallowed. "And now?"

Her sharp laugh was really more of a sob. "I don't have so much going on."

"Oh." Justin nodded and swallowed again. "I know how you feel. I was thinking about talking my grandparents into moving back east with my family."

"And you?" This time, it was Abigail's turn to swallow.

"I'd go with them."

"Oh." Abigail missed a step and reached out and clutched Justin's arm just before she would have fallen. He steadied her, and they stopped walking and looked into each other's eyes for a moment. Her eyes told him she hated that idea.

His told her the same thing.

He looked down at their hands, still entwined and sighed. "I think . . . I think that today is not the day to make big decisions."

"I," she whispered, "think that, too."

∞∞

When they finally made it back to Selma's house, they stepped into the living room only to find Heather and Bob Ray crying. Abigail's heart lurched as she looked into the dining room to find Selma and Guadalupe and even Elsa crying. Justin and Abigail froze and reached for each other, terror clutching their hearts.

"What?" Abigail demanded. "What happened?"

194

17

Daniel Strohacker was dead?

Selma motioned for them to sit down, but both Abigail and Justin remained standing, mouths gaping, eyes flashing, digesting this unthinkable bit of misinformation.

"No." Justin looked frantically back and forth among the tear-stained faces. "That can't be right. There must have been some mistake."

Selma shook her head. "No, honey. I'm so sorry, but they . . . they . . ." the elderly woman dabbed at her eyes with a tissue she'd plucked from her sleeve, ". . . they have identified the body."

Abigail felt light-headed. The lump in her throat was cutting off her supply of oxygen. The room seemed to tilt. She reached out and gripped Justin's arm for balance. He must have been seeing the same black spots dancing before his own eyes, because he clutched her back so hard it hurt.

His eyes were wild and his mouth worked but no sound emerged. At long last, he was able to whisper, "What happened?"

Bob Ray cast his bleary gaze on Justin. "They just now found his body. Under our . . . under . . . our place. Mrs. Carmichael called when a cadaver dog got a positive hit. It's him—" Heather rubbed Bob Ray's back and handed him a tissue. He took it and buried his face. "He was under there, to fix a leak. *I* should have been under there, man," Bob Ray cried, his voice muffled.

"Don't say that," Heather said and pressed her forehead against her husband's. "I'm the one who called him."

"Nonsense." Selma grabbed the tissue box on the coffee table, hobbled over to Justin and pressed it into his hands before she turned to eye Bob Ray and Heather. "This is no one's fault, do you hear me? Daniel Strohacker was killed in a terrible storm. Not murdered by you two."

"But . . . *why?*" Abigail finally found her voice. "What about Jen? What about their tiny son? What about *him?* That does not seem *fair or right!*"

"Honey," Selma said with a sorrow-filled sigh, "life is not always fair or right."

Abigail stared at Selma, unable to react. Unable to process everything that had happened over the last twenty-four hours. Numb now, like a computer overloaded and frozen up, she released her grip on Justin's arm. The icons in her brain were spinning. Receiving error messages. Unable to display pages. Woodenly, she turned and left the grieving group to descend the stairs to her new bedroom. Closing the door behind her, she paced the floor. What now? What? Do something. Anything.

Just. Don't. Think.

Eyes blank, she moved with an automated frenzy. She reached for her backpack, the bag from last night and the pants she'd worn yesterday. Dumping them out on the bed, she pawed through all her worldly possessions. Some jeans and tops. A pair of shoes. Some underwear and shampoo. And a whole bunch of tattered fabric. This *stuff.* These bits and pieces were all she had to show for her entire life. *Scraps. Don't think.*

She folded her clothes and stuffed them into an empty dresser drawer. The shampoo, her shears, and hair products she'd managed to salvage from the salon went on one of the shelving units under the window. She ran the carpet sweeper, dusted the bric-a-brac, fluffed pillows, and stacked books. The room, clean to begin with, was now spotless.

All that was left on the bed were the shreds of material.

Sinking to the edge of the mattress, Abigail slowly began to sort the bits of cloth. These were all fragments of people's lives, she reflected as she traced her finger over the various textures of satin and beads, wool and cotton, rough and soft. A wedding dress. A pillowcase. A suit jacket, a blouse, a prom dress, a tie, a dog's bed, some curtains, some upholstery, a choir robe, a stuffed toy, a costume . . . Abigail's head dropped into her hands. And . . . a baby's blanket. *Danny was dead.*

The man who loved God with all his heart and soul and mind. Dead. Before he ever got to touch his son.

No. Abigail inhaled a deep, angry breath. *No!* She thought of Jen, sitting there in that hospital with a newborn, grieving. Without her husband. This should be the happiest day of her life! She'd waited for it forever. She and Danny both! Her child would miss out on the best father ever to set foot on this earth. Where was the *sense* in that?

"*Where?*" she shrieked at the ceiling and then flopped to the bed and pounded on the tattered fabric with her fists. "Why would You let that happen?" she raged as she clutched the blanket in bunches. "Why didn't You save him? He was special! *He loved You!*" she shouted this accusation, not caring who was listening.

Behind her, the bedroom door softly opened and Bob Ray's wife stepped into the room. Without asking permission, she perched next to Abigail, so closely, their hips were touching. Crying herself, she handed Abigail a tissue, and then opened her arms. Though Heather was a stranger, Abigail leaned into her gentle embrace and allowed the younger girl to comfort her. And to quietly pray for her.

—∞∞—

Abigail woke to a knock at the door. Slowly, she sat up and pushed her hair out of her face thinking that was why she couldn't see. But, the truth was, the light outside was gone now. Not really caring, she guessed an entire day had passed. She'd worn herself out crying in Heather's arms. The last thing she remembered was Heather pulling a quilt off the other bed and covering her before she'd tiptoed out of the room.

"Abby?" It was Selma.

She cleared her throat. "Yes?" she croaked, her voice still rough from her tirade.

"Honey, I have some food for you here." The knob twisted and the door swung open. The smell of food permeated the air and made Abigail realize that she hadn't eaten since . . . she couldn't even remember. Selma set a tray on the dresser and then switched on a low glowing lamp by the door. Abigail blinked into the sudden light.

"I made a pot roast. The power went on and off all morning, so I decided to defrost a few things. I fixed you some potatoes and gravy and a salad . . ." She crossed the room and, gathering the pillows off the other bed, propped her great-niece up before moving to get the tray. "I checked on you several times . . . so did your friend, Justin. I think he's concerned about you, sweetheart. We all are."

Abigail rubbed her eyes first and then her face before she gave Selma a shivery smile. "I'm okay."

Selma peered through her glasses with bloodshot eyes. "Are you really?"

"Mm. I guess." She took the fork Selma handed her and began to pick at her food.

"Eat, honey. You'll feel better."

Too tired to argue, Abigail poked some roast into her mouth. The bits of cloth she'd spread out on the bed before Heather had come in had mostly fallen on the floor as she'd slept. Bending over, Selma picked those up and stacked them with the ones that still littered her quilt top.

"What are these?" she asked, fingering the different textures and sizes.

Abigail chewed for a second and then swallowed. "Remnants. Literally."

"Ah." Selma began to sort through them, arranging them according to color and size. Because she was a quilter, Abigail guessed. Must be habit. "These are not bits of fabric, you realize." Chin wrinkled in thought, lips pursed, Selma adjusted her glasses. "These are the pieces that need putting back together."

"Found them all over the place, after the storm. Right now, they represent all my worldly possessions." With a heavy sigh, Abigail scooped up a fork full of mashed potatoes and gravy and ate. The pot roast was tender and juicy and seasoned to perfection. Almost immediately she began to notice a difference in her attitude. In a blink, her plate was clean and her glass empty.

"There's more if you're still hungry," Selma offered as she settled the pile of scraps on the nightstand.

"No, thank you, though. I'm fine."

Selma took the tray, set it on the dresser, then returned to climb into bed next to Abigail. She was so bird-like she took up hardly any space at all in the twin bed. However, the warmth she generated, body and spirit, was large and slowly worked its magic. Abigail snuggled in next to her and whispered to her grandmother's younger sister, "Why, Selma? Why would God do that to Jen?"

"Honey, God didn't do it to Jen."

"Yes! He did. At the very least, He could have stopped it. Weren't we all praying for Danny? Didn't we ask Him to protect Danny? Didn't Danny just have a baby? Danny *trusted* Him!"

Selma plumped her pillow and made herself comfortable facing Abigail. "Did you like your hair salon?"

"Uh . . ."Abigail frowned and scanned the ceiling plaster as she tried to second-guess her great-aunt's weird line of thinking. Knowing Selma, she was going to take her on some circuitous route before she drove home a point. The road could be lengthy and sometimes convoluted, but usually ended up making sense. "Yes."

"Why?"

"Well, uh, it was pretty. It was stylish. I worked hard on it."

"You did?"

"Yes."

"God didn't do that to your salon? Make it pretty? Paint the walls? Sew the curtains?"

"I . . . well, no. I did."

"And the awards on the walls? Who won those?"

"Me."

"God didn't do that to you?"

"No," Abigail said and sighed. "I don't think so."

"Then why are you blaming Him now? Why do you take credit for the happy things and blame Him for the bad stuff?"

Abigail stared at the ceiling and sighed. The plaster made odd shapes in this light. One patch resembled a calf and another, an ogre. "Because it's not fair."

"Fair." Selma took Abigail's hand and held it up next to hers in the dim light. The differences between the smooth, supple young hand, and the gnarled, spotted one were obvious. "What would be fair?"

"Danny not dying."

"Danny had to die, honey. Just like me. And yes, even you. The mortality rate for human beings is 100 percent."

"But what about his son?"

"What about him? He is going to die, too."

"Without a father."

"I suppose pointing out that he has a heavenly Father would sound trite to you at this point, but it's true." Selma reached over and smoothed Abigail's hair behind her ear and cupped the young cheek with her hand. "When I was your age, I seriously thought I was placed on this planet to get a suntan. You know, to be happy. I was supposed to be happy. Clyde was supposed to be happy. All the kids were supposed to be— and live—happily ever after. We were supposed to accumulate stuff. Houses, cars, nice clothes, go on vacation overseas. Live the American dream. Get rich. Get slim. Get tan. Be happy. Happy, happy, happy. When we were done, we would go to heaven and be even happier. No stress, no strain, no thought, no pain. And no God. Didn't need Him, because I was so busy being happy. But there was something missing. I knew it, even then, in the midst of my supposed 'happiness.' Then, on June 8, 1966, we lost everything. In a tornado, of all things. And suddenly, I wasn't happy anymore. In fact, I was suicidal."

Abigail's eyes widened. "You?"

Selma nodded. "Me. I wasn't happy. Couldn't cope. Ended up in the hospital with what they used to call a nervous breakdown."

"Wow. I never knew."

"Yeah, well, that's because that was the old me. The woman who blamed God because she wasn't always . . ." Selma shrugged.

"Happy," Abigail finished for her. "What happened?"

"I went through the darkest period in my life up to that point. And guess what? Instead of shopping and tanning, I was flat on my face, wishing I was dead and crying out to God. And He came alongside me and nurtured me and educated me, and suddenly, I was grateful for my sorrow and my loss, because it was the one thing that brought me to Him. I won't kid you, Abby girl, it was hell on earth, but I'd do it all again because I'd been so lost in my sin before my Savior found me. I'd been looking for stuff and people to fill me up, when the only thing that could ever truly satisfy me was a relationship with Jesus. Because this life with all its stuff and activity is going to go away. For me. For you. For Jen and her baby."

The sounds of Guadalupe loading the dinner dishes into the dishwasher filtered down the stairs. Robbie cried. Rawhide barked. Then, it was still again.

"It's not about building our life here," Selma continued. "A lot of people think it is, and they are flat out wrong. It is about building your relationship with the living God. The God who sent His Son to suffer, even worse than you are suffering now, so that your sins could be forgiven and you could stand righteous before God one day. Now that's unfair. But He did it because he loves you so much. Can you believe that?"

Tears began to leak out of the corners of Abigail's eyes as she rolled to face Selma.

"Life is full of tests. We can pass or we can fail. It's up to us, how we react to the pain that comes our way. You can lie down and die, or with God's strength, you can get up and fight. You can blame God or you can join Him. You can reject or accept. When a curve ball comes your way, how are you going to handle it? On your own, or trusting Him to help? It's not easy to have faith, but then anything worth having never is. He never promised us that being a Christian would be easier than not.

He just promised us He would never leave or forsake his children. And because He is always with us, we don't have to be afraid. Of anything. Including death."

Selma swiped at a tear that rolled over Abigail's nose and hovered at its tip. "I think it was Corrie ten Boom who once said, 'When a train goes through a tunnel and it gets dark, you don't throw away the ticket and jump off. You sit still and trust the engineer.' And so now," Selma said, "when everything seems a mess, I can rest. He's on the job. He'll take care of Jen and the baby. And Danny is exactly where he wanted to be. With his Father."

In the quiet of early evening, Abigail closed her eyes and mulled everything Selma said, sorting, digesting, attempting to come to grips with it all.

And as she did, Selma began to softly snore at her side.

Justin stumbled out of the den and followed his nose to the kitchen where he discovered the aromatic pot roast. His eyes felt grainy and swollen and his throat sore. He'd been glad Abigail disappeared when she did. His meltdown hadn't been pretty. Thank God Bob Ray was as big a wuss as he was, when it came to the death of a friend, because they'd both bawled like babies. Justin still couldn't believe it was true. Danny.

Dead. It was stupid, but he felt almost betrayed. Danny had always been there for him. Danny was the go-to guy. For everything from advice about building materials and clients, to God and women and godly women. And it wasn't just the advice. It was the camaraderie. Danny was as much Justin's brother as his own brothers were. Danny had rescued him when he was homesick and lonely. He'd shared his friends and family and church. Now what?

Staying here in Rawston seemed impossible now.

Poking through the cupboards, Justin discovered a dinner plate and loaded it with the amazing-smelling stuff that simmered in the Crock-Pot. He was hungry as a bear. Slept the day away after his head and heart had nearly exploded from grief. He was sitting at the table finishing his second cup when Abigail came in. Like an idiot, he sat up and tried to fix his hair. He wished he'd taken a shower before he'd come in here to eat, but his stomach had been too hollow.

"Hey." Her smile was wan.

"Hey." He responded. Clearly, she felt as rotten as he did.

"I just made a fresh pot of coffee. Want some?"

"Love it." She sank into a chair and smiled. "Good pot roast, huh?"

"Must be. I had thirds." He set the mug before her and filled it with dark, hot coffee. "Cream or sugar?"

"Black. Thanks." She took a sip and smiled in satisfaction. "Mm. And he makes good coffee? I'm tellin' ya, Mister. Keep this up and I'm gonna marry you by sundown."

"I can do laundry, too," he bragged. He put the coffee pot away and joined her at the table.

She pounded her fist on the satiny oak. "That does it. Where's the parson?"

He chuckled and almost wished she was serious. "We've probably been through more in two days than most engaged people go through in two years."

"Weird, hmm? You can get to know a person pretty fast in a pressure cooker, huh? But interesting as it's been? I wouldn't recommend it."

"Me neither." He shrugged and before he could rein in his mouth, blurted, "Although, I've known people for more time . . . that I've liked less." He hoped she attributed the sudden redness in his cheeks to his newly steaming mug.

Lashes lowered, she blew across her coffee. "Me, too."

His pulse accelerated. If he was to stay in Rawston—big if—but if he did decide to stay, it would only be if she did. Getting to know her better might make it worthwhile. An hour whizzed by as they talked over their coffee. They mourned Danny. They grieved for Jen and the baby. They discussed their mutual survivor's guilt. They teared up. They shared a paper towel. And then another. They talked about Kaylee and Chaz's wedding.

Working up his courage, Justin looked at Abigail in the eye, loving the huge dimple that pushed a crevice into her right cheek and asked, "Will you go with me?"

"You mean, like a date?"

"Yeah. Like that."

"You sure? I can't promise I can dance the way I did when you first saw me, without Bob Ray trying to read me my rights."

"I'll take my chances." He angled a look at her over the top of his coffee mug.

"In that case? It's a date."

3:00 a.m.

They were still talking when Heather came in with a fussy Robbie. Abigail glanced at the clock and couldn't believe it was already so late. Where had the time gone? Selma continued to sleep down in her bed, but after all the coffee with Justin just now, she'd never be able to doze off. And at the moment, she didn't want to. "Hey, Heather," Abigail said and smiled at her new friend with affection. "Hiya, Robbie."

Robbie smashed his face into his mother's neck and squealed. "Say hello, stinker," Heather urged.

"No!"

Abigail tickled his foot as she walked by. "I was just going to see what flavors of ice cream Selma's got in her freezer this week. She is never, ever without. Anyone else want some?"

"I keem?" Robbie's head whipped around.

"Yep. Just for you," Abigail said and moved to the freezer.

"I will if she has any chocolate chip mint," Justin said.

"You're in luck," Abigail called over her shoulder. "She's also got some vanilla and some Moose Track stuff and some Marion Berry Swirl." She unloaded it all, got out some bowls and spoons, a couple of toppings, some bananas, and soon they were having a good old-fashioned ice cream social.

3:30 a.m.

Abigail looked up as Elsa staggered into the room and yawned.

"Did somebody say ice cream?" she asked, staring at the mess on the table.

Justin pulled a chair out for her and slid an empty bowl in her direction. "We wondered when you were going to show up."

She grinned and loaded her bowl. "My sweet tooth betrays me?"

Bob Ray stumbled through the doorway next, blinking and bleary-eyed. "Anybody else feel like they're going insane?" he asked, dazedly.

Elsa took one look at his crazy bed-head and burst out laughing. "You *look* insane."

Heather glanced up and laughed.

"What?" Bob Ray looked around. "What?"

Abigail turned around in her chair. Bob Ray's eyes were as swollen as Bart Simpson's and so red they seemed to glow, like two coals burning in his head. His spiky hair and five o'clock shadow and rumpled clothing only cemented the insanity impression. Both Justin and Abigail burst out laughing.

Insulted, Bob Ray pouted until he ducked down to check his appearance in the mirror that hung by the back door. He turned around, his eyes crossed and his mouth hanging slack and everyone lost it. Soon, he was laughing as hard as the rest, and they all doubled over until they were convulsing and holding their stomachs and dabbing at the tears that streamed down their cheeks.

5:00 a.m.

Carting a laundry basket on her hip, Selma came up the stairs to the sounds of Abigail and Justin loudly accusing each other of cheating at cards. Their laughter was the giddy stuff of too little sleep and more than a little flirtation. It seemed that when Abigail had stepped away to the bathroom, Justin had rearranged her hand. They were now wrestling and tickling and inciting the other players to riot.

Everyone dropped into their seats and looked sheepish when Selma stepped into her warm, country kitchen and slid her basket onto the kitchen counter. "Good morning," she sang, delighted with the mess and the noise and the first signs of healing hearts. She remembered laughing during some of the more stressful times in her life, including one hilarious barbecue party with the kids, right after the '66 tornado. Clyde had barbecued a shoe as a joke. It was that, or cry. And many times, a mixture of both. The tears and the laughter both were a healthy outlet for such overwhelming tragedy.

"Since you are all awake," Selma called above the resuming noise, "I will rustle us up some flapjacks."

6:00 a.m.

The stacks of pancakes disappeared nearly faster than Abigail and Selma could flip them, and soon everyone was sated and seated around the kitchen table, sipping coffee. They all seemed to have a tacit agreement that the TV would stay off until they'd had a chance to digest. Over breakfast, the discussion was filled with plans for the day. Justin and Bob Ray decided to head out soon and assist in the rescue effort. Guadalupe was going to try to find some fresh produce for their dinner. Abigail and Heather were thinking about going to the hospital to check on Jen and the baby, and Abigail wanted to look in on Brooke and Isuzu.

They all decided that if they were needed, they would stay on and volunteer to help wherever they might be asked. Everyone lingered over coffee, reluctant to leave the cozy safety of Selma's kitchen. As Abigail helped Selma and Heather tidy up the dishes, she lifted the laundry basket that Selma had brought upstairs earlier. "Did you want me to take this to the laundry room, Selma?"

"No, honey. Put it on the kitchen table, will you? I have a project I want to do and—before you all leave for the day— I'm going to show you all, since I'll need everyone's help. Bob Ray? Justin? Would you boys pop an extra leaf into the table? You'll find one in the pantry. Heather, grab another chair from the dining room. Abigail, wipe the table down, honey. And Elsa, I keep a high chair on the service porch for my little guests. Would you grab that for Robbie?"

Chairs scraped over the wooden floor, and everyone exchanged expectant glances as they hustled to do Selma's bidding. Guadalupe dried the freshly washed table, and finally they were all ready to gather and watch Selma unload the burgeoning basket.

First came the stack of scraps Abigail had collected after the storm. Then, Selma added Danny's Bible cover, some fabric she'd collected from her shop for working in the evenings, a beautiful quilt, and a paper pattern. With Guadalupe's help, she spread the quilt out over the surface of the table.

"Before you all rush off to your appointed rounds today, I wanted to take a moment of your time to plant some dream seeds, if you will. First," Selma turned to Abigail as she patted the stack of scraps Abigail had brought home. "Would you mind if I took these pieces and put them to good use? I have an idea for a quilt."

"You want to make a quilt? Out of this stuff?" Abigail asked.

"Yes. It will help me to give thanks."

"Thanks?" The crease between Abigail's eyes furrowed. "For . . . what?"

"Just bear with me. Doing this will bring answers to your questions. You'll see.

"Last time something devastating like this storm happened to me, I made this quilt." She patted the beautiful quilt now stretched across the tabletop.

"Why?"

"Because to me, the death of my son, Paul, was like a storm." Silence rocked the room for a moment.

"How did your son die, Selma?" Heather finally ventured.

"In a terrible mining accident, honey. He was with his best friend, who also happens to be your late father-in-law. Did you know that Bob Ray's dad, Robert, and my son, Paul, both died in the same mining accident?"

Heather glanced at Bob Ray. "I didn't know he was with your son."

Bob Ray shrugged. "Mom wouldn't talk about it and so I learned not to."

"That was just Rayne's way, honey. But if you ever have any questions, feel free to ask. Your father was a wonderful man, Bob Ray. As was my son, Paul. Too bad you kids didn't get a chance to know them. Do you remember Paul, Abigail?"

"Vaguely." Abigail did remember him washing his Mustang out in the driveway one time and threatening to squirt her with the hose. She'd thought he was handsome.

"They say," Selma began, "that death haunts the mines. It certainly seems true enough. Paul and Robert worked for the Laurence Krieger Mining Company, back in the early '90s together. It was—still is, to my knowledge—one of the most fertile coal seams in the country. I'll never forget, one time I traveled out there to Barlow to visit the boys, and they took me down in the elevator. That thing dropped fifteen feet per second, and in about three minutes we'd gone down about two thousand feet into the ground. I'd never been so scared and claustrophobic in all my life. How the boys could stand working down there, in that dark underground maze of tunnels, I'll never know." Selma shook her head, remembering.

Abigail shivered and glanced at Bob Ray and then at Justin. They were listening to Selma with rapt attention. As if Justin felt her watching, he glanced up and smiled.

"The day they died, the roof had collapsed in one of the tunnels and injured several of the guys. Word went out that they needed rescue help, and Robert and Paul were the first to volunteer. What they hadn't heard was that a small explosion had caused the accident. They were also unaware that methane gas had been building up in an adjoining section. If Paul and Robert had stayed topside, only the two men crushed in the roof collapse would have died that day. But, because of some communication glitches, twenty-eight men, all eager to dig out their co-workers, perished that day in an explosion that could have—should have—been avoided if the company officials had taken care of all of the safety violations on time. And if communication had been clearer."

"I'm so sorry, Aunt Selma," Abigail murmured as she stared at the quilt spread on the table with a new appreciation.

"Thank you, sweetheart. Me, too. Anyway, when the big explosion was ignited by some high voltage electrical equipment, it sent a ball of fire rolling through the tunnels, looking for a way to the surface. Paul and Robert didn't race away from the danger, but toward it, because I am told, miners have a creed; when trouble happens, you save your brothers first and then you save the mine."

"Man," Justin shook his head. "That's rough."

"It was even worse than losing everything back in the tornado of '66. Because then, I just lost stuff. In the mining accident—" Selma turned her liquid gaze on Robbie, "—I lost my baby."

"I'd have died," Bob Ray blurted out and cuddled his son close.

"I was pretty close," Selma said. "By this time in my life, I was what you'd call a church lady. Thought I had the tiger by the tail so to speak. My act was together." Selma pulled a comical face and rolled her eyes. "You could say I was sure I was so blessed because I was such a good Christian. Then, Paul died and it felt like the rug had been yanked out from under me again."

Abigail's chair creaked as she leaned back, but that and the ticking of the wall clock were the only sounds. Selma's voice held them all captive, rapt, waiting for her to continue. Even young Robbie sat quietly in his father's lap and listened.

"I was devastated and angry. I wondered how God could let something like that happen to me."

Abigail felt color flare in her cheeks.

"I used to be so glib," Selma said with a heavy sigh. "I had never experienced this kind of pain . . . because I was a good person. I went to church. I tithed. I prayed for Paul every day. I was the best wife and mother I knew how to be. And yet, my beautiful son was taken from me, before he ever had a chance to find a bride and give me grandchildren.

"And so I went into a deep depression," to Abigail she said, "—maybe even worse than after the tornado—" and then turned her gaze to the quilt. "My faith was seriously tested. For a long time, I couldn't even set foot in a church. I couldn't see what good it would do. After all, I'd done everything right and still I suffered. My dear Clyde was the one who helped me see. He started asking questions. And he was good at talking things out. And the more he got to know the families of the men who'd died in the mining accident the more he began to understand how Paul had affected their lives."

Hand's trembling with age and emotion, Selma smoothed the fabric beneath her fingertips. "So, I made this quilt here, after he died. As a matter of fact, it's the whole reason I got interested in quilting. I remember thinking that tragedy is like a quilt before it is put together. Fragmented, chaotic, in pieces. Putting the pieces of the quilt together helped me make sense of the devastation. And the loss."

Selma pointed to the center of the quilt. "This square represents Paul. This piece here? It's from his LKM jacket. See the name, embroidered there?" Smiling, she traced the words, *Paul Tully* with her fingertips. "And this was from his high school basketball jersey. That part is a little bit of his number. And here . . . some of his favorite pajama bottoms."

Moving around to stand behind Heather, Selma pointed out the square next to Paul's. "This square here? Bob Ray's dad. See? *Robert Lathrop*. This is his LKM shirt. And this is a bit of satin from his mother—Rayne's—wedding gown. And this is a piece of Bob Ray's baby blanket." A big smile lit her eyes and smoothed the wrinkles from her lips. "Bob Ray's daddy is in heaven with Paul today, because Paul invited Robert to Sunday school, when they were kids, and Robert gave his heart to Jesus."

Selma shuffled over to stand behind Elsa. Resting one hand on the girl's shoulder, she smoothed her silky hair and pointed with the other.

"And this square here? It's for Paul's good friend, Adam. When they were kids, Adam fell out of the back of a moving pickup truck and went into a coma. See? Here is some of the hospital gown. Paul sat with him everyday in the hospital. Never gave up on Adam. Read to him, prayed over him. Eventually, Adam was released from the hospital, but he was never the same. But Paul was steadfast and hung in there with Adam through physical therapy and beyond. When Adam finally died of a brain hemorrhage some years later, Paul was there for his parents. A surrogate son for them. These are their squares."

As Selma spoke, goose bumps roared up the left side of Abigail's body and down the right. Paul's life had such a powerful reach. Even today, as Selma told his story to the next generations, she could see the ripple effect. Absently, she watched as Robbie's eyes began to slide closed.

"Each of these squares, around Paul's center square, represents a person who was profoundly affected by my son. And changed, for the better, because of his life. God set him down here on this earth for a reason. And for a season."

Selma picked up the cover to Danny's Bible and smoothed it between her hands.

"Clyde finally helped me understand that a season is just that. A period of time. And how long that time lasts is not up to us. But up to the one who put us here in the first place. Paul's life, as I see it here, was perfect. He, like the apostle Paul of the New Testament, fought the good fight. And, at the end of the race, I am convinced that he stood before the Lord and heard, 'Well done, my good and faithful servant.'" Selma held up the scrap from the cover to Danny's Bible.

"And, I know Danny has, too."

18

That evening, after the sun had set, everyone gathered around the kitchen table. Selma reached for Abigail's hand on one side and Guadalupe's on the other and, in her spunky style, requested that they all join her in giving thanks.

"Father, it is such a blessing to have these precious faces seated around my kitchen table bringing so much life back into this house. It does my heart good to enjoy the fellowship of old family," she squeezed Abigail's hand, "and new. Thank You for Your gracious bounty and the tender mercy You have bestowed on us all. In Your name—" Before she could sum up and say Amen, Bob Ray jumped in.

"And, Lord, hi there, it's me, Bob Ray. I just want to give thanks for answering my prayer and keeping Heather and Robbie s . . . safe," his voice cracked with emotion, "even though I have been kind of a loser. But I want to be a good husband and man like my father was, but I need help, and I'm really sorry . . . and I want to change—"

While he was praying, Abigail peeked over at Bob Ray's face. His eyes were screwed tightly shut, and Heather was smiling to beat the band. Abigail felt her throat close at their sweet expressions. Sensing someone else's gaze, she darted a glance at Justin. He, too, was grinning and shot her a quick wink before he bowed his head again.

When Bob Ray was done, Heather started in. "And thank You, Lord, for Ms. Selma Louise Tully. Because without her, none of us would be together at all. Please bless her generous heart." Next, Elsa's sweet young voice offered prayers for Nick's family and for Brooke and Isuzu and their family. And, while Guadalupe haltingly remembered those who'd lost loved ones, Abigail cried. Their bittersweet prayers and their affection for each other touched her to the marrow.

So much liquid poured from her face, Abigail was beginning to fear she'd eventually just float away. By the final 'Amen' she was nothing but a soggy, gooey puddle of pudding. Her sinuses were killing her, but the load on her mind was lightening.

Something was happening in her heart. Something agonizing. Miserable. And more than just the ravages of the storm. Something she hadn't even been aware she needed to address was there, festering, clamoring for attention. And whatever it was, she suspected it was going to take a while to work through. Abigail pressed her aunt's precious hand—joints swollen with arthritis, skin spotted and paper-thin—to her lips. The kiss was warm and lavender-scented, wet with hot tears and oh, so healing. Lips trembling, she returned Selma's sympathetic smile. Selma understood.

"Grab a plate and eat up, because I have a quilting project that needs to be accomplished in a timely manner," Selma announced to the group. "Right after dinner, I want us to begin work on Danny's quilt. And I know some of you are probably thinking," she glanced at Abigail, "why on earth should we stop and make a quilt now? And my answer to that is because you need to begin putting the pieces together."

For the first time in her life, Abigail finally understood.

That evening, over a hearty plate of Selma's famous beef stroganoff, they all discussed the day's events. Bob Ray and Justin told of the horrors and triumphs of digging people out from the rubble, and they each found scraps to add to the quilt. Assisting a neighborhood rescue crew, they'd uncovered a mother and her weeks old infant who—aside from being shaken up and hungry—were fine. Another heroic digging effort yielded three generations hiding in a wine cellar, all fine. There were other finds, some tragic, some with life-threatening injury. Justin and Bob Ray had worked feverishly together, carrying the wounded on a pallet they'd fashioned from a door and some long boards.

As they relived the day, Abigail was touched by the respect and affection that Bob Ray was developing for Justin. It was obvious in the way the young man regarded him with awe and regaled them with tales of Justin's bravery and quick thinking.

"I never would have thought of carrying that one guy out on the door like that, but Justin ripped it off the frame and used a rock, man, *biff, biff, biff* and straightened out some nails and busted some boards and cobbled the thing together, it was awesome!" He held his hand up to high-five Justin, who was shaking his head and rolling his eyes. "We loaded that guy up and he was on his *way*, man!"

"Yeah, yeah. Give it a rest," Justin said, and waved his palms at Bob Ray.

"Aww, dude is bashful! But seriously, guys, he was a super-hero today. I was just the sidekick. Did Superman have a sidekick? I guess I was like Robin, man."

Heather threw back her head and laughed and Bob Ray grinned at her in delight. Their mood was contagious, and

Abigail felt a reprieve from the day's depression bubble up into her throat and spread to her lips in a smile.

As the conversation ebbed and flowed, Abigail was enveloped in the warm, wonderful bosom of family. How had she not seen what she'd been missing, living alone and working her life away? The laughter, the camaraderie, the empathy and concern was so sweet . . . no wonder Selma had wanted a big family. Abigail angled a quick peek at Justin's smiling face as he razzed Bob Ray. She couldn't think of a single place in the whole world she'd rather be at the moment than crowded around Selma's battle scarred table with each of these people. Not even time spent in her beautiful salon or in her breezy apartment or in LA with a high-paying client could trump what was happening right here. The odd thought stunned her as she glanced from face to sweet face. Strange how things that had seemed so important only a week ago paled in light of what they'd all just gone through. This, she was beginning to see, was what was important.

Relationship. With each other.

And—she acknowledged the niggling thought—God.

The raucous noises of a family docked in safe harbor continued while Guadalupe whipped up a batch of triple chocolate brownies. They ate those with ice cream after the last of the stroganoff had been polished off.

"How is Jen?" Justin was the one to finally put voice to the question that had been haunting them all. He glanced at Heather before his gaze settled on Abigail.

Abigail and Heather exchanged sober glances. "She's . . . coping." Abigail filled her chest with air and slowly let it escape. "I think she's doing a whole lot better than I would be in her shoes. What do you think, Heather?"

"I agree." Heather stood and went to the sink for a cloth to wipe Robbie's face and hands of the noodles and applesauce he'd smeared on himself and his high chair tray. "We couldn't stay too long because her entire family was starting to arrive and trying to get at her, but she made time for us."

"Uh-oh!" Robbie shouted and hung over his high chair, staring after the spoon he'd just dropped.

Abigail picked up the spoon and handed it to Robbie to pound on his tray. She spread a napkin out to quiet his racket. "She was amazing. Exhausted and grieving, but there was also some joy, I think."

"Mm. And she said some things that were so . . ." Heather rinsed the cloth with steaming hot water and then squeezed it out in the sink, ". . . so profound. Jen has always been a rock for me. And when we went in today," she darted a quick smile at Abigail, "I thought we'd be a rock for her, you know? But she ended up cheering *us* up. Can you believe that? And Bob Ray," Heather paused and pressed the cloth to her mouth for a second, using it to stave off the tears, "she doesn't blame us."

Bob Ray stood and, quickly crossing the room, swept Heather into his arms, and rocking her back and forth, buried his face in her neck.

"She said it wasn't our fault." Her words were muffled by sorrow and the cotton of Bob Ray's shirt. "It wasn't our fault . . ."

Abigail swallowed at the lump that surged into her throat as she listened to Heather, remembering the poignant scene of Jen, holding her tiny baby and bravely facing a life without Danny.

"Oh," Heather said, leaning back in her husband's strong arms and dabbing her eyes with the washcloth, "and she wants a simple burial as soon as the funeral home can arrange it. They're swamped now, and it'll be family only, but she hopes that we'll all help her plan a really special memorial service for

Danny. In a few weeks. You know . . . after the dust has settled around here and everyone can come."

⸺⟋⟍⸺

"Many hands make light work, and the same goes for quilting. That's why, in the olden days, women would gather together for quilting bees. So you are all now part of my tornado quilting circle."

"Whoa," Bob Ray joshed, "I think my biceps just shriveled up and died."

"Did she say *man* hands make light work?" Justin grinned as the entire household gathered around the kitchen table to help Selma with her project. Behind them, the dishwasher sounded like a monster truck rally, and the smells of pine cleaner radiated from the still damp floor.

"Welcome to the quilting bee, my man." Justin and Bob Ray tapped their knuckles together across the top of the table. The women all just sat there and rolled their eyes, feigning long-suffering forbearance at their tomfoolery.

"We know you are looking forward to this enriching experience," Guadalupe deadpanned and eyed each one in turn with a quelling stare.

"I'm here for the party," Justin said. "Show me the bee and I'll quilt it."

"Okay, boys, I'm grateful for your willing hearts. Remember, this is a labor of love for our dear friend, Jen Strohacker." Selma grabbed a shoebox from tonight's laundry basket. "Pass these scissors out, if you will, Justin. And, Bob Ray, give everyone one of these pieces of cardstock."

As the guys did her bidding, Selma began to explain. "I found a pattern for our quilt," she announced. "I figured since most of you are new to quilting, it should be something simple, and you'll never believe what I found." She held up a pattern. "This one is called 'Storm Signal.' See how the triangles and squares are light and dark and it sort of resembles a lighthouse beam? That was Danny, don't you think? Like a beacon. You could always see the light of the Lord just beaming on his face."

There were murmurs of agreement as everyone inspected the pattern.

"I've given each of you a piece of cardstock, printed with the pattern. Go ahead and cut it out and write your names on the back. And, while you are doing that, I want each of you to think about the bits of fabric you want to include in your square. I think this piece," Selma held up the woven bit that had been part of Danny's Bible cover, "will be part of the center square and will represent Danny. The surrounding squares will represent the lives that Danny influenced. Kind of like a pebble dropped in calm water, the squares will ripple outward. I have already spoken to several other friends of Dan and Jen's who want to contribute squares. The fabric that Abby found the night of the storm will be used both in the squares and in the border. I'm hoping to complete the project in time to present it to Jen, from all of us, at the memorial service."

Brow puckered, Abigail stared at the pattern and thought about all the lives that Danny had touched. This quilt could be huge. But it would be beautiful. She looked up to see the tops of heads as everyone bent over their scissors, and a giggle squeaked from between her lips, surprising her.

"What are you laughing at," Justin asked, suspiciously.

"This reminds me of kindergarten," she admitted.

"If we were in kindergarten, I'd have cut my bangs off by now," Heather said.

"I seem to remember that look," Bob Ray mused. "It was very sexy."

The silly conversation continued as they worked. When they'd finished their patterns, Selma showed everyone how to select the colors to best highlight the design. They all sorted through her remnant basket and looked for ideas. Justin got the shirt that he'd worn the night Jen had the baby and cut a big chunk out of the center of the back.

Abigail stared at the gaping hole and laughed.

"What?"

"Well, you can't wear that again," she chided.

"Why not?" he asked, feigning ignorance.

"Next time, you might take a small piece off the tail, or something," she advised.

Justin rolled his eyes. "Oh, yeah. Like there's gonna be a next time."

"I don't know, my man," Bob Ray said. "This is kind of fun."

Abigail was amazed at how much everyone was enjoying the project. The hours flew by and when bedtime rolled around, even though everybody was exhausted from a long, emotional day, they were all reluctant to stop and head off to bed.

Early Tuesday morning, before they each set off to lend the community a helping hand, Abigail spread out her storm scraps and mulled them over.

Justin sat next to her, watching and offering his thoughts. "Since Danny was in the military, that piece of the flag would be good in his square, huh?" he asked.

"What's the rule on dealing with a flag after it's been ruined? I mean, don't you have to dispose of it in some special way?" Abigail wondered as she walked her fingers over raised threads of the stars.

"I think it would be fine to make an exception with this small piece. Danny loved his country and this would symbolize that."

"Mm. I think that's really nice."

Later, Abigail realized that if a time-lapse camera had been set up over the table, it would have told the tale of the numerous comings and goings of Danny's loved ones. Word of the quilt had spread, and people came by with stories and bits of fabric. Over iced tea and cookies, they would share their thoughts and memories as they selected fabrics from Selma's yardage to go with their offerings.

When Kaylee stopped by, she spotted the shreds from the bodice of her wedding dress. "Abigail told me she found this over by the cleaners." She fingered the lavishly beaded crewel work with a soft smile. "The plastic must have kept this part clean." From her purse she pulled several pieces she'd found in a drawer at the new house. "The black satin was leftover from Chaz's cummerbund and I also brought some of the wool that the tailor trimmed from his cuffs." Making herself at home, Kaylee picked up a pair of scissors and went to work cutting and pinning the middle of her square.

Kaylee's ideas inspired Elsa, and she began to work with the scrap that Selma had torn from the bottom of her prom dress the night of the storm. "This piece is a little bit stained with mud, but I like that," Elsa mused. "It tells a story. Sometimes beautiful things get ugly, before they get beautiful again."

Brows raised, Guadalupe and Kaylee stared at the child before they exchanged glances that spoke of how impressed they were with the depth of her thought process.

"Beautiful, Elsa," Selma murmured and kissed the girl's temple.

Tuesday evening, after another grueling day working the neighborhoods and searching for fewer and fewer survivors, everyone gathered after dinner to work on the quilt. As they pinned and basted their pieces together, they talked. There was a little bit of good news to celebrate, families reunited, people found, some rescued, help arriving in droves from out of state. But mostly, it was bad. Death and destruction and broken hearts everywhere.

The conversation twisted and turned and always seemed to flow back to Danny. Elbows resting on the table, Abigail cupped her chin in her hand and listened to Justin pour his grief out to Selma as they bent over his square, easing the material into the proper shape. "I feel guilty because I feel sorry for me. It's weird but I'm almost mad at Danny for getting under a trailer in the middle of a tornado. Talk about stupid."

"I think your feelings are pretty normal, honey. But I also see something else going on here," Selma said as she guided his hand. She was teaching him to baste.

"Tell me. Please." Justin tossed his square down and, leaning back in his chair, looked to Selma for answers.

"Well, I know you and Danny were very close and he was a great mentor for you. But, now that he's gone, I think maybe the Lord would appreciate your full attention. Sometimes, in the midst of the most serious trouble, we can't seem to reach the ones we usually depend on and I think it's because God wants us to talk to, and depend on, *Him*. Another of my favorite Corrie ten Boom quotes is 'You may never know that Jesus is all you need, until Jesus is all you have.'"

Justin slowly nodded and his eyes grew glassy with thought. "Um-hm."

"You know, sometimes the Lord will use the circumstances to help you lean on Him. Why do you suppose Danny was so close to the Lord? Maybe it was because he had no siblings or family to turn to for most of his childhood, so he had to turn to the Lord. And, the better he knew Him, the more he wanted to know Him. Interesting, don't you think?"

———

Wednesday morning, Isuzu brought over some swatches to contribute to the quilt; pieces of the kids' skating costumes, some red and gold fabric from the Sakura Garden's window dressings, among other bits and pieces that symbolized her family's connection to Danny. "Tyler want this in quilt," Isuzu said and held up a bit of ribbon from a medal the kids had won in a recent skating competition. "Because he say Danny was champion youth group leader. Tyler say nobody tell a Bible story the way Danny bring it to life."

As she spoke, she began to blink rapidly and her lips quivered. Losing battle with sorrow, Isuzu buried her head in her hands and cried. "This morning, they find Nick's body. Brooke say, Auntie Zuzu, I am glad that Danny go with Nick up to heaven . . . together. She feeling very much depressed and crying hard about Nick. She send this ribbon from corsage Nick give her. She want it in her square."

Abigail's heart squeezed as she rubbed Isuzu's back with one hand and fingered the satiny smooth strip of pink with the other. Again, she was impressed by the love Danny inspired. If it had been her, what kind of legacy would she have left? Shame kindled her cheeks. It would be nothing compared to Danny's. Her relationships tended to be superficial because she preferred it that way. That, she had told herself more than once, was all she had time for. She'd been too busy building her career to care about the people in her life enough to even ask after them when they were suffering. That was going to change. Starting now. "How are your brother and sister-in-law doing?"

Isuzu sniffed and dabbed at her eyes. "We all move into nice rental house. Share for now." As she described the house, Isuzu finished cutting out her pattern and wrote her name on the back of each square before she began to sort her fabrics. "This sound strange, but my sister-in-law, Mieko, is good. Very, very good. No restaurant, no skating, no school. She stay at hospital today, like big mother chicken, with wings spread over chicks. She tell me she happy for no more pressure. Perfect excuse. No Olympics because kids are broken. She say to me, 'Zuzu! For first time, I feel like kids are *my* kids and not belong to public. I never am so happy.'" Isuzu pinned a piece of her pattern to a bit of fabric and began to trim the edges. "I think this very good. I think Jesus happy that Mieko get her babies back. Haruo still in shock over restaurant, but like to cook at home, too. They will make new restaurant."

"They are going to rebuild? That's really brave."

"New restaurant will be nice. Maybe better. So. Will you make new salon for Zuzu?" She was staring so hard at Abigail that Abigail had to laugh.

"I'm thinking it over . . . I don't know. My mother wants me to move out to California. And Zuzu, it's safe there. They don't get tornados."

"True. Get giant earthquake. Knock you house over flat."

Abigail pondered that for a second. "Yeah. I guess so. On the other hand, I do have a job offer there . . . but, you know Zuzu, the more I think about what I used to believe was important— beauty and beautiful people—I just don't crave it anymore. It all just seems so silly now. On the other hand, I don't have anything here, really . . ."

Isuzu stared at her. "I am chopped liver? You have big business here. Cut hair now in Selma kitchen until you build new shop. Okay. Good. I will rent a space from Selma for now and go back to work. Soon, huh?"

"But—"

"Shh. I think you stay here. In Rawston," she whispered. "Marry Handsome-guy and you fight all day on phone." Isuzu's face scrunched and she laughed herself half silly.

Abigail groaned. Arguing with Isuzu was futile, so she changed the subject. "Zuzu, I was just thinking about something nice you and I might do for Brooke."

Isuzu stopped laughing and looked up from the fabric she held in surprise.

Abigail tossed her scissors into her sewing basket. "It sounds like she's going to be in bed for a while and I was thinking. Let's go to the beauty supply up in Southshire and get some nice lotion and facial stuff, and we'll make her feel pretty. What do you say?"

Smile wide, Isuzu got to her feet and grabbed her purse. "I say, let's go."

∽∾∽

That evening after dinner, while Selma set up her sewing machine on one side of the kitchen, Abigail set up a swivel chair and her new hair supplies on the other, near the sink. There was a knock at the kitchen door and Isuzu came in with a leather satchel and a TV tray. "You tell them yet?" she whispered.

Finger to her lips, Abigail shook her head as she helped Isuzu unload and set up. That afternoon, they'd gone a little overboard at the beauty supply. Brooke had been so grateful for her pampering that they'd decided to do it for everyone.

Abigail came home loaded down with specialty hair products for everyone in the household, and Isuzu had loaded up on nail supplies. They were both as giddy as children listening for Santa's sleigh bells on Christmas Eve.

When they were ready, Abigail used a spoon to tap on the bottom of a saucepan.

"Excuse me!" she called over the sewing hubbub at the table, "May we have your attention please? The Doo Drop-In and Zu-Zu Nails are open again for business!"

"We here to make you beautiful for wedding," Isuzu explained.

Heather and Elsa stared at each other for a second before they leapt to their feet and squealed, *"Yes!"* Chairs a-scraping, they charged at Abigail and Isuzu with open arms. After Abigail managed to emerge from their barrage of kisses and hugs, she handed them each a hairstyles magazine. "Why don't you girls pick a doo, and I'll start with Robbie."

Abigail brainstormed with Heather while she worked on the toddler's hair and Elsa discussed hair styles and nail colors with Isuzu and her mom.

The lopsided lengths of her son's thick curls had Heather wincing. "I've been doing it myself, because it's all I can afford," she said, embarrassed. "I used to go to my mom's salon at the country club when I was in high school. Started dying my hair when I was in the fifth grade. Isn't that ridiculous?" Her dismay was audible as she exhaled. "I haven't had a good haircut since I got pregnant."

"That's the part I think is ridiculous," Abigail teased as she buzzed up the back of Robbie's head with a new pair of clippers. The child sat stock still, his eyes wide, his lips curved into a slight smile.

"Ticky," he said and laughed.

"I don't suppose you could do this one on me?" Heather held the glossy spread open so that Abigail could see and pointed out a trendy hairstyle in the magazine.

"Sure. You'd look great in that."

Heather squealed and clasped her hands together and, once again, Abigail found her heart growing softer. When Robbie was done, she handed him off to Bob Ray and recommended a shower, then turned her attention on mama.

"Time for some pampering, huh?" Abigail studied the picture and discussed the length of the various layers and the wispy bangs. "You want some color?"

Heather was jittering with excitement. "You could *do* that?"

"Highlights? Like this?" Abigail asked. She'd have thought the girl just won the lottery, Heather was so excited. Over the next hour, Abigail cut and colored and shampooed and blow dried and flat ironed. Before Heather was allowed to look in the mirror, Elsa put some mascara and lip gloss on her and Isuzu gave her a manicure. When they finally handed her the mirror, Heather burst into tears of joy. Bob Ray gave her a wolf whistle and insisted on dancing her around the kitchen. "Is my wife gorgeous, or what?"

They all agreed. She was. The haircut had completely transformed her, and she looked like a young girl again, rather than an exhausted mom. With the exception of Selma and Guadalupe, Abigail cut and styled everyone's hair until it was Justin's turn.

He eyed her warily as she pulled him from his seat at the table and led him to the sink. "What are you planning to do to me?"

She took the opportunity to freely study his handsome face. "I'm just going to give you a good cut. C'mon. I'll wash your hair. It's easier to cut when it's wet." Somewhat dubious, he followed her to the sink, where she stood, tucking a towel around his neck. They were standing face-to-face and he grinned at her, eyes twinkling. Her stomach tingled. *Oh, my.* This was better than dancing. To hide her suddenly nervous hands, she turned the water on and waited for it to warm, testing it with her fingers.

"Head in the sink," she ordered, and clearing her throat, reached for the spray nozzle. His hair was thick and soft and she first soaked it, and then filled her hands with her favorite shampoo.

"Suddenly I get why the girls spend the big bucks getting their hair done. I love this!" Justin shouted from the depths of the sink to Bob Ray as Abigail scrubbed his scalp, lightly running her nails through his hair as she massaged.

"Oh, yeah." Bob Ray ran a hand through his new haircut. "I'm a believer."

"I'll give her about a year to knock this off," Justin called back to Bob Ray.

Abigail laughed as she rinsed the soap from his head. Though she didn't really need to, she lathered him and rinsed once more, then she applied a good conditioner before the final rinse. While he was still bent over she wrapped his head in a towel and rubbed it half dry.

"Take a seat," she directed and, shaking out her cape, fastened it around his neck. Using a longer guard on the clippers, she trimmed up the back and sides, taking her time, enjoying the perfect excuse to touch his head and allow her hands to linger on his neck and shoulders. When she was satisfied with the results she took scissors and comb to the top, thinning and trimming and shaping until he looked ready for a photo shoot. Man, she thought as she lightly shaved the line at his neck and sideburns, he was handsome. Crazy handsome on the outside, but even better on the inside. There was a goodness about him. Like Danny.

When she was done, she blew the hairs off his face and he grinned and asked, "Am I good?"

She could feel her goofy smile light her eyes and tingle her toes. "Yeah." She tipped his chin up and studied his face for a long moment and considered how it reflected the sweetness of his heart. "You're good."

19

Bright and early Saturday morning, Heather and Bob Ray fixed a hearty breakfast for the entire household. The savory smells of onion and garlic frying in butter, potatoes browning, bacon sizzling, and coffee perking summoned sleepyheads from their beds and drew them to the kitchen table for both food and family. While they all ate, the chatter was festive as the talk of Chaz and Kaylee's wedding that evening buoyed their spirits. Everyone was eager to put the storm and its atrocities out of their minds for a little while and get out of the house and celebrate life.

"Hey, you know what?" Abigail cradled her coffee mug between her hands. "It just occurred to me that I don't have anything to wear to a wedding." Everyone glanced around as that realization dawned for them all.

"I don't think anyone is going to care if we wear jeans," Justin said with a shrug, "you know, all things considered."

"Yes, but it would certainly be nice to have one good Sunday-go-to-meetin' outfit for times like this, don't you think?" Selma said as she pinned a row of completed quilt squares together. "Why don't you kids take the Olds and run up to the mall in Southshire? I have some money in the cookie jar that the kids sent me for my last few birthdays, but to be honest, I just haven't needed anything and so I've been saving it for a rainy day. I think a tornado counts. Take it and go shopping."

"Oh, no," they all demurred, but the longing expressions on their faces claimed that they were oh-so-tempted.

Selma stood and moved to her cookie jar. Without ceremony, she brought it to the table and dropped it in the center with a thud. "Haven't you ninnies learned anything from the storm? Seize the day, kids! Life is short! Get out there and live it. For me?"

Grins and eyes huge, Guadalupe and Elsa, Bob Ray and Heather, Justin and Abigail all exchanged excited glances. "We'll pay you back," Bob Ray promised.

"Okay, it's a deal," Selma agreed. "I've got a bunch of storm junk in the backyard that needs hauling off—" Before she'd finished her thought, chairs rumbled across the wood floor as everyone leapt to their feet to kiss Selma's face, and then rush pell-mell out the door. "Leave Robbie here," Selma called after them, and then turned her attention to the child who was still seated, forgotten, in his high chair. "They're not gonna get too far without the jar, huh kid? So. It's just you and me and the VeggieTales, how about that?"

"Meggie Tay!" Robbie shouted. "Bob!"

"Bob the Tomato is my favorite, too."

Heather popped back into the kitchen, her face flushed and her eyes bright with excitement. "Sorry, Selma. I got a little over anxious to be on my way. Be good, Robbie." Heather kissed her son and Selma waved the girl off. Heather bolted, squealing like a kid on her way to the candy store, the cookie jar in her arms.

That afternoon, after a full morning spent buying wedding togs, the doorbell rang and Rawhide scrambled to loudly announce Kaylee's arrival. She'd brought her brand-new veil and tiara and Heather and Elsa watched as Abigail deftly wove her hair and headpiece into a work of art that had her looking every inch the princess bride. When she'd gone, Abigail turned her attentions on everyone else in the household and shampooed and conditioned and gelled and sprayed and flat-ironed and blow-dried until they were all spit-shined and ready for a night out.

"You have a servant's heart, sweetheart," Selma murmured, admiring Abigail's handy work around the room. Abigail beamed under the praise. For the first time ever, Abigail was more satisfied with the status of her heart than the nature of her art. It had been fun, washing their heads and listening to their sighs of contentment and basking in their satisfied smiles.

It took two trips with Justin driving the Olds, but they all made it to the church on time. Because of some unexpected repair work that the Midwestern General Electric Company was doing on a substation just outside Rawston, the Prairie Central Bible Church lost power about two hours before the wedding. Undaunted by this minor inconvenience, Kaylee and Chaz relied on dozens of emergency candles to light the sanctuary for their sunset ceremony. The sparkling beauty took Abigail's breath away as she and Justin stepped inside the vestibule. A young usher lent Abigail his arm and led them both to their seats behind Selma, who had Bob Ray and Heather on one side and Guadalupe and Elsa on the other.

Bemused, Abigail glanced at Justin's profile as she took her seat. A week ago she'd known she was attending Kaylee's wedding, but she'd never have guessed it would be in the company of this particular group. And, at the moment, she couldn't imagine attending with anyone else. Odd as it seemed, they were a little family now.

The delicate strains of a stringed quartet playing Pachelbel's "Canon in D" filled the air as Kaylee's bridesmaids came down the aisle before her, carrying candles—dressed in beribboned lace paper doilies to protect their hands from the wax—instead of flowers. Then the stringed music faded and the pianist played the prelude to the wedding march and they all stood as Kaylee walked down the aisle on her father's arm. She was positively glowing, and the dress—her father brought it from Seattle—had belonged to her mother but looked as if it had been made for Kaylee. The cast on her broken arm had been painted and then beaded and sequined to match the glove on her good arm. Instead of a bouquet of flowers, she, too, carried a candle, as did Chaz, his brother, Davon, and the two groomsmen. Up at the altar, a unity candle waited for her and Chaz to light as a symbol of their marriage bond.

Everywhere, candlelight flickered. On window ledges, table tops, railings, the piano and organ tops. It was absolutely breathtaking. The shadows muted out any repair work that needed to be done because of the tornado and gave the ceremony a feeling of splendor. Through the arch that had held the stained-glass window, the last vestiges of the setting sunlight only added to the ethereal mood.

Sniffles began to ripple across the assemblage as Kaylee's father tenderly kissed and handed his only daughter off to her groom. Chaz's flickering and shadowed expression was one of adoration for his bride as he drew her to his side. Oh, how handsome and tall he stood in the tux that had been stored in the new house. Love seemed to spark and shimmer between them as warm and bright as the candles they carried. Once Mr. Johnson had taken his seat next to Kaylee's mom, the minis-

ter—whom the wedding program listed as Pastor Caldecott—
welcomed the guests.

"Welcome, beloved. I know I speak for both Kaylee and
Chaz in extending our gratitude to you for joining us to bear
witness to the exchange of their wedding vows. On the heels
of a devastating and tragic storm, it is a privilege and an honor
to be able to unite these two young people in holy matrimony."

Pulse pounding, breath caught in her throat, Abigail could
almost feel the collective smile of the congregation, for it was
a live thing, blooming and spreading and generating warmth.
Justin took her hand and tucked it into the crook of his arm.
That such joy could flow on the heels of such horrific chaos
amazed Abigail. And yet, as she watched and waited, her
heart was suddenly so full. Eyes creasing at the corners, Justin
glanced down at her and she knew by his tender smile that he
felt it, too.

"This service is a blessing to our beleaguered community in
so many ways. It is a new beginning. A fresh start. A symbol
of hope. And a symbol of God's unending grace. I know there
are a number of you out there with us tonight who might be
questioning how a supposed God of love could allow such
tragedy to come into our lives. And believe me when I tell you,
you are not alone."

Abigail felt her mouth drop open, and in her peripheral
vision, she could feel the glances and knowing smiles of those
in her household darting in her direction. Leaning forward,
she wriggled around in her seat and stared hard at the pastor, as if by doing so, she could not only hear better but also
absorb the meaning behind his words.

"This is a question of the ages, is it not? And there are
no simple answers. However, I think the words of beloved
nineteenth-century pastor and writer J. C. Ryle sum it up best
in a message that is appropriate, considering what Chaz and

Kaylee have so recently lived through. It is also relevant to the storms that every marriage will encounter at one time or another over the years."

The pastor cleared his throat, adjusted his glasses and began to read. "In his sermon entitled *We Shall Thank God for Every Storm*, Pastor Ryle says, 'If we are true Christians, we must not expect everything smooth in our journey to heaven. We must count it no strange thing, if we have to endure sicknesses, losses, bereavements, and disappointments, just like other people. Free pardon and full forgiveness, grace by the way and glory to the end—all this our Savior has promised to give. But He has never promised that we shall have no afflictions. He loves us too well to promise that.

'By affliction He teaches us many precious lessons, which without it we should never learn. By affliction He shows us our emptiness and weakness, draws us to the throne of grace, purifies our affections, weans us from the world and makes us long for heaven. In the resurrection morning we shall all say, "It is good for me that I was afflicted." We shall thank God for every storm.'"

Tears spilled down Abigail's cheeks, and of course, she had left the house without so much as a tissue tucked in her sleeve. Shouldn't she have known better? This was, after all, a wedding. Crying was on the agenda. She sniffed and swiped at her nose and eyes, the words of the sermon chipping away at the stone that had encased her heart since she was eleven years old. Was it good that she had been afflicted? Even though it had been terribly painful, she had to think that it was. She'd definitely changed. And she believed . . . *knew* it was for the better. Would she have learned so much about herself without the storm? Probably not.

In the past week, she'd spent more time considering her priorities and searching her soul than she had in all of the other thoughtful moments of her life combined. Looking back, if she were honest, she didn't exactly admire who she used to be and what she'd deemed important. Like a cold front sweeping in from the north, she could feel a storm brewing in her soul. More change was on the horizon. Would her metamorphosis continue to be this painful? This emotional? Eyes squeezed tight, she took a deep breath. She would be stronger because of it. A better person, by far, than the vain, rather vapid girl she'd been only a week ago. Feeling Justin jostling around at her side, she watched, bleary-eyed, as he reached under the pew in front of them, plucked several tissues from a box that had been stored near his feet for just such occasions, and handed them to her.

Directly in front of her, Bob Ray and Heather were sitting together. Hearing Justin find the tissues, Bob Ray reached down and grabbed several and handed one to Heather and one to Selma. One he kept for himself and proceeded to loudly blow his nose.

Pastor Caldecott turned to Chaz. "Chaz, you and your bride have made it no secret that you and Kaylee have waited to give the gift of your virtue to each other for after the wedding. For this obedience, I believe the Lord will bless you. And for this reason, I'll make every effort to keep what follows short and sweet."

Laughter rippled through the audience as Chaz winked at Kaylee. Bob Ray slid his arm around Heather and pulled her close and kissed her temple.

"And so, Chaz, please repeat after me. I, Chaz Edwards, do take you, Kaylee Johnson, to be my lawfully wedded wife—"

Bob Ray's expression was solemn as he silently mouthed the vows along with Chaz into Heather's ear. "I, Bob Ray Lathrop, do take you, Heather Bancroft, to be my lawfully wedded wife . . ."

Abigail felt her eyes welling up all over again and this time, Justin grinned and handed her the entire box of tissue. Her shoulders shook with silent laughter.

". . . to have and to hold, for better or for worse, for richer, for poorer, in sickness and in health, to love and to cherish, from this day forward until death do us part."

Kaylee repeated her vows next, her voice as clear and strong as Chaz's had been. "Chaz, I give you this ring as a symbol of my love and faithfulness. As I place it on your finger, I commit the rest of my life to you."

"Do you, Chaz," Pastor Caldecott asked, "agree to wear this ring as a reminder of the vows you have spoken today, your wedding day?"

"I do."

When they had both agreed and the rings were in place, Pastor Caldecott turned to the book of Ruth in his Bible and read from the first chapter: "Wherever you go, I will go; and wherever you stay, I will stay. Your people will be my people, and your God will be my God."

Eyes shining, Heather smiled at the earnest expression in Bob Ray's red-rimmed eyes as she whispered the words along with Chaz and Kaylee. After a beautiful prayer and a song by a soloist, the couple lit the unity candle, and Pastor Caldecott happily proclaimed, "By the powers vested in me by the laws of this great state, I now pronounce that you are husband and wife. What God has joined together, let no one put asunder. Chaz, you may now kiss your wife as often as you like for the rest of your lives." A happy whoop went up as Chaz swept Kaylee into his arms, bent her over backwards, and planted a joyful kiss on her lips.

"It is my honor to present to you for the first time ever, Mr. and Mrs. Charles E. Edwards! Please join us across the street at the Rawston Community Center for the reception." Wild applause roared across the room as Chaz set his wife back on her feet and escorted her down the aisle.

❦

The reception was even more fun, if possible, without the benefit of electricity. Held in the Rawston Community Center's enormous community room, Bunsen-burners kept the food piping hot and all of the tables had candles in the centerpieces. Someone had set patio torches up in iron floor stands and decorated them with ribbon and flowers. The string quartet traded in their various instruments for guitars and drums and Chaz pulled a reluctant Kaylee out on the floor for their first dance as man and wife. There was plenty of teasing between the two. Chaz spent considerable time limping, which had Kaylee going after his feet on purpose. Finally, her father cut in on the fun and the two of them danced off while Chaz hobbled over to his laughing mother. As plates were cleared, people filtered to the dance floor to dance in the twinkling candlelight. Standing, Justin extended his hand to Abigail.

"Dance?" Eagerly, she nodded and allowed herself be pulled through the candlelit throng. "Just like starlight, huh?" he murmured.

"Better almost." She nodded. It was absolutely enchanting. Everyone agreed, the power going out had only added to the beauty of the evening. "I can't believe it's only been a week since I danced with you the first time."

"I know. This is gonna sound like a really bad pick-up line, but I feel like I've known you all my life."

"Me, too. Weird, huh? Okay. Since we are old friends now, can I ask you a personal question?" Abigail asked and angled a mischievous smile up at him.

Justin tilted his head toward her. "Shoot."

239

"I couldn't help but notice when I cut your hair that you clean up rather nicely."

A crooked grin tugged at his lips. "And?"

"Well, the wedding got me to wondering how you managed to avoid getting married and having kids, like your brothers did, for so long."

"What, so long?" He pulled a funny face. "I only just turned thirty."

"In ten short years, you'll be forty."

"Wow! When you put it that way it makes me sound old or something." He laughed. "Seriously?"

"Yeah. Seriously." Abigail shrugged. "I really don't get it. You've got all the Boy Scout virtues, plus you're hard-working and good-looking . . . I mean, I don't want to stick my nose where it doesn't belong, and you can tell me to mind my own business but, like Selma says, time is short, and I figure, if you want to know something you should just ask. So. I want to know. Why haven't you allowed some filly to lasso you into the barn?"

A half-smile crossed his lips as he ruminated over her question. "A bunch of reasons, really, but they all boil down to one thing."

"What one thing?"

"The thing on the list."

"The list? What kind of list?"

"The list of things I am looking for in a wife."

"And you haven't found someone who is everything you're looking for yet?"

His shadowed gaze found hers. "Maybe. I'm not exactly sure."

Abigail swallowed at the suddenly serious look in his eyes. "What is on the list?"

"Well, she has to be at least 5'6"."

Abigail grinned. "What else?"

"I like crazy, curly hair. And green eyes. I insist on a great sense of humor and someone who will be willing to cut loose and just have fun. But at the same time, she needs to be enterprising and a hard worker. I am also looking for a loving spirit, a soft heart, a tough cookie, a helpmate, a best friend, and one other, extremely important thing. In fact, to be honest? It is the only thing."

Breathlessly, Abigail looked at him. "What?"

"The woman I marry will just know." A new song began and Selma tapped Justin on the shoulder to cut in, leaving Abigail to ponder his mysterious words.

20

The weeks that followed Chaz and Kaylee's wedding passed in a flurry of activities for Selma's household, interspersed with time spent together in the evenings working on the quilt . . . and healing. By day, Bob Ray, Justin, Abigail, and Heather volunteered for various clean up and recycling task forces. By Monday, it was clear that everyone who could be rescued had been, and when at last all rescue efforts had been called off, it became a gut-wrenching search for bodies. The list of deceased continued to grow and the cost of the damage mounted, but there was progress, too. An army of heavy equipment and their operators descended upon Rawston and slowly cleared the debris away. Temporary housing arrived in the form of trailers. Government assistance trickled in and insurance adjusters were overworked and overwhelmed.

It was also clear that Rawston would be digging out from under for years to come.

Even so, the beleaguered community was enjoying a spirit of camaraderie and brotherly love that most American cities would never know. The storm brought out the very best in people, and more than one Rawstonian was heard to say they'd had no idea just how rich they were in love, until they lost everything they owned.

In as little as two weeks after the storm, Danny's quilt top had been pieced and sewn together, and Selma asked Justin and Bob Ray to carry the old quilting frame that Clyde had built up from the basement. After the dinner dishes were done that evening, everyone helped to drag the heavy oak kitchen table up against the far wall. Then, they pulled Clyde's frame into place and Selma loaded the quilt top together with a thin layer of batting and the quilt's back onto the roller arms. The atmosphere was party-like as everyone dragged chairs around the frame for Selma's most popular lessons on "Hand Quilting" and "Tying Your Quilt."

Abigail settled in next to Justin as they listened to Selma teach and watched her work with rapt attention. It was just as if she'd stepped backwards into another century, she thought, reveling in the simple pleasures that her new life offered. She wasn't the only person who was eager to thread their needles and start quilting the beautiful piece. They were all fairly giddy with anticipation.

"I'm going to ask the girls to do the needlework, and you boys to do the tying," Selma explained. "Tying takes strong hands. Watch, while I demonstrate the double-twist square knot." Once she'd guided them through several knots, Selma hovered behind Bob Ray as he and Justin loaded large quilting needles with heavy thread and plunged them into the dots she'd drawn. The elderly woman's small hand rested lightly on Bob Ray's broad shoulder as both he and Justin grunted and fought to get their needles through the heavy layers. But the needle was slippery and unwieldy in their large, unskilled fingers.

"If that's too hard for you, Selma could probably help you, Bob Ray," Heather goaded and bit her lip to keep from laughing.

Eyeing her crossly, Bob Ray snorted. Justin did, too.

"You still struggle with arthritis in your fingers, huh Aunt Selma?" Abigail asked innocently, after Selma had successfully demonstrated another tie.

At that, Justin got up and left. No one said anything at first, and then Abigail ventured in a hushed tone, "Do you think he's mad?"

"Gracious, that would be odd now, wouldn't it?" Selma said, clearly befuddled. "I've never had a student just up and leave without a word like that."

"I hope he comes back," Bob Ray said, still grappling with the slick needle. His tongue peeked out from between his teeth and his muscles bulged. "I could use the help."

Heather giggled. "You don't need the gym anymore, honey. Just look at how you're getting a good workout yanking on that needle and getting all sweaty like that."

"Shut up," he snapped, but he was laughing as he said it. Everyone giggled.

Justin returned a second later holding up two pairs of pliers. "A man's tools are needed for a man's job," he announced with a grin and tossed a pair to Bob Ray who pulled them out of the air like the star football player he was. For the men, the quilt tying job suddenly became less of a battle.

"Thank you, Justin. For a minute there, we thought you'd given up."

"And miss the fun?" He seemed truly surprised that Selma would even suggest such a thing as he took his place and winked at Abigail. "Never."

The women all exchanged broad smiles. No one doubted that the men were enjoying the quilting bee as much as the women were.

Over the evenings that followed, the chairs around the quilting frame became the household gathering place to sew and tie, to talk and to drink coffee and to share the day's activities with each other. As one day blended into another, the quilt, as well as their lives, began to take shape. Pieces had been picked up and put together, and the beauty began to emerge.

Once the rebuilding efforts began, Justin had more work than he could handle most days, which was good because it served to distract him from his losses—most especially, Danny. Justin's *J.G. Construction Company* not only had to hire Bob Ray on as an assistant, but a half-dozen carpenters as well, because Justin had contracted so many rebuilding projects. Justin and Bob Ray's first team effort was a run up to Southshire to buy a company truck. For both men the work was rewarding, but Bob Ray felt a special sense of purpose.

"I think perhaps the Lord blesses those who make an effort to live according to His will," Selma told Bob Ray one night as he sat alone in the kitchen with her, eating a sandwich as she quilted his and Heather's quilt blocks.

"Totally." Bob Ray bobbed his head into his napkin as he wiped his mouth. "You know, Aunt Selma, I never was much of a pray-er, until I found myself crammed into a refrigerator under a bar in the middle of a tornado. But something huge happened to me then. I can't explain it. It was like suddenly, *kablam*-o. I could see! Life was like . . . a twinkling. Just like Danny always said. And here I was, about ready to take that big ride into the great beyond without knowing . . ." his voice cracked with the emotion that was so ever present in all of them these days, ". . . without *knowing* . . . where I was going. My mama used to talk about Hell and how it was a real place and everything, and I always just sort of blew that off as a myth until I looked it in the eye, you know? And," Bob Ray hung his head, "I didn't want to go there."

Selma placed her hand on his wrist. "Amen," she whispered.

Abigail set up a mini hair salon in Selma's laundry room and set back to work servicing her old clients and adding a steady stream of new. Hair, it seemed, didn't stop growing simply because a storm had come to town. Business, if not exactly booming, was at least steady. One afternoon Abigail was between clients and wandered into the kitchen to scare up some lunch and found Selma quilting. "Beautiful, Auntie Sel," she murmured, as she watched Selma draw the thread into perfect rows of perfectly spaced stitches. "Jen is going to love this."

"I hope it helps her heal." Selma's smile was wistful. "It certainly helped me."

"Really? How has it helped you this time?"

"I love to see the ways the Lord finds to use us. Each of us, like Danny here," she pointed out the bright center patch, "is the center of our own quilt. Our lives are made up of bits and pieces, some good, some bad. And isn't it amazing how God, in all His infinite wisdom, can use even our mistakes and what we might consider chaos, to His glory? Take the storm, for example." Selma ran out of thread and tied a knot as she ruminated. "Consider how it revealed things to each of us that would have otherwise remained hidden and left us in our ignorance if the winds had not blown them into view."

Abigail watched her aunt's hands shake with the benign tremor of age as she snipped off a new length of thread and began another arduous row of stitches. The fabric, each piece so different than the next, all pointed to Danny's willingness to share his life and love of Jesus so unselfishly with others.

"Yes," Abigail finally said at length and sighed. "I see."

These days, the house was also ringing with the shouts of small children as Elsa and Heather landed a plumb baby-sitting job for some working moms who'd lost their day care in the storm. The money they made not only filled the cookie jar; it helped to fill the pantry. When they weren't caring for small children, they could be found working together with Guadalupe and Selma doing housework and planting a big garden. But in between these efforts, the teenaged Elsa had time to carefully work stitches into the fabric of her own square, as Rawston High School had closed for the year.

"I almost went outside, on prom night," she confided in Justin one evening, when it was just the two of them sitting in the quiet kitchen after everyone else had quit stitching and gone off to watch a movie in the next room.

"Really?" Justin reclined, shoulder blades to chair back and rubbed his sore fingers. "What stopped you?"

"Tyler, you know, Brooke's brother?"

"The skater?"

"Yeah. He was looking for his sister, Brooke. I told him that I saw her go outside . . . with . . ." Elsa stopped sewing for a moment and turned her limpid eyes on Justin, "you know, Nick. Tyler was going to follow her out there . . . but, I knew that Brooke wanted to talk to Nick. Alone. Because she wanted to tell him . . ." Tears spiked her long, heavy, dark lashes, ". . . she wanted to tell him that she loved him, you know? So, I asked Tyler to dance so that he wouldn't bug her. But, if I hadn't done that, maybe she wouldn't have been hurt. Ah . . . ah . . . and Nick . . . you know?" Elsa dipped her head and the sounds that came from behind the quilt were those of grief.

"Or," Justin said softly and patted her back, "maybe Nick wouldn't ever have known she loved him, and maybe Tyler would have died, too." Elsa's sob came on a quick intake of air and her unsteady smile was appreciative. "You—sweet girl— may have saved Tyler's life with your bad dancing self."

She giggled and sniffed. "Danny tried to teach me to waltz. But it was so lame."

"Danny was lame sometimes. That's why we loved him, huh?"

"It's why I did. Yeah."

—⸱⸱⸱—

As one day melted into the next, Selma claimed she couldn't remember ever feeling so vitalized. And happy. And needed. And . . . blessed. A full house was her bliss, but Abigail knew that her aunt was not the only one benefiting from the communal living arrangement. For now and into the foreseeable future they all were not only grateful for a roof over their heads, but for the new beginning that the arrangement afforded them all. And for the comfort they offered each other as they began the difficult healing process.

The work on the quilt redoubled.

Especially now that Jen had called Abigail and let her know that she'd set the date for Danny's memorial. She'd decided it should be held in a week and a half, at the Rawston Christian Church on the first Saturday afternoon in June. Jen told her that she'd organized some music and a number of speakers, but she got the impression that Abigail and Heather had something up their sleeves and left a slot in the program for them. Would they be ready in only eleven days? Would fifteen minutes be enough? *Fifteen minutes.* Long after she hung up, Abigail pondered. Fifteen minutes to pay tribute to a man like Danny? It would take a lifetime to do him justice. On the other hand, fifteen minutes in front of an audience? Seemed like a lifetime to simply point at squares in a quilt.

After dinner had been eaten and the kitchen cleaned the night that Jen had called, Abigail joined Justin on Selma's sprawling wrap-around porch. Years ago Clyde had hung two wooden swings by chains from the porch ceiling, at opposite ends of the house. With Rawhide snoozing at their feet, Abigail and Justin sat drinking iced-tea in one swing while Heather and Bob Ray giggled and snuggled in the other.

The pink-orange twilight grew purple and closed in on them, surrounding Rawston and shutting out the rest of the world in a velvety blanket of crickets' song. It was rumored that the rate the insects chirped could tell the temperature. Abigail didn't know about that, but it was very warm and the steady music was peaceful. Through one screened window, the strains of Elsa and Robbie watching a movie in the living room filtered out, while the low conversation of Selma and Guadalupe working on the quilt wafted out another

"Jen called me today. About the memorial service," Abigail said. The sweat on her glass began to drip so she touched it to her knee where it left a perfectly round watermark on the denim. Even her glass seemed to be sorrowing. In her peripheral vision she could see Justin's head dip under the heavy news.

His Adam's apple bobbed as he swallowed and nodded. The grief over losing his best friend was a daily struggle. "Today must have been her day for taking care of some business. She called me, too."

"What about?"

He trailed a drop of condensation on his glass of iced-tea with a fingertip as he spoke. "She wants to talk to me about buying the lumberyard from her."

"Are you thinking about doing that?" Could he be considering staying here in Rawston? She pressed her damp glass to her throbbing heart.

"I don't know." Brows lifted, he shrugged. "With the rebuilding needs of this town, it would be a lot of work. I'd need help. Could be prosperous. I'm praying."

Praying? What did that mean? What if God said no? What then? There was so much he wasn't saying. So much that was connected to his feelings for Danny. She didn't feel comfortable pressing him, so she instead shifted her gaze to the spooled rail that surrounded Selma's porch. The floorboards creaked as Bob Ray and Heather slipped unobtrusively into the house, leaving them alone.

After a long moment Justin's eyes slid closed and he said, "I miss him. Danny should be there, running the lumberyard. Doesn't feel right, Jen and me . . . talking about me taking over something that he'd worked so hard to build."

"Yeah. I know. But I can't think of anyone he'd rather have had take over."

"I still can't believe he's gone." Chin to chest, Justin looked sideways at her. "Did you know," he paused and wet his lips, "that the last conversation Danny and I had was about you?"

"Why?" Abigail squirmed around to better see him.

He attempted to curtail his grin. "I wondered what you looked like. I didn't know that I had just danced with you, the night before."

Abigail rolled her eyes. "What'd he say?"

He took a sip of his tea, then chuckled. "Something about a tall Tinker Bell."

"What on earth?" She leaned back and laughed. "A tall . . . Tink?"

"I have to agree, now that I know you."

"What? No way! She was mean!"

"Nah. She was . . ." He looked her face over. "Feisty."

"Is that on the 'list'?" she blurted and then wished she could hit the rewind button on her mouth. *Oh . . . no.* She didn't want him to know she cared at all about the list.

"Should it be?" The creases that bracketed his lips deepened.

The swing slowly came to a stop as they neglected to keep it moving. Their eyes flicked over each other's faces, gauging each other's expressions.

"I don't—" she spoke at the same time he did.

"It's not—"

They stopped talking and laughed.

Abigail decided to change the subject, although ever since the wedding, she'd puzzled over his list. Wondered about the one thing he felt was so important. "What else did he say about me?"

"He told me you were raised by a single mom after you turned eleven. And he told me a little bit about your . . . father."

"Oh. What'd he tell you?"

"That you had some forgiving to do before you found peace."

A flurry of anxiety set her heart to pounding. That was the last thing she wanted to hear. Probably because it was true. "He said that?"

Softly, Justin said, "Yeah."

Abigail's eyes burned. "I think maybe he was . . . right."

"He usually always was."

"I'm . . ." a hitch in her voice had her stumbling over the words, "I'm scared."

The swing jostled as Justin draped an arm around her shoulders and pulled her head against his shoulder. "Facing the demons from your past is a scary thing. But you said yourself that family is priority one."

They talked long into the evening about the memorial, and Abigail felt as if they'd come up with a fledgling presentation plan that would please Jen and, at the same time, honor Danny. By the time she reached her room, a case of the jitters about confronting her father and decisions about the rest of her life had her feeling restless. Where was a crystal ball when she needed one? Endless questions buffeted her mind as she began to undress and found a long T-shirt to sleep in.

Living with Selma couldn't go on forever. And, though the laundry room was fine for now, eventually she'd need to find a real place to work. The idea of moving to LA was losing its appeal, but was still an option. As she folded her clothes, she wondered how she could ever find the nerve to face her father. To forgive him. And to ask forgiveness. The idea was just so daunting.

Lord, she prayed, *why is life so hard?*

Once her room was tidy and she'd turned off the overhead light, she threw back her covers, crawled into bed, and attempted snuggle down, but . . . there was something in there with her. Something cold and sharp. Snapping on the bedside lamp, she felt around and retrieved a book with an envelope taped to the cover. It was a note. From Heather.

Abigail, this book was in the rubble at my house and Bob Ray rescued it for me.

Once, a long time ago when I was really struggling, I found some answers here.

It helped me a lot. I hope it will do the same for you.

Love, Heather

The words on the cover blurred and a smile trembled at her lips. It was some kind of leather-bound devotional. Curiously,

Abigail turned it around in her hands and flipped through it, until she landed on that day's date and began to read:

Very early in the morning he came to his disciples, walking on the lake. When the disciples saw him walking on the lake, they were terrified and said, "It's a ghost!" They were so frightened, they screamed.

Just then Jesus spoke to them, "Be encouraged! It's me. Don't be afraid."

Peter replied, "Lord, if it's you, order me to come to you on the water."

And Jesus said, "Come."

Then Peter got out of the boat and was walking on the water toward Jesus. But when Peter saw the strong wind, he became frightened. As he began to sink, he shouted, "Lord, rescue me!"

Jesus immediately reached out and grabbed him, saying, "You man of weak faith! Why did you begin to have doubts?"

When they got into the boat, the wind settled down. Then those in the boat worshipped Jesus and said, "You must be God's Son!" (Matthew 14:25-33)

Abigail stared at the page, realization slowly dawning.

She'd been in a storm! Not the Rawston tornado, but a figurative storm, years ago. When she was eleven, her father left her mother for a new wife and a new daughter. That event had affected her life as surely as the tornado, for she'd lost her home when Karen moved them to the other side of town. She'd lost all of her old friends in the move to a different elementary school. And, though she hadn't realized how it had affected her at the time, she'd lost her father as surely as Jen's baby had lost Danny.

Very clearly now, Abigail could see how—because of these losses—she'd taken her eyes off the Lord and had begun to sink. And she'd been sinking ever since.

Bowing her head, she poured her heart out to Jesus.

Pushing the doorbell had to be as frightening as aiming a gun and pulling the trigger, Abigail thought, three days later as she stood on Dave Durham's porch. For if her father was home this afternoon, there was no turning back. He lived in an attractive tract home in a modern neighborhood that had fared quite well way over on this side of town. The house was a nondescript beige with black shutters and a cranberry front door. There were twin black rockers on either side of the door and some beautiful brickwork wainscoting the lower half of the house. A silver milk can held a handful of sunflowers, and on the door, a whimsical placard proclaimed that this was the Durham Family's Residence. Dave's new family. The replacement family. Abigail battled a wave of resentment that urged her to rush back to the Olds. But, just as she took the first, tentative step backward, the door swung open and she was trapped.

An attractive blond woman—Mindy must be in her late thirties by now if Abigail's memory served—answered the door with a smile. "What can I do for you?"

Abigail cleared her throat. "I'm Abigail Durham."

Mindy's face registered surprise, and her smile froze for a nanosecond before she recovered and said, "Well, hello. Of course. You're Dave's daughter. Won't you come in?" Her smile morphed into the real thing.

"Is my, uh . . . dad home?" The word was foreign and oddly large in her mouth.

"He's in his home office working on his computer," Mindy stepped back and glanced over her shoulder. "Would you like to speak to him?"

"I . . . yes. Please." She hesitated on the threshold. Awkward. Uncertain. If Mindy felt any such discomfiture, it didn't show.

"Great, come on in, and I'll just let him know you're here."

Fighting another compulsion to bolt, Abigail stepped into the cheerful foyer. Slowly, her gaze moved across her father's world. It smelled much the way she remembered him, and the warm, spicy fragrance pulled her backward in time as surely as a photograph might. A nicely appointed living room was on the right and the formal dining room, on the left. Straight ahead was the kitchen, where a young woman sat on a barstool at the counter. Abigail's heart clutched because it was like looking at a picture of herself from about ten years ago. This girl was her half-sister. Last night she figured the girl must be eighteen by now. Probably, she'd just graduated from the newer North Benton High between Rawston and Southshire. There was so much she didn't know about these people. So much she longed to discover now that she stood looking into the girl's clear, smiling eyes.

"Lindsey? Honey, this is Dad's daughter, Abigail. She's your half-sister," Mindy announced as if they'd discussed it and happily accepted it years ago.

Abigail didn't know what reaction she'd expected, but it wasn't the delighted, nearly giddy response she got.

"*Are you serious?* I have *so* always wanted to meet you!" The girl nearly toppled her stool as she leapt to her feet. She took a step, held out her hands, dropped them, lurched forward and launched herself into Abigail's arms. "I always wanted a big sister," her exuberant confession was muted some by Abigail's shoulder. Leaning back, she said, "I used to pretend that we knew each other. I'd have little conversations with you, and you'd give me advice and stuff . . . Dorky, I know, but I feel like I know you."

"I'm flattered," Abigail admitted and couldn't stall the smile that shanghaied her mouth and eyes. It was like talking to herself as a teen. Lindsey's enthusiasm was infectious and worked wonders on her tightly wound nerves. Instantly, Abigail liked her and regretted not being there so those conversations could have happened. "I always wanted a sister, too." It was true.

Lindsey stepped back and her eager gaze drank Abigail in, starting with the shoes and traveling to her hair. "Dad says we look alike. I think he's right. Oh! And guess what? I want to be a hairdresser, too! You are so *good*. Dad made a scrapbook for me of all the articles about you and the contests you've won and . . . like everything."

Abigail was completely taken back. Dave knew so much about her career? Dave had included her in his new life? Dave . . . cared? She stared back at the girl with wide eyes and was just about to reply when her father walked into the room.

"Abby?" he said the single word, but it was loaded with so much more. Her head snapped around and their gazes met. The expression in his eyes was vulnerable and filled with everything from remorse to love. He spread his arms and Abigail rushed to him and returned his fierce, emotion-packed hug.

Later that evening, Abigail parked the Olds at the curb in front of Justin's house and cut the engine. Arms braced on the steering wheel, she sat for a moment, contemplating the glorious tangerine clouds that streaked the horizon, announcing the onset of twilight. Soft, golden light bathed their corner of the prairie, diminishing the damage done by the storm and giving the neighborhood an otherworldly feel. She could hear the sound of Justin's chainsaw biting through the bark of a tree that had fallen in his yard. When he saw her, he cut the power and his expression told her how happy he was to see her as she climbed out of the car. The smell of sap and freshly cut wood greeted her along with his words.

"What brings you here?" he asked, dabbing at his brow with the back of his wrist as he set the chainsaw on a stump. He was months from moving back in, but the house already looked a hundred times better than it had, the night of the storm.

She pushed the car's door shut behind her and crossed the yard. "I . . . know," she said simply.

"You . . . know." His grin was lopsided with confusion. Tugging off his stiff leather gloves, he gestured for her to join him on his stoop. "Good. I'm glad somebody does."

She took a seat beside him and reached up to brush away some of the sawdust that clung to his nose and cheeks. "I saw my father today."

His brows shot up in surprise. "You did?"

Pulling her lips between her teeth, she nodded and plucked a woodchip from his hair. Holding it between her fingers, she felt its rough texture and smelled its fresh scent.

"And?"

Rawhide trotted across the yard and joined them on the porch. Tail thumping, he crawled up beside Abigail and laid his head in her lap, sniffing at the woodchip she held, examining it for chewability. "And . . . it was amazing. They were all—" she tossed the chip on the lawn and gathered the dog's head in her hands as she groped for words in the human language that could describe her experience. But there were none. Not really. What had happened had been the kind of thing that only God could have orchestrated. With a storm.

"They," she started again, blinking in amazement, "they were nothing like I expected. They were incredible. Awesome. A gift from God." Rawhide nudged her hands, urging her to resume her massage with a canine groan. She laughed at him and scratched his ears. "Both he and Mindy were so sorry for the way they broke up our family. They've lived with a lot of regret, and it hasn't been easy. My sister is a hoot, sort of like a mini-me. They say they pray for Mom and me every day. Isn't that amazing? And, I never, ever would have believed it, but I think my father finally helped me figure out just what the thing on your list is, and that, my dear, is what I *know*."

His smile was both quizzical and amused as Rawhide flipped on his back for some attention to his belly. "Do tell."

"He said," Abigail blinked rapidly and swallowed. She *would* get through this without crying. "He said Danny Strohacker taught him, over a decade ago, that the best marriage is a cord of three strands. And Dave wanted me to know it now. Because he wishes he would have known it when he married my mom. And, because," she turned and looked him in the eyes as she spoke, "it's the strongest. And so, knowing you the way I do now, I know that the number one thing on your list—and on mine now, too—is Jesus." She slipped her arm through his and leaned her face against his shoulder. He smelled of earth and motor oil and gasoline and Armani for Men and warm flannel and fresh air, and she wondered if it was possible that she'd fallen in love with him already.

"So, am I right? Is that it? Jesus is number one your list? Because, ya know, if He's not, then you need to let me know so that I can start looking elsewhere for someone to come a-courting."

Chuckling, he buried his nose in her hair and whispered, "Yes. You're right." And then, much to Abigail's relief and delight, he took her—ugly dog and all—in his arms and kissed her. First on her blushing cheeks and then full on her lips. Neither of them noticed the wild tattoo of Rawhide's tail against the porch's floor.

And, for the first time in a year, Justin finally felt at home.

21

Daniel Strohacker's memorial service was standing room only. Jen's many brothers stood in the vestibule of the enormous North Rawston Community Church, surrounded by floral wreaths and pictures of Danny, welcoming people, directing them to the guest book and handing out programs with Danny's smiling face featured prominently on the cover. At the doors to the sanctuary, Jen Strohacker stood holding her baby and looking beautiful, smiling and accepting hugs and condolences from friends and family as they headed into the auditorium to find their seats.

"It's awkward, huh?" Jen murmured to Abigail and Heather as they hugged her and kissed the baby's head. "I keep telling everyone that they don't have to tell me they're sorry, because I know. We all are."

"We don't really know what else to say," Abigail admitted, her expression rueful.

"And, we *are* so sorry," Heather blurted into her tissue and she blew her nose. "I'm sorry." She laughed. "Sorry."

"I know, honey," Jen said, and laughed sympathetically. She kissed Heather's temple. "I don't know what to say either, to tell you the truth."

"Well," Selma reached up and touched the baby's tiny hand, "I'm betting Daniel wouldn't want us to sit around with long faces today. This is a celebration of his beautiful life, after all. And, just because he moved to heaven before us doesn't mean that is the end of Daniel Strohacker. We'll see him again soon enough. And, when you get to be my age, you realize that the more people up in heaven there are waiting to greet you, the more excited you are to get there."

Jen grinned. "I love the way you think, Selma Tully."

"Beautiful baby, by the way," Selma said. "You and Danny did good."

"Thank you! I feel shameless about agreeing." Her eyes crinkled with appreciation as they swept the group clustered around her and the baby. "I'm so glad you are all here and I'm looking forward to what you all have done for Danny today."

Once they'd all found the seats that Bob Ray and Justin had saved for them, the program started with some music that Danny had loved, performed by several gifted artists. When everyone had arrived, his pastor welcomed the throng, gave a short but inspiring message about God's plan of salvation and then introduced Jen's brother—and Danny's best friend growing up—Brett. Brett's sorrow lurked just beneath the surface of his wide grin as he cleared his throat and began to speak.

"Danny liked to tell everyone he had the world's smallest family. We think he did that to get sympathy from old ladies and my sister." Laughter rippled. "But, if being an only child means not having brothers and sisters, then I'd like to refute his claim with a little slideshow from my childhood."

The lights dimmed and a picture of a family at Christmastime was projected on two huge screens on either side of the podium. "This," Brett turned toward one of the screens, "is Christmas at our house in 1970." Using a laser pointer, Brett pointed at a kid under the tree. "This is me. This one is Jen.

The rest of the kids are our siblings. This here is Mom. And Dad. And wait a minute . . . could it *beee* . . . Danny? Yes! See there? We're seven. Wearing matching sweaters? Yeah. Gifts from my Aunt Marge."

The next photo was also of Christmas. "Here we are in 1971. See the sweaters? There's Danny, under the tree. Those are my Lincoln Logs. I think he sawed several of them in half, sort of foreshadowing his lumberyard thing. And here? In '72? Yeah, uh . . . there he is. We're nine. Matching sweaters, thanks, Aunt Marge. He's holding my Hot Wheels? Never saw those again. 1973 . . . let's see . . . oh, right, that's us. More matching sweaters? Marge? Please? This was the year of the G.I. Joe. Look at Dan's 'fro." The laughter was regular now as every single Christmas featured Danny in the middle of Jen's huge family wearing one of Aunt Marge's specials.

"Here we are at Yellowstone on a family vacation. Danny is the one in the swim trunks. He had great legs. Us at Disneyland. Danny and me on the Matterhorn. Thanksgiving. Danny is the turkey on the left. This is our family at Easter. That's Danny with the full basket of eggs. And that kid next to him there with the mouth open and the empty basket? That's Jen crying."

Dozens of pictures spanned the years and Abigail hadn't laughed so hard in months. After Brett had finished and the lights were still dimmed, a musician friend of Danny's stood and introduced the music video he had written and produced.

It seemed that Danny was renowned for his love of moto-cross. Apparently, he was equally renowned for his many and painfully splendid wipe-outs. The first familiar notes of the famous Irish song, "Danny Boy" accompanied some of Dan's more spectacular accidents. The lyrics had been changed to suit the topic. *"Oh Danny boy, the bikes, the bikes are calling, From glen to glen, and down the mountainside. The summer's gone, and off the bike he's falling. 'Tis you, 'tis you must go—UH-OH—*

and I must ride." The song went along in that vein for a number of nutty verses and eventually ended in thunderous applause and laughter and the overhead lights coming back up.

One after another, people offered heartfelt tributes, some funny, some poignant, all acknowledging Danny's passion for the Lord. When at last it was their turn, Abigail's knees were knocking as she headed to the podium with the rest of her and Selma's storm family. Justin and Bob Ray carried the quilt to the stage in a box, took it out, and unfolding it, stretched it up and over a frame they'd built and assembled for the occasion.

Abigail nervously cleared her voice. *Lord,* she prayed, *please don't let me cry and ruin this.* As she began speaking, a peace seemed to descend and her knees stilled. "Today, we have all heard how Danny was the only child of only children. So, not only did Daniel Strohacker have no siblings, he had no aunts and uncles, no cousins nor second cousins once removed.

"His parents were older when they had him so he also had no grandparents. In the '70s, when he was only thirteen, Danny's father passed away from a heart attack. Four short years later, when he was seventeen, he lost his mother to ovarian cancer.

"From outward appearances, it would seem that Daniel Strohacker was doomed to be alone. But as we have already heard today, nothing could be further from the truth. Danny was a family man, and right now, this room is filled with his family." A smattering of applause quickly grew into a roar.

"Most of you probably can't say that you ever saw Danny without this."

Abigail picked up the laser pointer that Brett had been using earlier and pointed out the center square. "This is the fabric from Danny's brilliant red Bible cover and the heart-beat of this quilt. It is the bloodline through which we are all related, in one way or another, to Danny. And this beautiful quilt, unfortunately, only illustrates a small fraction of Danny's massive family. To do it justice, the quilt would fill the parking lot and beyond. And so we are limited today to this quilt, built from pieces of the lives of Danny's brothers and sisters, his aunts and uncles, his grandparents, his cousins, and his sons and daughters. And of the storm that finally took his life." Abigail moved the beam across the rows of fabric that she and Justin had gathered the night of the storm.

"Growing up, I always told people that I could identify with Danny because he was an only child. So was I, said I. We were loners in a lonely world. But this storm proved me wrong about so many things. Danny wasn't an only child. And neither was I. It took an EF5 tornado to point that out to me, and for that, I am truly thankful."

Amazingly, applause resounded throughout the building for a solid minute. Teary-eyed, Abigail continued. "Danny always lamented that he didn't have a family of his own. But his legacy cries otherwise. And so, for my square, I chose mostly tattered bits of fabric I'd gathered in the storm. Disjointed pieces, like a family, coming together to form something that, to me, anyway, is beautiful. I think Danny would agree that family can come from unlikely places in unlikely circumstances."

Abigail stepped back and one by one, each square—as different and beautiful as the members of Danny's family—was presented by its maker. Kaylee and Chaz presented their square together and spoke to the inspiring Strohacker marriage.

"When Chaz proposed to me," Kaylee said, "he said, 'Kaylee, I want what Jen and Dan have,' and so our square has pieces of our wedding clothes to symbolize how Danny's love for Jen inspired us."

When it was Guadalupe and Elsa's turn, Elsa operated the pointer and Guadalupe spoke. "Elsa's Daddy, Miguel, is in Mexico. He was deported because of some problems with his green card. But he will be back here next month, if the Good

Lord is willing. The day before he left us, Miguel tells Danny, 'Please, take care of my little girl and do some things for her that I cannot do, while I am away.' So, Jen loans Danny to us sometimes for bike-riding lessons, and then swimming lessons, and then math homework and youth group and finally . . ." she glanced at Elsa and they giggled. "Some terrible dancing lessons." Guadalupe paused and looked at the floor, unseeing as she gathered her words in English. "He was a good father figure to my daughter when she needed a daddy, and I can never give these minutes back to Jen. But we give her the gift of knowledge." She craned around and looked at Jen sitting in the front row. "Knowledge that Danny Strohacker was a fine daddy. And in Elsa he has . . . *una hija*. A daughter."

Next, Heather pointed out the square she made with the laser pointer. "My piece here looks really weird. I know. But even though it looks like an old washrag and some other scraps, it's a symbol that probably only Danny would understand." She cleared her throat. "The day Danny died, he was . . . he was . . . he was helping me. My baby stuffed a washcloth down the toilet and some towels into the tub and he flooded the house. Danny came over to help me unplug my drains and dry the house out. The washcloth might seem inappropriate to some people. But to me it symbolizes Danny's willingness to help anytime . . . anywhere . . . anyone. That was Danny. Loving his neighbor. The washcloth also symbolizes forgiveness. This red velvet here is a bit of a baptismal curtain that protected me and my son the night of the storm. To me it says, my sins are washed away by faith in the Living Water, Jesus Christ. Danny taught me that."

The Nakamura family followed, Tyler on crutches, Brooke in a wheelchair, Isuzu speaking for them all, rousing the crowd to laughter and tears. After several others, Bob Ray was up next. "This is my square, over here." He took the pointer and drew loose circles around it with the tiny red light. "It's a little messy, but I'm still learning the finer points of needlework."

The laughter flowed in appreciative waves. "Selma here—" grinning, Bob Ray grasped the podium, leaned into the microphone, and nodded at the tiny woman at his side, "—her seam ripper was smokin' sometimes while I practiced, but we finally got my patch right-side up. Anyway, in the rubble I found some clothes I wore to baseball games, back when I was in high school. The thing I remember most about Danny from those days is how he was never afraid to pray in public. And he never swore. And he always praised his team. And . . ." Bob Ray exhaled and blinked, ". . . if the other team did something cool, he'd cheer for them and no one ever thought he was like, a traitor, you know? Danny modeled what it meant to be a man. I learned a lot from watching him over the years, about being a good coach and a good husband and a good man. I hope to one day be all of those things and make him proud up there."

Finally, it was Justin's turn. Slowly, looking up at the video screen as he walked, he made his way to the podium. He braced his palms on each side of the podium, gripping it, head down. Abigail thought for a moment he was praying. Finally, he shook his head, sniffed, and looked out over the crowd.

"Danny would have laughed himself sick, to see me hunched over a sewing machine." Amid hoots and catcalls and laughter, Justin glanced up at the ceiling. "I did it for you, big guy. And I want you to know I ruined a perfectly good shirt in the process . . . this here?" He picked up and pointed with the laser. "It's the shirt I was wearing when I delivered Danny's son right after the tornado, in the middle of a parking lot while being coached by a homeless man and a hairdresser with a flashlight." He waited for the applause to die. "Yes, I have to say that was a moment I'd never anticipated enjoying, but it will go down in history as one of my all-time favorite experiences."

He moved the laser's beam. "This is the material we wrapped the baby in that night. And this is a piece of the dog bed, you had to be there, and . . . this is a prayer pocket I made . . ." Justin had to stop and gather his wits for a moment. "Sorry," there was laughter in his sob. "And I put a prayer in there for your son, big guy. And a promise to be there for him. The way you were always there for me."

He glanced at Abigail, and his smile said it all. He was staying.

Tears gathering in her throat, Abigail's heart threatened to pound out of her body as she stood, staring at him and smiling. When the lights came back up, the applause thundered, and Justin stepped into Abigail's outstretched arms.

When the memorial service was finally over, the skies overhead were black and roiling and rumbling with the spirit of another supercell. Rain began to fall in earnest, driving everyone home as soon as humanly possible. No sooner had Abigail and Justin chauffeured their clan to Selma's place in the new truck and the Olds than the newly replaced storm sirens began to wail. Another storm was on the way. *What would it bring?* Abigail wondered, reacting first with dread. And then fear. And then chagrin, as she parked the Olds and Justin parked his truck in Selma's driveway. If they were all going to live in Rawston without sinking, the way Peter had, they needed to keep their eyes on the Lord in the midst of the storm. No matter how scary. Together, they hustled everyone into Selma's storm shelter, lit the emergency candles, reached for each other's hands and began to pray that their Creator would help them beyond every storm.

Epilogue

Good morning, Rawston, heart of the American Midwest! We've got 7 a.m. straight up on your Thursday, May 3rd, and you are listening to Mike and Julie on 101.5 K-RAW. Keep it right here for another installation of our special weeklong tribute: **Rawston: One Year Later**, featuring the guys from Dan the Handyman Lumberyard. Today's special guests are co-owners, Justin Girard and Bob Ray Lathrop. Good morning, guys!"

"Good morning, Mike and Julie."

"Let's start off by having you tell us how your lives have changed since the storm. Bob Ray?"

"This is gonna sound really weird, Mike, but in many respects, they've gotten better. For starters, my man Justin here is going to be getting married next month, to Abigail Durham, from the new Doo Drop In Hair Salon in Old Town."

"Congratulations, Justin!"

"Thanks! We're thrilled. And, Bob Ray should mention that he and his wife just welcomed a baby daughter into their family, Danielle Louise. And she's a beauty. Looks just like her mama."

"I'd love to show you all pictures of her, but since this is radio . . ."

"Speaking of babies, I hear that immediately after the storm, you delivered a baby, Justin! How is everybody doing today?"

"As well as can be expected. Today, that baby is now walking and talking some. His father, my best friend, Daniel Strohacker, was killed in the storm, and we all still feel his loss. But we know that Danny would be happy to see the way his wife and baby are coping, and how the business at his lumberyard has flourished because of the massive rebuilding efforts."

"Bob Ray, is it true that you guys had to move into a group home of sorts?"

"That was a total blessing, Julie. Justin's fiancée's great aunt— Selma Louise Tully—opened her home to a bunch of us right after the storm, and we've all been living together for a year now while we rebuild Justin's house and Abigail's business among other projects."

"You know, Mike and Julie, I think both Bob Ray and I can say that this time together as one big family has been one of the best times in our lives."

"Oh, yeah. Justin's right. We're really going to miss him and Abigail after the wedding. But the rest of us are staying put, for now. We all help each other out, and we're in no hurry at the moment. In fact, my wife and I are in the process of buying Selma's house and annexing off an apartment for her."

"So busy! You've both been instrumental in the rebuilding process here in Rawston. How's that going, Justin?"

"Everybody has been working like maniacs, and the results are impressive. The high school and hospital are bigger and better than ever, and Old Town is beginning to reemerge from the chaos. In fact, everyone is going to take the weekend off and celebrate at the annual Rawston Quilt-o-Rama in two weeks. We've got people coming in from all over to celebrate and to view the 'Rawston Storm Quilt' that the community put together this last year with some of the tattered fabric that was salvaged from the storm."

"Kind of a special symbol of rebuilding, huh, guys?"

"Yeah, bit by bit, we're putting the pieces back together. And it's . . . beautiful."

Discussion Questions

1. Abigail Durham seemed to be living the American dream, at the beginning of the book, as a young, successful business owner. How do you see that she needed God's direction in her life?

2. Some people would think that a storm would ruin your life forever. What were the positive things that came from the storm?

3. How did Selma help Abigail deal with the losses that the storm brought?

4. Quilting is not just Selma's work—it is an activity that helps her make sense of chaos and stay centered on God's sovereignty. What activity do you use to stay centered?

5. Abigail is afraid to give her heart to Justin and find hope after the storm. If you knew Abigail, how would you help her learn to trust God? Have you ever experienced something similar? How did you cope? What did you learn?

6. Jen Strohacker was widowed at a young age. Why do you think God would put two people together only to take one away?

7. Have you lost someone you loved? How did you deal with the loss?

8. Bob Ray seemed to change overnight. Do you think his changes were permanent? Why? Why not?

9. Isuzu's family lost their Olympic dream and suffered great loss. How, in the scheme of things, might this have been good for the children? For the parents?

10. Do you think Dr. Bernard Blumenfeld was a real doctor? A homeless man with a real story? An angel unaware?

11. What was the ripple effect of Danny Strohacker's death? How do you see that his life might have been used? His death?

12. Have you ever questioned God's plan in the midst of a life storm? How have you come through and seen His hand on your life?

Want to learn more about author
Carolyn Zane and check out other great
fiction from Abingdon Press?

Sign up for our fiction newsletter at
www.AbingdonPress.com
to read interviews with your favorite authors, find tips
for starting a reading group, and stay posted on what
new titles are on the horizon. It's a place to connect
with other fiction readers or post a
comment about this book.

Be sure to visit Carolyn online!

www.carolynzane.net

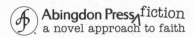